More praise for

AIN'T GONNA BE THE SAME FOOL TWICE

"A funny, poignant, and fractured look
at an uncertain era."
—*Dallas Morning News*

"A sassy, savvy protagonist . . .
While calling up evocative cultural touchstones
crossing race and gender lines, Sinclair turns up the
amp on the black boomer experience—the '60s and '70s
with hide-nor-hair of the Beatles . . . She's breathed life
into an Everyteen/woman: A big city girl who struggles
with the usual coming-of-age quandaries, then dusts
herself off—attitude intact."
—*Los Angeles Times*

"A story of personal exploration and discovery . . .
From the get-go, Sinclair hooks you with Stevie's story
through the creation of colorful characters so down-to-
earth and real that they feel as if they've leapt off the
page and are right next to you."
—*St. Petersburg Times*

"It takes a keen, unblinking eye to look through the
lens of nostalgia and see the past for what it was.
April Sinclair has that kind of vision."
—*Philadelphia Daily News*

"A novel of identity politics . . .
This tale has verve and readability."
—*The New Yorker*

"Exciting . . . a fast-reading and interesting novel . . .
Sinclair has clearly staked out her place among the
best young novelists."
—*Virginian Pilot and Ledger-Star*

Other Avon Books by
April Sinclair

COFFEE WILL MAKE YOU BLACK

APRIL SINCLAIR

AIN'T GONNA BE THE

SAME FOOL

TWICE

AVON BOOKS  NEW YORK

AVON BOOKS
A division of
The Hearst Corporation
1350 Avenue of the Americas
New York, New York 10019

Copyright © 1996 by April Sinclair
Cover illustration by Zita Asbaghi
Back cover author photo © Robert Trachtenberg
Published by arrangement with Hyperion
Library of Congress Catalog Card Number: 95-33051
ISBN: 0-380-72794-3

First Avon Books Trade Printing: February 1997

Printed in the U.S.A.

OPM 10 9 8 7 6 5 4 3 2 1

for my friend, sue holper
my catalyst for change

acknowledgments

Time to round up the usual suspects and thank them. First, I want to acknowledge my manuscript consultant, Susan Holper, and also thank Judy MacLean for her feedback on the manuscript. Thanks again to my supportive family and friends for being there during this process.

Cheers for my occasionally tough, mostly sweet, always insightful editor at Hyperion, Leslie Wells. And my wisecracking, ex-biker chick, agent, Winifred Golden (Margret McBride Literary Agency) who helps me to bring home the tofu. Thanks also to the staffs at Avon, my paperback publisher, and Hyperion for their enthusiastic support.

I appreciate the valuable residencies provided by the Djerassi, Yaddo, and MacDowell artist colonies during the writing of *Ain't Gonna Be the Same Fool Twice*. And thanks to René Rossi at seventies radio station, KBGG in San Francisco, for her research assistance.

I have countless wonderful memories, due to the many fans who touched my heart through letters and personally at my readings around the country. I'm also grateful to the international audience who bought the Spanish, German, Dutch, and Korean editions of *Coffee Will Make You Black*. Love knows no boundaries.

summer 1971
to
spring 1975

1

You meet the same peoples over and over again in life," Grandma warned from the doorway.

I didn't give her my full attention. I was too busy cramming wool sweaters into a suitcase full of jeans. Despite my sweaty, well-toasted skin, I knew I'd need warm clothes in a month or so.

"They names and they faces might be different. But they will be the same peoples," Grandma insisted. Her words hung in the humid Chicago air like the smell of chitterlings cooking on a stove. She pulled a paper towel from her apron pocket and wiped the sweat off her fudge-colored forehead. Grandma wore one of those serious aprons that you had to stick your arms through. There was nothing prim and proper about her.

I was the first person in my whole family to go away to college, and I was excited. But I knew that "book learning" wasn't everything. Grandma says experience is the best teacher. And she is no one to take lightly.

Mama joined Grandma in the doorway. The two of them could barely fit. They were both big women. Neither of them were fat, just big in the way grown women are supposed to be, according to Grandma. She'd often say, "Chile, don't nobody want a bone but a dog." But I was content with my slim figure. Thin was in, especially in white America, where I was headed. After all, Twiggy was the model of the hour. And besides, I certainly wasn't anywhere near that skinny. I did have titties and booty to speak of.

There sure were a lot of memories in this bedroom. The walls had been yellow, pink, and finally blue, my favorite color. I shook my head at the now worn-out-looking white bedroom furniture that had looked so magnificent the Saturday afternoon they carried it home in my uncle's truck. Mama and Daddy bought it used from a house sale in Lake Forest, a rich northern suburb. I'd thought I'd died and gone to heaven. Aunt Sheila took one look at the gleaming white furniture and declared that we'd arrived.

I gazed at my bed. The quilt that Grandma made me years ago was almost in tatters now. I'd bought a brand-new, lime-green corduroy bedspread with some of the money I'd made this summer helping Grandma at her chicken stand.

Mama looked sad, like she hated seeing her only daughter go. You'd never know by her puppy dog expression that Mama had swung a mean switch in her day. She'd also done a lot of preaching over the years. And I'd been the mainstay of her congregation. My two younger brothers could never be held hostage long enough to listen to her sermons. Boys were "out-side children," they "liked to go," as Mama would say. I won-dered if David and Kevin would finally have to help her out in the house. She might make them wash a few dishes, but that would probably be about it.

"Well, Mama, you won't have me to kick around anymore," I teased.

"Just don't let some man make a fool out of you and you'll

be all right." She sighed. Her smooth pecan complexion only showed wrinkles when she frowned.

I didn't have a boyfriend right now. I'd gone to the senior prom with a dude from the school band who'd asked me at the last minute. I'd barely known the shy, husky trumpet player drew breath until he'd mumbled, "Stevie, will you go with me to the prom?" They call me Stevie at school. My family calls me Jean. My name is actually Jean Stevenson. I'd swallowed and answered, "Yeah, I'll go with you." Paul was shy and quiet, but kind of cute. At least he wouldn't expect me to put out, I figured.

Our date had been pleasant enough. I even had fond memories of resting my head on Paul's shoulder as we slow-danced to the prom's theme song, "We've Only Just Begun." It was a white tune by the Carpenters; and our class of 1971 was all-black, except for a couple of Puerto Ricans and a Chinese girl. Some people had complained about the honky theme, but the prom committee prevailed. Only three other white songs were played during the prom, Carole King's "It's Too Late" (which everybody agreed was hot, white girl or no white girl); Bread's "I'd Like to Make It with You"; and Bob Dylan's "Lay, Lady, Lay." Of course no dudes could complain about the last two.

Paul and I had gone to the Indiana Dunes for the senior class picnic the day after the prom. And Paul had been a perfect gentleman, lightly brushing my lips only when he'd said good-bye. It would give me a sweet feeling, just thinking about it. Something might have come of our connection if we'd had more time to get to know each other. But we didn't; Paul's draft number was pulled. He jumped up and joined the navy and shipped out right after graduation. Paul figured if he was in the navy, he'd have a better chance of staying out of Vietnam.

"Jean," Grandma said, interrupting my thoughts. "We're expecting great things outta you."

I chuckled as I stuffed underwear in the inside pocket of the large suitcase. "Grandma, I'm just going away to a state university, so don't y'all expect me to come back a Rhodes scholar."

"I know you'll do us proud," Grandma said, dabbing her eyes.

Suddenly, I felt a lump in my throat. I was sad to be leaving everything familiar, even Mama.

"You just keep your head in your books," Mama admonished. "And don't let men distract you. Men are nothing to get excited about, remember that." It was obvious that Daddy no longer excited Mama. The two of them reminded me more of business partners than lovers. She often passed Daddy like a vegetarian walking by a steak house. I wondered if the earth had *ever* moved.

"I don't know what you talking about." Grandma winked. "Men *are* too something to get excited about! Jean, if you can't be good, be careful."

Mama folded her arms. "You oughta be ashamed of yourself, talking like that at your age!"

"*You* the one who should be shamed," Grandma insisted, stepping into the bedroom and swinging her full hips.

"Chile, there might be snow on the chimney," she laughed, pointing to her Afro. "But, there's sho' nuff fire down below!" She snapped her fingers and did a boogaloo step.

"Get it, Grandma!" I laughed, clapping my hands.

"Poppa must be turning in his grave," Mama sighed.

Grandma rubbed her nose. "My left nostril is itching. Some man is talking about coming to see about me right now. And if he cain't cut the mustard, he kin least lick the jar!" Grandma rushed out of the room.

Mama shook her permed head in horror.

Grandma said her good-byes in Chicago. She shoved a twenty-dollar bill in my hand and then we hugged for the longest time.

As soon as my brothers, my parents, and I were out of Chicago good, we saw corn for days. I don't mean that literally, it was only a four-hour drive. But I don't care if I ever see another cornfield again, no matter how much I like eating it.

I've been assigned to a coed building, modern twin towers with twenty floors. Mama says she would've preferred for me to be in an all-girl's dorm. Daddy agrees with her, like he usually does on matters involving us kids. I don't know why Mama's tripping. We're on two different sides of the building. We even have different elevators.

It got a little emotional in the parking lot for us and plenty of other families. Everybody hugged me, Mama, Daddy, tall, lanky David—who will be a junior on Southside High's basketball team—and cute, chubby Kevin, who I can't believe will be a freshie this fall.

There wasn't a dry eye among us, including my father's narrow dark eyes. He's due for a dye job, I thought, noticing the gray around his temples. But Daddy still looked strong and athletic in his bowling shirt.

Grandma says white people are born actors. So, I'm not sure how my roommate and her family really felt when they discovered that I was black. I'd moved into the room first. My family was long gone by the time Barbara, her parents, big brother, and little sister trooped in with her stuff. Everybody was cordial, none of them tripped out like they'd seen Godzilla or anything. But who knows how they *really* felt?

Anyway, thank goodness, my roommate seems like the sweet type. Maybe because she's so homely. She probably figures she has to be extra nice. I hate to be cold, but the girl's face is hurting. Barbara is tall and skinny, downright gawky. She's got long, stringy, brown hair and pinched features. I don't have to worry about any latent homosexual tendencies being aroused by the sight of her, that's for damn sure.

I know that I can be attracted to a girl. I got a crush on the school nurse back in high school. Nurse Horn said it was normal for adolescents to develop same-sex crushes. But it still bothered me that good-looking girls turned my head.

Barbara is from a small town—Quincy, Illinois. She goes to bed at nine o'clock and plays a lot of Barry Manilow and even some classical. I'm thankful that she plays it real low. I try to be considerate, too. I don't blast my Motown sounds unless she isn't here. I made up a riddle. Why do white people go to bed so early? The answer is, because they're "tired." If you don't get it, that means you're "tired" too.

Today, I finally found the ivy. I'd always pictured a college having old, stately, brick buildings with ivy hanging from them. But I've only seen one place like that on this campus. The newer buildings outnumber the older ones, about two to one.

I like most of my classes. Only one of my teachers seems racist. Not anything overt, just a feeling I get. But that's nothing new. I can't trip on it. I have to keep my eyes on the prize, like Daddy says.

In class, my answers better be right. I feel like I have to represent my race. If I look dumb, we all look dumb. It's a burden. Sometimes I envy the white students, who can just blend in.

It's a trip suddenly to be surrounded by wall-to-wall white folks. And it's really strange living in the same room with one. It's a mindblower to look over at a pink face sleeping in the bed across from me. I keep waiting for the girl to go home, but then I remember she lives here.

In the cafeteria, when I sit with white girls from my floor, I cut my chicken with a knife. And I surely don't suck on the bones. I pretty much avoid watermelon altogether.

In the second week of September, I made my first trip into town. The place reminded me of that song "I Wanna Holler, But the Town's Too Small." There are no signal lights or busy intersections. But there is a statue in front of the courthouse of some dude on a horse. Every small town probably has one, I thought.

I was sitting on the bench waiting for the campus bus. I'd just finished buying a flashlight and some tampons. The weather was perfect, about seventy-five degrees and very little humidity, for a change. Suddenly, I heard somebody shouting "Nigger!" Then I felt wet spit on my arm. I looked up as a truckload of men passed by, leaving a cloud of gravel dust. It all happened so fast, I was stunned.

I felt anger, fear, and humiliation all rolled into one. The white people walking by and the campus bus pulling up to the curb became a blur. Since I couldn't kill the assholes in the truck, I simply wanted to disappear. Somehow, I gathered my composure and boarded the bus. And, I was able to stare out of the window at the postage-stamp-size town just like anybody else.

But tears ran freely down my face when I told Mama on the phone what had happened. She said in a calm but concerned voice, "Baby, I'm sorry that happened to you, but you will just have to tough it out. Lord knows, we as a people have come through slavery, survived the KKK, and the dogs being set on us in Birmingham. And you will just have to survive getting a college education in rural Illinois, so long as they're giving you a four-year scholarship. It's too bad, but that's just the way it is." Mama paused. "Sometimes, your soul looks back and wonders how you got over."

I'm thankful for the camaraderie I feel with the other 500 or so black students on this campus of 20,000. Most black folks speak to one another, whether we know each other or not. The few who don't are scorned as "Uncle Toms" by the rest of us.

I met a sistah named Sharlinda in the dorm bathroom. She had Noxzema all over her face. We nodded and introduced ourselves before I brushed my teeth. Then Sharlinda said that it was hard getting used to not seeing roaches running every which way when you turned on a light.

I could've turned my nose up and acted insulted. Just because I'm black doesn't automatically mean I'm acquainted with roaches, does it? But despite Mama's vigilant efforts, we keep us a few roaches in residence. Not to mention occasional mice and a rat every blue moon.

So, instead of copping an attitude, I laughed and said, "Girl, I know what you mean."

Sharlinda confided that she'd never slept between two sheets before in her life. She said it had taken her a whole week to figure out what the second sheet was for. I laughed and told her I could relate.

It seemed like by the time I'd rinsed the toothpaste out of my mouth, Sharlinda and I had become fast friends.

Sharlinda is cute and "healthy," not a size eight like me. She's light skinned with sharp features and curly hair that you could barely call a 'fro. You might think she was born to purple until she opened her mouth. Sharlinda talks like a stone sistah. She can butcher the king's English with the best of them. She was probably raised on a boot and a shoe.

Sharlinda grew up on the West Side of Chicago. I came up on the Southside. She says the West Side is the baddest side of town. I don't disagree with her.

I'm a journalism major. Sharlinda's major is undeclared. She's in the "Reach Out" program. Mama would say that they had to reach *way* out to let Sharlinda into somebody's college.

Mama seldom likes my friends, and I know she wouldn't approve of Sharlinda. She prefers seddity people and I don't. I like it that Sharlinda is funny and down-to-earth. I'm often drawn to people like her. Mama would say that's my downfall.

Anyway, it's nice having a friend to hang out with. Especially since I don't have a boyfriend yet. The competition for brothas is a little stiff because more than half of the black students are female. A few of the dudes have been checking me out, especially a handsome, clean-cut type named Myron. But so far nothing has materialized, just a couple of smiles and one long, lingering look in the campus bookstore. Maybe I'll give Myron some play soon. Blood seems nice, I just hope he isn't too square for me.

Yesterday, Sharlinda and I went shopping in town. I was nervous, but at least I wasn't alone. Besides, I knew I had to conquer my fear. There were almost no other black people in sight. We felt like aliens until we found this cool store run by hippies. Sharlinda bought a black light and a reefer pipe. That's how I know she smokes dope. I've still never even tried it. But I'm ready to.

I bought two posters for my room, one of a woman with a big rainbow Afro and another of a peace sign.

Speaking of peace, I marched in my first demonstration against the war last night. A few dudes even burned their draft cards. That's when the campus police ordered us to disperse. When we didn't disband fast enough, they sprayed us with tear gas. I hated that shit. My eyes and throat were burning all the way back to my dorm.

There was a long-haired photographer taking pictures at the demonstration. I told Sharlinda that I might end up in *Life* magazine. She said, I'd be more likely to wind up in a CIA file. That worried me a little. But Sharlinda said, "Don't trip. You're small potatoes, ain't like you're Bobby Seale or somebody."

Tonight, my roommate and I were interrupted from our studying by a big commotion outside. We stuck our heads out the window into the warm Indian-summer night to find out what the deal was. I thought it might be another antiwar demonstration.

But to my surprise, what I saw was as traditional as the Fourth of July. I'd heard about panty raids but I never thought I would actually witness one in 1971.

Girls were sliding the window screens open and panties were raining down on white boys' heads. They sniffed them like they were fresh-baked rolls.

They talk about us being wild, I thought. I swear, white folks are something else.

"I have half a mind to throw my funky drawers down there," I said aloud. I forgot I was talking to square-ass Barbara.

"Let's do it!" She smiled wickedly.

I was as surprised as if a nun had invited me to an orgy.

"Who knows? This may be the last panty raid. It's the end of an era." Barbara sighed. "This will at least give us something to tell our grandchildren."

"Yeah, we won't be able to say we were at Woodstock, but we can say we were in a panty raid."

"Well, it beats swallowing goldfish or stuffing yourself inside a phone booth."

"OK, let's go for it then." Barbara and I reached under our long nightshirts and pulled off our drawers.

We giggled as our panties, still warm from our body heat, were quickly snatched up.

2

Sharlinda and I were sitting up in the room of this girl named Today, waiting for her to come back from town. Today had gone to the Prairie Star Diner to apply for a job as a cashier. Last week we started this tradition of playing gin rummy and ordering out for pepperoni pizza on Thursday nights. None of us had Friday morning classes.

Sharlinda had gotten Today's roommate, Becky, who was working down at the desk, to let us inside the room. Becky and Today got along well enough to coordinate their room. They had matching red corduroy bedspreads and each had a stack of beer cans over her desk.

Today was more Sharlinda's friend than mine. They were both Kappa Kittens, little sisters of the black fraternity Kappa Alpha Psi.

"Damn, Today know it's Thursday night." Sharlinda dumped several albums on the bedspread.

"Maybe they're showing her how to use the cash register. You know it's Spaghetti Night at the Prairie Star Diner. The joint is probably jumping. They might have had to put her to work right on the spot."

"Whatever," Sharlinda muttered. She put Marvin Gaye's dynamite album on the box.

I shuffled the cards for Solitaire. Sharlinda stuck the other albums back in their stand.

"Girl, I didn't tell you I saw you over by the Union this morning," I said.

"How come you ain't say nothing?" Sharlinda opened the beige, vinyl-covered bolster over Today's bed. She pulled out a bottle of Boone's Farm and some paper cups.

"Sharlinda!" I raised my eyebrows.

"Today won't mind. You don't understand. We're both Kittens."

I decided not to trip. Sharlinda knew Today better than I did. Maybe she *would* understand. And hadn't Grandma always said, "People would rather buy you a drink than a sandwich?"

"Anyway, girl, you were making tracks so fast. I didn't want to yell out and sound all ignorant. You weren't late for a nine o'clock. Why were you booking like that?"

"I was rushing to get to my math class." Sharlinda handed me a paper cup full of wine. "We had a test today, girl."

It wasn't like Sharlinda to be racing to get to a class. A party yes, but not a class, and certainly not to take a test. I sipped my wine.

"Why were you breaking your neck to take a test?"

"I wasn't rushing to take a test, fool."

"Wait a minute." I demanded my propers. "You see a fool, you knock her down!"

"OK, sorry. Anyway, I was trying to get a good seat by this white girl whose paper I could cheat off of."

"Did you succeed?"

Sharlinda stretched her hand out for me to give her five.

"I had a bird's-eye view."

I slapped Sharlinda's hand. "You think you passed?"

"Sho, if she passed, I passed."

"The girl know you were cheating off of her?"

"She'd have to be a new kind of fool not to have known."

I picked up a card. "What if she'd gotten pissed off and covered up her paper? Then you'd 'a looked like a fool."

Sharlinda leaned back against the bolster.. "Look, the chick was cool. I cheated off of her once before and made a B. She knew what time it was. Miss Ann was hipped to what was happening."

"The instructor still could've caught you, girl."

Sharlinda gulped her wine. "Yeah, but he didn't, did he? Coulda-woulda-shoulda don't cut it, do it?"

I pointed toward the bedspread. "You spilled some wine." I was being careful sitting at the desk. I was raised not to sit on somebody's bed without being invited.

"The bedspread is red and the wine is red." Sharlinda rubbed the liquid into the corduroy fabric. "So, it ain't no biggie."

I glanced at the poster on Becky's wall advertising a Grateful Dead concert. "I'd rather study, myself. For one thing, I wouldn't want to give a white person the satisfaction of thinking that the only way I could get over was to cheat off of them." I looked back at my cards. "They probably think we're all dumb anyway. You just confirm their suspicions."

Sharlinda pushed up the sleeves of her school sweatshirt and folded her arms. It was a sure sign that she was getting pissed.

"Well, I would rather give them the satisfaction of helping some po' dumbass nigga get over, than my black ass not being able to pledge Delta next year. I have to bring my grade point up to a two point five."

The door swung open and Today dragged in, huffing and

puffing. She threw her heavy coat on the bed. Today was tall and striking with a vanilla-bean-colored complexion. She seemed neither surprised nor happy to see us. And she didn't appear fazed that we were drinking her wine.

"Well?" I asked searching Today's high-cheekboned face.

"Well, what?" she replied, changing out of her skirt and blouse.

"Did you get the job?"

"Yeah, did you get the gig?" Sharlinda asked.

"What y'all talking about?" Today asked, running her fingers through her short Afro.

"You know, the cashier job at the Prairie Star Diner," I answered in disbelief.

"What makes y'all think the Prairie Star Diner was hiring?"

"Today, the HELP WANTED sign was in the window just as big as day. No pun intended."

"Yeah, and you told me that you were on your way to town to apply," Sharlinda reminded her.

Today pulled on her T-shirt and zipped up her jeans. She glanced up at her poster of President Nixon sitting on the toilet.

"Ooh, that sign. 'Gertrude, didn't I tell you to take that sign out of the window, two days ago?' 'Oh, Ruth, I forgot.' " Today mimicked the white townies. " 'Why, the new girl starts Monday. Nice girl, too, from one of the Quad cities.' "

"Yeah, sure," I groaned.

"Yeah, like fun," Sharlinda rolled her eyes.

"But wait." Today held up her hand. "Y'all haven't heard the killer."

"What's that?" I asked.

"Pour me a taste while I tell you what the real killer is."

Sharlinda handed Today some wine and freshened our drinks.

"Honey, the real killer is, I had Becky call the diner from the desk a few minutes ago."

"No, you didn't, girl!" Sharlinda said.

"Girl, yes I did, too. And wait til you hear the stone killer."

"What's that?" I wanted to know. "The stone killer is the woman at the diner told Becky to come on down. The cashier job was still open."

"No she didn't!" Sharlinda shouted.

"Yes she did!" Today sipped her wine like it was a really good year, steada some cheap stuff.

"Umph, umph, umph," I shook my head.

"Well, then, Aunt Jemima, what took you so long?" Sharlinda teased.

"I'm gonna let that slide. Anyway I hit every store on the square to see if anybody was even thinking about hiring. I mean I pounded the hell out of the pavement, and ended up missing the last bus. I had to walk from town."

"You couldn't hitch a ride?" Sharlinda asked.

"I don't like to hitch by myself."

I nodded, I felt the same way. "Any luck, anywhere?"

"Not really. I made the mistake of going into Tumbleweed Liquors. And the guy behind the counter patted my butt as he handed me the application!"

"Did you give him a piece of your mind?" I asked, fuming.

"Did you go upside his head with one of them whiskey bottles?" Sharlinda hollered.

"No, but I read his behind from *A* to *Z*. And then he had the nerve to tell me that he was only a red-blooded American responding to a negress in heat!"

"A negress in heat!" Sharlinda screamed angrily.

"Check the calendar—is this man really saying 'negress' in 1971?" I marveled.

"Girl, if I hadn't seen the courthouse and the jailhouse out of the corner of my eye, I would've done serious damage to him. But then I would've just been another nigga behind bars. I didn't want to add to the country's black jail population."

"You need to go to the NAACP," I suggested. "I think the closest branch is in Peoria."

"Wow, Stevie, the NAACP, in Peoria, Illinois." Sharlinda rolled her eyes. "They will really scare somebody."

"Well, we should get people to boycott the Prairie Star Diner, then."

"This town is almost a hundred percent white. Our business is just a drop in their damn bucket." Today poured herself some more wine. "What do they care? They don't want us in the Prairie Star Diner, no way."

"They'd care if enough white students and professors joined in with us. If the newspaper supported us, we could make a difference then."

"Stevie, these white students ain't gonna get bent out of shape behind this. They done put civil rights on the back burner, chile. All they care about is smoking reefer, women's lib, and staying out of Vietnam."

Today nodded in agreement. I wish I had me a joint," she sighed. "Anybody got any weed?"

"Not me." I shrugged. When have you *ever* had any weed? I asked myself. I had yet to buy my first nickel bag. I was on a tight budget. Mama sent me spending money every week. But it barely covered the laundry, snacks, and the quarter movies they showed at the Student Union.

The real deal was, I'd only smoked dope a few times with Sharlinda. The truth be told, she'd taught me how to inhale. I liked it. It made me laugh. It made me horny. Unfortunately, it made me hungry. And I was almost a size ten now.

"I ain't got so much as a roach, and all my connections went to Chicago for the weekend already." Sharlinda sighed.

"Plus, my money is funny and my change is strange. Unless y'all want to forget about the pizza."

"No, I'm starving, after walking damn near two miles. Pour me another taste, girl."

"I'll pour all of us another taste." Sharlinda held up the half-empty bottle. "Let's kill this bad boy."

Today got up and turned the album over. "Let's order the doggone pizza—see if the line's free."

I was the closest to the phone. "I know the number by heart."

"Hello, hello." I didn't hear a dial tone. I wasn't surprised that someone was on the line, because we all had party lines. But I couldn't understand why nobody was talking. I just heard breathing.

"Hello. How come you're not saying anything?" There was no reply.

"They're not talking, just breathing."

"I'm sick of their shit!" Today shouted.

"You know who it is?" I asked.

"Damn straight. It's this hoogie down at the end of the hallway. They call themselves having an argument by just breathing on the phone, lately."

Hoogie was a word for white people, like *honky* and *peckawood*. Although hoogie usually referred to middle-class-white folks. I'd only heard it used by black students here on the Illinois prairie.

Sharlinda frowned. "This is some really tired-ass shit."

I decided to talk some sense into these people tying up the line.

"I need to use the phone. Please give up the line if you're not gonna talk." Now, who could resist that request. I'd been polite but firm. I listened for an apology or a click, but there was no response. I stared at the receiver in disbelief.

"This is beyond ridiculous!" Sharlinda yelled. "This is *rodiculous!*"

I hung up the phone.

"You should've *slammed* that mothafucka down!" Sharlinda shouted.

"Have you complained to your R.A.?" I asked.

"Yeah, and it hasn't done shit. I've had it up to here with these hoogies! Do you hear me? They've gotten on my last nerve. They think they own the whole damn world. The only one I can stand right now is Becky."

"Stevie, girl, you too nice, trying to reason with them and shit. 'Please give up the line if you're not gonna talk.' " Sharlinda mimicked. "You let these hoogies run all over you."

I gulped my wine. "Nobody runs over me."

"Yes they do, too. You can't even make a simple-ass phone call."

"Well, let's see if you have any better luck."

"OK." Sharlinda grabbed the receiver. "Hang the mothafucka up, if you ain't gonna talk. Goddamnit! You know this is a goddamn party line, shit!" Sharlinda yelled, leaving the receiver dangling from the wall.

"Well, if that don't work, nothing will," Today sighed.

I listened for a dial tone. "Sharlinda, looks like they're still breathing. You wanna go downstairs and call from the desk?"

"Hell no! I don't want to go downstairs and call from the goddamn desk! I have a constitutional right to use the mothafuckin' phone!"

"A constitutional right?" I laughed. "The telephone hadn't even been invented when the Constitution was written."

Sharlinda folded her arms and twisted her neck.

"The Constitution guarantees me the right to freedom of speech, goddamnit! These hoogies are interfering with my right to speak. And I'm gonna fight for my goddamn rights. Now, can I get a witness?"

Today waved her hand like they do in church.

"I think you might be stretching the Constitution a little bit far, myself," I said.

"Stevie, there you go, acting like a Libra. Well, you can't always see both sides," Sharlinda insisted. "Not if you've got soul."

"I've got plenty of soul, Ms. Leo," I shot back at Sharlinda. I picked up the phone. If I were lucky, I'd get a dial tone. And at least, I would appear tough. But instead, I heard the breathing again. "Now look, I'm gonna give y'all two minutes to get off this phone or else your ass is gonna be grass!"

I turned toward Sharlinda and Today, cradling the receiver in my hand. "How do you like me now?"

"Did you hear her? My girl went 'Chicago' on 'em. She got hipped to her constitutional rights, honey." Sharlinda and Today gave each other five.

"Sho did!" Today agreed. "She told 'em their ass is gonna be grass!"

"You see, Stevie might act all educated, but you better not fuck with her. They done made her show her color now. She's still a sistah from the Southside," Sharlinda bragged.

I prayed for a dial tone. I hoped that my mouth hadn't written a check that my behind couldn't cash.

Today grabbed the receiver. "Ain't this a blip! They *still* breathing."

"Stevie, you said they ass was gonna be grass," Sharlinda reminded me. "It's been two minutes and I still ain't heard no dial tone."

"OK!" I shouted into the phone. "You've left me no other choice. Now, your ass *is* grass!" I slammed down the phone.

"She's in Room Five Thirty-two," Today said calmly.

Sharlinda slapped my back, excitedly. "If you gon' kick some ass, let's go kick some ass!"

For some reason, I lacked Sharlinda's enthusiasm. "What about her boyfriend? What if he runs over here?"

"Fuck her boyfriend. We got boyfriends too," Sharlinda insisted. I knew that she was braiding Kenny's hair, but he hadn't asked her to go with him yet. And as for me, yeah, I'd gone to the quarter movie with Myron twice and he'd even paid. But we were technically still in the talking stage. He was at least three movies away from getting over. Maybe one, if he produced a joint. I didn't know Today's business. She seemed to be in love with anybody tall, dark, and Greek.

"Plus, we got the whole Kappa line," Today interrupted my thoughts.

Maybe so, but none of these people were here now. I gulped down the rest of my wine for strength. I crushed the waxy paper cup in my hand.

"OK, I'm ready." I stood up and headed for Room 532 with Sharlinda and Today at my heels.

My fist was raised to knock on the girl's door.

"What you fixin' to knock for?" Sharlinda groaned. "Would you invite somebody to come in your room who said they were gonna kick your ass? Just open the goddamn door!"

I dropped my hand and turned my head. "I just can't run up in the girl's room. It might be illegal or something."

"Yeah, this is a legal ass kicking," Today answered sarcastically.

"What if the door is locked?" I asked hopefully.

"Well, we can't stand here all night wondering. Let's get this show on the road!" Sharlinda reached in front of me and tried the doorknob. To my horror, the door swung open easily.

A stocky white girl stood planted with her back to us, holding the telephone. She was wearing a long denim work shirt and her head was wrapped up in a towel.

"That's right, it's all my fault! *You* had nothing to do with it!" she shouted in a French accent. "Everything is all my fucking fault!" Suddenly, the white girl turned and faced us. "Pardon me, but I'm utilizing the phone. What do you want here?"

We continued to stand in the doorway, but no one spoke.

The girl turned her attention back to the phone. "Matthew, you're nothing but a male chauvinist pig!" She slammed down the receiver.

I couldn't help but appreciate the way "chauvinist" had rolled off of her tongue. But this was no time to admire her French accent.

"Well, I guess she told him," Today whispered.

I shuddered to myself. Maybe this girl was tough. Perhaps she'd descended from peasant stock.

"You have no right barging into my room like this!"

Sharlinda nudged me. "She's got the nerve to jump bad, now."

I found my voice. "You had no right to tie up the phone like that. You know it's a party line."

"Look, I really don't have time for this shit."

"We don't have time for *your* shit, bitch!" Sharlinda shouted.

"You've been pulling that breathing routine for over two weeks now." Today sighed. "You need to quit."

"Look, I'm off the phone now. So, will you just go." She waved her arms like she was shooing away pigeons.

"Naw, Mademoiselle, we ain't going nowhere!" Sharlinda insisted.

"We're not?" I gulped.

"No, it's too late for her to grip." No, it's not, I wanted to protest. Let her beg, so we can leave.

"She should've gotten off the phone when homegirl first asked her to," Sharlinda continued. "Now, the shit done got funky."

Let's not get technical, I thought. "She's off the phone now," I argued. "Let's just order the damn pizza."

Today ignored me. "Didn't you hear her say your ass is grass?" Then she elbowed me. "Right, Stevie?"

"My ass is grass? Does that mean the three of you plan to attack me now?"

"Oh, no, just her," Sharlinda pointed.

"Don't worry, it's gonna be a fair fight," Today promised.

"This is crazy. Look, I'm not in the mood. So, please remove yourselves from my doorway at once."

I stood frozen.

"Oh, she's really selling woof tickets now," Sharlinda nudged me. "Your shit ain't shaky, is it, homegirl?"

"You can whup a hoogie," Today chimed in.

I appreciated her vote of confidence. But what if this white girl descended from a long line of grape stompers? People who'd just as soon stomp your ass as make wine. And what if she freaked out and called security and I was arrested? I might even lose my scholarship.

The girl walked toward us. I glanced into her killer blue eyes. It was obvious that she meant business. I sized her up as we faced off. We were about the same height, but she was quite a bit stockier. My stomach began to churn. My mouth felt dry. It would be just my luck for her to be a P.E. major, I thought.

Why wasn't this white girl acting scared? I'd never planned to hit her, just scare her. Why didn't she just grovel and get it over with? Did Sharlinda and Today expect me to just grab her and start hitting her? It had been years since I'd been in a knock-down drag-out fight. The situation suddenly seemed absurd. It would've almost been funny if I didn't feel my stomach tightening into knots.

The girl stared me down. "Move, so that I can close my door."

"Tell her to make you," Sharlinda snarled.

Miss Ann should be trembling, begging for mercy, pleading for us to accept her apology. Didn't she have sense enough to be afraid of three black girls with Afros? Didn't a person's color mean anything anymore? What planet was she from?

The girl reached for the doorknob. It felt like every hair on the back of my neck was standing up and saluting. It's funny how certain situations make you aware that you even *have* hair on the back of your neck.

"Tell her to make you!" Sharlinda repeated.

"Make me," I whined.

"No, make yourself!" The girl tossed her head back, the way white girls do. Her towel began to unravel.

"You came here to kick my ass. So, if you're going to kick my ass, then go ahead and kick it, if you think you can. Otherwise, move so I can close my door." The girl tossed her head again and the towel finally fell to the floor revealing shoulder-length black hair.

I stood glued to my spot. How could I back down without losing face? The girl picked up the towel and threw it on one of the beds. She sighed and reached for the doornob again. Did she dare try to move the door against me?

"Hey." Sharlinda held her hand up as Miss Ann reached around me. "Wait just one mothafuckin' minute. Don't I know you?" she asked.

"Yes, certainly," the girl shot back. She reached for her glasses on the dresser. I felt myself breathe again.

"You're in my math class!" Sharlinda exclaimed. "I didn't recognize you without your glasses."

I relaxed considerably and moved aside so Sharlinda and the girl had plenty of room to inspect each other.

"So, she's in your math class. What's that got to do with the price of neck bones?" Today wanted to know. "What does that make y'all, long-lost cousins?"

"This chick was kind enough to let me copy off of her paper this morning," Sharlinda smiled, lounging against the dresser.

Now the girl was blushing.

"You cheated off of her?"

I was pleased that Sharlinda's dishonesty had paid off. Otherwise I would've had to hurt Miss Ann.

"If it hadn't been for her," Sharlinda said smiling, "I don't know how I would've got over."

"Well," the girl replied. "I'm not so sure I did very well on the test."

"Hey, don't sweat it. Last time we got a B.

"I recall *we* did, didn't *we?*"

"In class, we go by last names, but my first name is Sharlinda."

"I'm Celeste."

"Celeste, this here is Stevie, the one who was gonna kick yo' ass. Her real name is Jean Stevenson, but everybody calls her Stevie." Celeste and I nodded. "And this is Today, she's got a twin sister back home in Maywood, named Tamara. Dig up, they were born a few minutes apart. But one was born one day and the other was born the next. That's how come they're To-day and Tamara.

"Anyway, we just wanted to order a pizza and I guess one thing led to another. I just had no idea it was you."

Celeste made a sheepish face. "Well, I know I haven't been appropriate about the phone."

That's an understatement, I thought.

"But things have been alarming between me and my boy-friend lately."

"I know how that can be," Sharlinda nodded. I rolled my eyes. All of a sudden now, she's Miss Congeniality.

"Hey, you don't mind if I check your phone line to see if it's free, do ya?" Today asked politely. "You know at night the lines stay jammed. We still have to order our pizza."

"Sure, go ahead, help yourself. The phone book's right there.

A passerby shouted "Hi, Celeste" from the hallway. The girl noticed us and did a double take. I figured Celeste had earned several "cool points." People would be saying she had joined some militant black organization with French connections.

"Why don't all of you have a seat, make yourselves com-fortable?"

I looked up at the turquoise fishnet decorating the opposite wall. Today leaned back against one of the bolsters.

"The line's free," she announced happily.

"You don't need the phone book." I rattled off the number.

Today held up some Zig Zag papers that had been lying on top of the bolster.

"Celeste, you don't happen to have any weed?" she asked sweetly.

Celeste shrugged from the opposite bed. "Just homegrown."

"Hey, beggars can't be choosers," Sharlinda said, sitting down next to Celeste.

"I can get into some homegrown," Today agreed.

"Hey, it's cool with me," I said, nonchalantly. "Can't always be Mexican or Jamaican or Colombian." I shrugged, impressed with my own hipness.

Life was now beautiful. The black light was on, magnifying every little speck of dust. We were digging the Woodstock album. Celeste was rolling a couple of joints. And the door was closed with a towel stuffed under it. This was more of a ritual, just part of being cool. We weren't really worried about getting busted.

Today called down to the desk and told Becky to have the pizza guy ring Celeste's room when he came. I was groovin' on the psychedelic poster of Jimi Hendrix while he played on the box. Then a poster of Angela Davis over one of the desks caught my eye. Maybe Celeste's roommate was a sister we hadn't heard of, I thought. "Is that your roommate's poster?" I pointed.

"It's mine," Celeste answered casually, licking the ends of the freshly rolled joint.

"Angela Davis, right on." Today nodded approvingly.

Celeste passed Sharlinda the joint. "You sho' know how to roll. I likes 'em fat."

"Yeah, California style." Today smiled. "None of those skinny New York joints."

"My joints always come out like that. I wasn't even trying to roll them any special way."

"New York stuff be thin, they stingy with they pizza crust,

they reefer, and the city still on the verge of bankruptcy." Sharlinda sighed.

She exhaled and passed the joint to me. I sucked in the weed and tried not to cough. I took it in sucking air, the way Sharlinda had taught me. I blew out the smoke big time.

"Celeste, don't you want a toke?" I asked, proud of my drug vocabulary.

To my surprise, she shook her head. "I'm taking a holiday from it for a while."

I handed the joint to Today. "For me, this is just what the doctor ordered. Let me lay my burdens down."

"This is some good shit for homegrown. Celeste, you sure you don't want none?"

"Yeah, I'm cool."

Sharlinda hit the joint. "I've already got a little bit of a buzz, y'all."

I took another hit and felt it go to my head. Why didn't Celeste want to get high? It was awfully strange. What if she's a narc? She could be undercover. What if that wasn't a black light? What if it was really a hidden camera? What if we were being photographed? We didn't know where she was coming from. We didn't know this girl from Lassie.

"There's really a mellow vibe in here, now." Sharlinda smiled, her eyes shining.

"Thanks," Celeste said as she turned the album over.

Sharlinda pointed to the box. "I digs that album."

"Yeah, I'm digging it too," Today added. "Thanks for hipping us to it."

"Celeste, what's your major?" You're not in law enforcement, are you? I thought.

"I'm an art major." She pointed to a small sculpture of a naked woman on the desk.

"That's beautiful," I breathed.

"Do you do men?" Sharlinda wanted to know.

"Yeah," Today echoed.

She and Sharlinda laughed and gave each other five.

Celeste shook her head. "Actually, I find the female form more beautiful."

"Well, to each his own, said the woman who kissed the cow," Sharlinda said, shaking her head.

I found Celeste's answer intriguing. I remembered I used to sneak and look at my father's *Playboy* magazines as a child. It wasn't that the half-naked women were so tantalizing, but it was the only nudity available. Except for this boy named Leroy who used to show us his dick on the way to school in the second grade. But there was always a crowd around him, so you couldn't get a really good look.

Sharlinda asked Today to give her a shotgun. Today turned the joint backward inside her mouth. She held it between her teeth and blew smoke out through the other end into Sharlinda's mouth. I wanted to learn how to do that.

"Celeste, did it bother you to have Sharlinda cheating off of you?" I asked.

Celeste looked surprised, and Sharlinda choked on her inhale.

"Stevie can't help herself. She's a journalism major." Sharlinda rolled her eyes. "She interviews everybody."

Celeste cleared her throat. "I think a more pertinent question is, Did it bother Sharlinda?"

Sharlinda took a long hit off of the joint. "Sharlinda is feeling no pain, y'all."

"Sharlinda, you might not graduate magna cum laude. But you can make it without cheating," I assured her.

"Girl, Sharlinda will do well to graduate, 'laude' have mercy!" Today said.

We laughed and I gave Today five. Even Sharlinda cracked a smile.

"Look, all kidding aside," I said with a drawl (I was a little high), "I have faith in Sharlinda."

"You know what I got faith in?" Sharlinda tilted her head. "I got faith in her. I got faith she pulled a B on that test, maybe even an A. That's what I got faith in."

"Hey, don't put your faith in me. I'm no brain or anything," Celeste said.

"You say you ain't Chinese, huh?" Sharlinda laughed.

I felt uncomfortable. It was embarrassing enough to sit there and listen to Sharlinda put so much faith in a white person. Hadn't I made the Dean's List my first quarter? And Today was no dummy; she was majoring in business administration. Now, Sharlinda had to throw in that remark about Celeste not being Chinese.

Today was quiet. She put the roach between two matchsticks and handed it to me. I managed to inhale without burning my mouth.

I exhaled and found my voice. "Sharlinda, you're stereotyping Chinese people, just like people stereotype black people."

"Thank you," Celeste spoke up. "I'm glad you said that."

"Stevie, you tripping. I was just making a joke."

"Stevie does have a point," Today said.

"Whatever." Sharlinda sighed, reaching for the second joint.

"Look, I didn't do jack shit in school, back in Paris," Celeste said.

"I love April in Paris." Sharlinda cut in.

"You know Paris?"

Today and I came to attention. Sharlinda better not twist her mouth and say she's been to Paris, I thought. Not unless there's a Paris, Mississippi, or something.

"No."

"You mean the song?" Today asked.

"I'm talking about the perfume, y'all."

I shook my head. "Sharlinda, you're not ready."

"She's not ready for what?" Celeste asked.

"Not ready for prime time," Today laughed.

Celeste still looked confused. It was an insiders' remark. It meant that Sharlinda wasn't ready for proper, white society. I was too high to try to explain it to Celeste. And not high enough to give a white person I barely knew insider information.

"Anyway, Celeste, you were saying?"

"I was saying?" Celeste gave me a puzzled look.

"About not doing jack shit in school," I reminded her.

"Oh, yes, well, when I came here to the States, I decided to make a fresh start. I just began applying myself. I don't have any magic formula. If you'd like, we could study together, Sharlinda."

"What have you got to lose?" I asked.

"Yeah," Today agreed. "Worse come to worst, you can always fall back on cheating."

Sharlinda gave her a fake smile.

"Think how much better you'll feel if you get an *A* or *B* on your own," I said.

"Yeah," Celeste agreed.

"Girl, you know you need to bring your grade point up if you want to pledge," Today reminded her.

"OK, OK, goddamn. Y'all ain't got to run it into the damn ground. I'll do whatever y'all say. Just get off my case!"

The telephone rang and Celeste picked it up.

"Finally, well, it's about time. I'd just about given up on you."

"The pizza's here?" Today asked hopefully.

Celeste put her hand over the receiver. "I'm getting married!" Celeste looked all happy, like she'd gotten a contact from the dope we'd been smoking. We stared at her with our mouths open.

"The pizza man proposed to you?" Sharlinda asked.

"No, it's Matthew. He finally agreed that we should get married. That's what we've been battling about."

"Why you want to get married?" Today asked.

"Y'all ain't gonna live together first?" Sharlinda sounded disappointed.

Celeste shook her head and patted her stomach. "I'm almost eight weeks pregnant."

"Eight weeks pregnant!" Sharlinda shouted.

"You're pregnant?" I echoed with surprise.

Celeste nodded.

"Damn, Stevie," Sharlinda groaned. "You was fixin' to jump on a pregnant lady!"

Ain't this a blip, I thought. Like she wasn't the main instigator. "I didn't know she was pregnant, Dodo-brain."

"Would it have really mattered?" Sharlinda asked.

"Yes," I snapped.

"Look, you guys, I'm just so excited. We're going to sign up for married housing. It's gonna be so fantastic!"

"Congratulations, yeah, congratulations," we said with a reasonable amount of enthusiasm. I mean, it *would've* been cooler if they were going to live together.

Celeste talked to Matthew a few more minutes, and hung up the phone. "You know, you should do natural childbirth," I suggested. "I mean you oughta have the breathing down pat by now," I winked, "after all that panting into the phone."

Everyone couldn't help but crack up, even Celeste. I smiled. I didn't joke with someone unless I liked them.

The telephone rang again and Today answered it. "Good, it's about damn time. I've got the munchies bad. We'll be right down."

"Celeste, want us to stop by and bring you a piece of pizza on the way back?" I offered.

After all, we'd smoked the girl's weed. Not to mention that I'd almost kicked her ass. The least we could do was feed her.

"Remember, you're eating for two now," Sharlinda cut in.

"Oh, no, thanks, you guys, I'm too psyched to eat right now."

Today fingered what was left of the nickel bag.

"Now that you're having a baby you might not want this weed around."

"Yeah," Sharlinda agreed. "It might be too much of a temptation."

"Oh, you guys can have it," Celeste smiled.

"Thanks. Hey, I'm glad we gave peace a chance," Today said.

"Yeah, me too." Sharlinda made a V with her fingers. "Peace, y'all."

We all held up our fingers. And we all said "Peace" with Woodstock playing in the background.

3

Skip to the beginning of our senior year. Dudes had come and gone, pounds had been gained and lost, naps had been straightened, but Sharlinda, Today, and I had remained tight. We'd rented a car and driven to Galesburg to see *Jesus Christ Superstar* and to Peoria to see *The Exorcist.*

Sharlinda and Today had both pledged Delta Sigma Theta. Sharlinda had gotten tutoring through the Reach Out program and had maintained a C average. She and Today worked together in the dorm cafeteria. I had a job in the campus bookstore.

Celeste had become one of our hanging buddies. We'd even taught her how to play a mean game of Bid Whist. One night Celeste looked up from her hand and shouted, "I can't let a three walk!" And she proceeded to take the bid with a downtown four, coming in clubs.

"We ran a Boston on their rumps!" Celeste shouted when she and I won the last book. We gave each other five. Running a Boston was like pitching a no-hitter.

In case you're wondering, Matthew turned out to be jive. He got cold feet and Celeste ended up going to New York City and having an abortion. Abortion had been illegal in Illinois at the time. I had mixed feelings about it. I would've hated to have to make the decision myself. That's one reason I insisted on rubbers in addition to my diaphragm the times I've done it. I'm scared of the pill and the IUD. Ultimately, I feel the decision to end an unwanted pregnancy belongs to the woman. So, I guess you could say I'm pro-choice.

Celeste is convinced now that most men are chauvinist pigs. She wears a big ERA button, even on her nightshirt. I went with Celeste down to Springfield when the Equal Rights Amendment came up for a vote in the Illinois legislature. It went down in defeat. I was disappointed, since I do consider myself a feminist. But I didn't break down and cry like a bunch of white women did. I've been black too long to trip that hard on the ERA.

Today is all for women's rights so long as men and women won't have to use the same bathrooms. Even Mama supports equal pay for equal work. Sharlinda says she can't get behind the ERA, because she still expects men to pay on dates. Grandma insists black women want to be white women and white women want to be white men.

When Sharlinda and Today broke it to me that they planned to become roommates for senior year, I'd asked Celeste if she wanted to be my roomie. She'd answered, "Very much so."

In the back of my mind, I was thinking Celeste would be a good person to finally confide in about my interest in women. After all, I'd personally sold her a copy of *Our Bodies Ourselves* by the Boston Women's Health Collective. And I bet I wasn't the only one who read the section "In Amerika They Call Us Dykes."

"Stevie, it's natural to notice attractive women, just like it's natural to appreciate beautiful works of art."

That's what Celeste said when I confessed to her that sometimes I checked out women more than men. Celeste should know because she's an artist and besides, she's French. You would expect her to be more sophisticated than most other people, now wouldn't you?

Celeste said the fact that I'd done the do with three dudes, a total of fifteen times and had never come, didn't mean diddly-squat. (She'd picked up some black slang from her hanging buddies.)

"Plenty of women don't really get into sex until they're in their thirties," she'd explained. I was only twenty-one, so there was still time.

I was lucky to have Celeste. Sharlinda and Today were cool, but I couldn't talk to them about my fears around my sexuality. I suppose you could say I had the best of both worlds. I had my "sistahs" to hang out with and Celeste to get deep with.

But I don't want you to think that I am living in a utopia or anything. This place is still over 95 percent white. And although it *is* 1975 and people are usually cordial, at times you can still feel the racial tension. When floor mates chip in to buy a keg of beer for a party on a Saturday night, black folks, including me, might give fifty cents, but we have no intention of partying with them. Hey, not everybody wants to be around a bunch of no-dancing white folks chugging beer and blasting "Bye Bye Miss American Pie" over and over. Especially not last night when our floor kegger conflicted with the black fraternity Omega Psi Phi's (commonly known as the Q's) pledge party. Even though I'm not in a sorority—I am a GDI (God Damn

Independent)—I still dance at every set. (Black folks on the Illinois prairie call parties "sets." And if you dress up we call it "jumpin' clean" or "gettin' clean". And like I told you before, white folks, "hoogies." If you're dating a white person, we refer to you as "going Greyhound" or simply "riding the bus.")

The morning after the floor party, I was sitting on my bed listening to War on my eight-track player. The door was cracked open, but I still didn't appreciate Kelly barging in without knocking.

"Stevie, where's your floor spirit?" the Resident Assistant demanded in an anguished tone. Her baby face was contorted as she twisted her ponytail.

"How are we ever going to come together if you people keep segregating yourselves?" She continued before I could respond. I knew that Kelly was referring to my not showing up last night. I was the only black girl on the floor, so my absence had been conspicuous. But what about the hippies down the hall? I was sure K.C. and Feather hadn't attended the party either. And Celeste had gone to visit friends in St. Louis, but nobody asked about her. I resented Kelly being up in my face now. It's not like she really cared about me. Kelly was just a rah-rah type. All she was tripping on was some phony-ass floor spirit. She didn't understand my dilemma. Black people would think I had a hole in my soul if I chose my floor party over something sponsored by one of the black fraternities or sororities on campus.

"Turn that nigger music off!" a male voice down the hall shouted as War sang "The World Is a Ghetto."

"Does that answer your question?" I asked. Kelly's pudgy face got all red and she looked like she didn't know what to say. I just asked her to kindly close my door on her way out.

So, you see, being black down here is a potato salad short

of a picnic. I've even had to put up with overhearing a store clerk whisper loudly in the five-and-dime, "You've gotta watch them, they'll steal anything that's not nailed down." It doesn't matter that I've never stolen anything in my whole life. And that I know white girls in my dorm who steal the place blind. Who cares, I'm black and I swear that's all most people ever see.

Like when I was in the grocery store last week and this white woman looked at me and reminded her friend not to leave her purse in the shopping cart. Now that was good advice, but would she have said it if she hadn't looked up and seen me? I doubt it.

Despite experiences like that, I still try to see this place in balance. I'm a Libra, what can I say? I've had both positive and negative things happen. I've met good and bad people, both black and white. And although I'm a card-carrying member of the Black Student Association, I also value my friendship with Celeste.

The most militant black person, high on weed, might admit that not all hoogies are bad. But a close friendship between a black person and a white person is still pretty rare, and perhaps even suspect. Yet, little by little, Celeste and I have become just that, close friends.

It was interesting when we compared our lives, my childhood as the oldest of three on the South Side of Chicago, and her growing up an only child in Neuilly, a Paris suburb. We advised each other about clothes, classes, and dates. She's even dragged me to some foreign films. Now, I've grown to prefer them.

After Celeste and I became tight, most of the other white girls on our floor pretty much ignored her. Only the hippies ever come in our room. Celeste sometimes finds herself eating alone in the cafeteria. Sharlinda and Today serve food during most of the dinner hour. And I almost always eat at the "black table." I occasionally eat with Celeste and the white hippies. And sometimes I've even brought Celeste to the black table. But I've been careful not to wear out Celeste's welcome. It's an unwritten rule that you can't bring a white person to the black table one time too many. Nobody said how many times were too many.

One evening, I came straight to dinner from a newspaper meeting. I was taken aback when I saw Celeste sitting at the black table! All eyes were on me when I sat down. I barely acknowledged Celeste's cheery "Hello." I imagined what the six other sistahs and brothas were thinking. How dare this hoogie come to the black table unescorted? The mashed potatoes tasted like glue, yet I managed to mumble through them, "Celeste, I didn't tell you to meet me here."

Celeste looked confused. I ignored the hurt in her dark eyes. Instead, I concentrated on the collective sigh of relief I was hearing from the brothas and sistahs at the table. I imagined that they were thinking, Stevie pulled the white chick's coattails. Stevie's cool. We can count on her not to let that hoogie get out of hand.

Back in our room, Celeste and I sat across from each other on our matching turquoise bedspreads in silence. How could I explain to her the politics around the black table?

"Celeste, can't you understand why it was more important for me to be cool than to show my real feelings?" I pleaded.

Instead of nodding, Celeste burst into tears. I couldn't help but feel bad. But it wasn't my fault things were the way they were.

"Why can't we all just love one another?" Celeste whimpered.

"I do love you, Celeste," I heard myself say.

I walked over to her and sat down beside her.

"I love you too," Celeste said.

I wiped her tears away with my hand. "I'm sorry, Celeste. I'm sorry I hurt your feelings."

Celeste whispered in her French accent, "What I'll remember most about America is you, and San Francisco."

Celeste's words were still echoing in my ears a couple days later when Today, Sharlinda, and I were deciding where to go to celebrate our graduation. We were all getting money as gifts from our families. I suggested San Francisco. Today had an aunt in Oakland, and Sharlinda was dying to ride the cable cars. So it was settled.

Graduation was just around the corner, and I was excited about getting out there in the real world. My mother and father and grandmother were all thrilled about my graduating. I was proud to be the first one on both sides of my family to get a college degree. My brother David was a sophomore at Iowa State on a basketball scholarship. And my other brother, Kevin, was about to graduate from high school, with no plans in sight.

Overall, I couldn't wait to get out of the sticks. But I still had mixed feelings. Sure, I'd encountered racism, but I'd also made the Dean's List twice, been Features Editor of the school newspaper, acted in *Purlie*, developed friendships, dated, hitchhiked, learned to give great shotguns, and partied hardy. And I would miss the abundance of stars in the night sky, the train's whistle, and the sound of crickets.

Celeste and I spent the night before graduation together. We were both between boyfriends. We sat on my bed and got high on reefer like we'd done on other special occasions.

Carly Simon's song "Anticipation" played on the stereo. By the time Celeste turned the album over, I felt high as a kite and seriously horny. I asked her if the French French-kissed differently than the Americans. Celeste laughed and told me she would be happy to demonstrate and I could be the judge.

"OK," I agreed, my heart pounding.

I felt scared and excited about the prospect of kissing Celeste. I was in the mood to be daring. What the fudge, I was twenty-one and graduating.

Celeste wasted no time in plunging her lips onto mine. I felt my body tingle as I tasted her tongue. I kissed back, and my heart suddenly felt open and full. Our lips finally parted. I gazed into her midnight-blue eyes. Wasn't it natural to have warm feelings for Celeste? She wasn't a lesbian, she was just my friend. And being high had just made me want to be closer to her.

Celeste interrupted my thoughts. "Let's push our beds together," she suggested.

I couldn't help but raise my eyebrows. "Huh?" I asked, unsure of what Celeste had in mind.

"It's our last night together. I just want to be close to you, that's all."

"OK," I agreed, thinking about how much I'd miss Celeste after she returned to France and I went back to Chicago.

We were lying side by side in the dark in our nightshirts. I was wearing panties, unlike Celeste. She seldom wore panties; she didn't believe in them. I was barely breathing, even though we weren't touching.

"We should've pushed our beds together a long time ago," Celeste giggled.

Suddenly, I felt her bare toes against mine. I froze as her flat, cold foot rubbed against my ankle. I was afraid that Celeste's foot might go too far. Don't be ridiculous, I told myself, she's not that way. The weed is just making you paranoid. I decided to breathe.

"Your foot is cold," I complained, trying to hide the fact that Celeste's toes were beginning to make my body tingle.

Celeste withdrew her foot. "I'm sorry," she apologized.

Now you made her feel bad, I told myself. Why are you pretending you didn't like having your foot touched? You're only human. You need affection just like anybody else. And what could be more innocent than playing footsies? So, just relax. Quit making everything sexual.

"Celeste"—I swallowed—"give me your foot, I'll warm it up."

I bravely rubbed my toes against Celeste's foot until we both felt warm.

"We've got a big day tommorrow. We'd better get some sleep," I said, turning over on my side. "Good night."

"Thanks, Mademoiselle."

"You're most welcome."

"Sweet dreams," Celeste mumbled.

Graduation itself had been rather boring. The best part was grinning with my parents, grandmother, and brothers afterward.

"I do declare," Grandma exclaimed, after posing for a picture with me holding my diploma. "I dare you to mention a subject now that Jean doesn't know something about. I dare you," she repeated while the rest of us laughed. I knew enough to know that I had a lot to learn about life that wasn't in a book.

My parents beamed when I introduced them to Sharlinda and Today in their black caps and gowns. I was also excited to see Celeste when she waved her cap with a peace symbol on it. But I decided not to subject her to Mama's scrutiny when I noticed the raggedy jeans sticking out from underneath her gown and her worn, Indian-style sandals. When Celeste starting walking toward us, I knew I had to head her off.

Celeste hugged me and groaned. "Graduation was so fucking boring! I wished I'd had a joint." I was glad that my family wasn't within earshot. Celeste and I hugged each other goodbye with tears in our eyes. We'd already exchanged addresses and promised to keep in touch.

"Think of me when you're in San Francisco. Say 'hello' to the Golden Gate Bridge."

"Think of me when you're back in Paris. Tell the Eiffel Tower I said 'hello.' "

I'd been offered a job with a newspaper in Monmouth, Illinois, but I'd postponed my decision until after my trip. Who could think about Monmouth, Illinois, when they were planning a trip to San Francisco!

In the meantime, reality had set in within the walls of our caramel-colored bungalow back in Chicago. My bedroom had never looked smaller. And Mama, who was only pushing forty-five, looked tired. Her job as a bank loan representative had once been a source of pride. But now she dragged in from work like an old cleaning woman. My father had gone from being a janitor at the hospital to a clerk at the post office. He occasionally complained about the pressures of the job, but most nights he just sat in front of the TV and drank beer until he fell asleep.

I couldn't get over my little brother Kevin coming in at two in the morning, smelling like reefer with his cute, baby-faced self. Kevin had the nerve to call himself a player. He seemed only to want to party and have a funky good time. I could hardly use the phone to plan my trip because he was always on it, talking to one of his fast girlfriends. But if nothing else, Mama was proud because at least Kevin didn't go for white. All the pinups on his bedroom wall were black.

"Kevin doesn't even go for light," Mama had marveled. "Every girl he's introduced me to has been brown-skinned, not a high-yellow one in the bunch. The only thing a white girl can do for Kevin is tell him which way a black one went," she'd said proudly at the coffee hour after church this morning. Mama's words soothed every woman in earshot who worried that white women were taking all of the good black men.

After church I followed David into our dark, cool basement. He had to duck his head going down the stairs. It was a relief to be out of the blazing hot sun. David and Daddy had built him a room down here. It had a door and everything. David called it the cave. I thought that was an appropriate name for the hideout full of dirty clothes, record albums, and empty beer cans. I suppose it looked all right when David turned on his black light and you noticed every speck of dust glowing in the dark instead of the clutter.

I'd just finished telling David about Mama bragging on Kevin at coffee hour.

"It's easy for Kevin, he's not a basketball player surrounded by white girls smiling in his face like I am at Iowa State," David said, sipping a beer.

I nodded as I looked for a place to sit down. I threw David's old funky sweatshirt on the bed and settled into the old beanbag chair.

"Kevin's not under the kind of pressure I'm up against," David continued.

"Poor baby. All those white girls grinning up in your face. It must be hard." I pretended to play a violin. "What's a brother to do?"

"Come on, Jean," David whined. "Cut me some slack." He tossed me a can of beer.

"David, you know I'm not gonna really bring out the violins for you." I popped open the cold can. "There are too many sistahs sitting home alone on Saturday nights."

David pulled an album from the rack. "This is in your honor, Stevie."

David played Santana's *Black Magic Woman* on the stereo.

"Whoopey do do," I answered sarcastically, between sips.

David turned on his red lava lamp. "How's this for atmosphere?"

My eyes were drawn to the flow of the red mixture inside the lamp. A person could be hypnotized by it.

"Stevie, didn't you ever cross over in your four years at college?"

I shrugged my shoulders. "I went on a few dates with a couple of white dudes." I remembered Jeremy on the school newspaper. He was a stone hippie, love beads and the whole bit. We'd seen *Easy Rider* at the Student Union together. Afterward we'd hugged. I liked Jeremy, but he wasn't big on soap and water. He was overdrawn at the funk bank. So, I'd turned my attention toward a brother named Skylar.

"Did you ever kiss one?"

I remembered Daniel, this white dude I'd gone to dinner with while traveling with the debate team. Outside my hotel room, Daniel had pressed me against the wall and forced his tongue inside my mouth. I had to fight to get away from him. Daniel hadn't kissed me, he'd attacked me.

"No," I answered. Then I remembered my French kiss with Celeste. But that didn't count because she wasn't a man.

"Would you ever be involved with a white dude?"

"I don't know, it would all depend on how I felt."

"I heard that. Let's get high with my bong. I've got some dynamite weed, Jamaican."

My eyebrows shot up. "David, you get high down here?"

He nodded, producing a wide glass tube.

"Mama and Daddy would kill you if they knew."

"Look, Mama and Dad have their own problems. They're tired and worn out. All they want is a little peace these days. They don't look for things to get upset about. Hey, as long as I burn some incense and stuff some towels underneath the door, everything is cool."

"You don't think they suspect?"

"Sometimes people see what they want to see."

"Yeah, that's true," I agreed. "You know, bro, I don't want to end up like them."

"I don't want to end up miserable either."

"I appreciate all the sacrifices they've made. But it's like I never remember them *ever* being happy," I added.

David sighed as he went to fill the bong with water.

4

The night before our trip, I was almost too excited to fall asleep. Sharlinda, Today, and I had looked over the brochures and finally agreed on a small, romantic-looking hotel that was supposed to be a stone's throw away from Nob Hill. I was enchanted by the fog, cable cars, steep hills, and Victorian houses that I read about in my tour guide. I imagined San Francisco to be more like a foreign city than an American one.

Sharlinda, Today, and I cheered as our 747 took off under partly cloudy skies. I said a prayer as we rose high above Chicago. I was nervous. I'd only flown a few times with the debate team. And we'd encountered turbulence on our trip to D.C. last year. I didn't even mind that Sharlinda had talked us into letting her have the window. I was sitting on the aisle, but that was OK. I'd get to see plenty, once I got to San Francisco.

We'd already planned a deluxe bus tour tomorrow that would include Chinatown, Twin Peaks, Golden Gate Park, Fisherman's Wharf, you name it. Sharlinda wanted to go to Alcatraz Island and see the prison where Al Capone and the Bird Man of Alcatraz had served time. But Today and I thought it would be too depressing. I said I'd rather see the giant redwoods, and

Today was more interested in walking across the Golden Gate Bridge. Too bad we weren't rich, 'cause then we could go down the coast to Monterey and Carmel. I'd wanted to go there ever since I'd seen the Clint Eastwood movie *Play Misty for Me*. I also wished we could afford to go wine tasting in the Napa Valley. I had champagne tastes; too bad I was on a beer budget.

"Honey, you need to put your seat in its upright position for landing." The stewardess' soft, husky, southern accent interrupted my thoughts. I looked into the face of a sistah. It was nice to see a black stewardess in the friendly skies. Her rich color reminded me of the inside of a chocolate truffle. Celeste had given me one from her box of Valentine's candy last February.

"Sorry," I said, "I forgot." I felt embarrassed that I might have made this sistah's job more difficult. But I didn't regret the opportunity to look into her soft brown eyes.

"You don't have to be sorry." She patted my shoulder reassuringly. "It's my job to keep you safe." I moved my chair up, but I hated to see the stewardess go. In those few seconds, she really made me feel taken care of. I caught myself checking out her sleek figure as she moved gracefully down the aisle.

"Look at the sunset. It's beautiful," Sharlinda exclaimed as our plane descended over the San Francisco Bay Area.

"Yeah, it's gorgeous," I agreed, craning my neck to see the hills and water and sky tinged in shades of orange.

"Enjoy your stay in San Francisco." A blonde stewardess smiled at the front of the plane as we exited. I thanked her, but I was disappointed not to be able to say good-bye to the sistah.

Suddenly, I heard her velvety voice. "Is the Bay Area your home, or are you visiting?"

"We're on vacation."

"Well, have fun."

"Thank you," I smiled.

"Stevie, you haven't heard a thing I've said, have you?"

"Huh?" I asked Today.

"I was asking you what I should wear Saturday night. Remember, we're going out with my cousin Brian and two of his friends."

I felt ashamed that I had been grinning up in the stewardess' face when Today was nice enough to have set up a hot date for me.

"I'll help you pick out something to wear when we get to the hotel," I promised.

"What about you, Stevie?" Sharlinda asked as we walked through the terminal. "What are you going to wear?"

"I don't know," I answered. But I realized that I hadn't even given it a minute's thought.

The hotel was a disappointment. It was old and plain. The creaky elevator took forever to get from the first floor to the third, and the hallways were a dingy yellow.

"It sho' ain't the Ritz," Sharlinda said as we walked into a nondescript room with gold draperies and brown plaid bedspreads that looked straight out of the fifties. The canvas cot could've come from an army surplus store.

I plopped into a chair. "Well, how much time did you plan to spend in the hotel room anyway? I mean, I came to see San Francisco."

Today and Sharlinda each sat on a bed. Surely they didn't think I was going to sleep on the cot for a week. I looked around the room at the small dresser and chest of drawers. I hoped there would be enough space for all of our stuff. It was suddenly important to me to stake out my territory.

"Let's see if we even have a view." Today sighed, jumped up and peeked through the draperies.

"Well? So, do we?" Sharlinda asked while I counted the drawers in the dresser.

"Yeah," Today answered. "We have a view of the side of a tall building."

"I want a damn refund!" Sharlinda shouted. "Everybody is supposed to have a damn view in this town. Today, how did your aunt steer us to this dump?"

"Remember we're on a tight budget," I said, not wanting Today to feel bad about her aunt. We were already here; we might as well make the best of it.

"Yeah, it was this place or the YWCA. At least here, we have a private bathroom," Today reminded Sharlinda.

"Yeah, but how can we go back and hold our heads up if we didn't even have a view. What are we going to tell people in our postcards?" Sharlinda wanted to know.

"I don't know about y'all, but when Miss Thing finishes describing this place, folks will swear we were at the Mark Hopkins, up on Nob Hill, honey," Today laughed.

"Well, I just hope this bad boy don't have no roaches. Then I can share your fantasy," Sharlinda smiled.

"We're taking turns sleeping on the cot. So don't you all get too comfortable," I warned, getting up to unpack.

The Deluxe City Bus Tour had kicked my behind. We'd gone some of everywhere: Chinatown, Golden Gate Park, and Twin Peaks. The next day we rode a ferryboat over to Sausalito and bought souvenirs. On Thursday, Today visited with her aunt over in Oakland. Sharlinda and I rode the cable cars out to Fisherman's Wharf. And today we took a bus tour over to Muir Woods in Marin County. The giant redwood trees were spectacular. It had been an exciting week. Tomorrow we were hooking up with Today's cousin Brian and two of his friends for a night on the town. Come Sunday, we'd fly home.

I knew that Today was self-conscious about the ten pounds she wanted to lose. But in my opinion, wearing a tight skirt that looked like it had been painted on drew even more attention to her weight. The bottom line was, we were all in competition. Sharlinda had lost weight recently, but she piled on the makeup, partly to cover up her zits and also, I suspected, because she was nervous. At one time, Sharlinda's light complexion would've given her an edge over Today and me. But this was 1975, and there was no guarantee that every brother would prefer Sharlinda's pale complexion to our brown ones.

The room smelled like fried hair. Today was straightening her naps in the bathroom mirror with a hot comb. She didn't travel anywhere without it. Sharlinda had fine, limp hair that she swore she couldn't do anything with. She'd recently traded her natural in for a perm.

"Stevie, you think they'll like naturals?" Today yelled from the bathroom.

I continued to pick out my Afro in the dresser mirror.

"How would I know? I've never met them. Brian is your cousin."

"But I haven't seen my cousin since I was ten."

"The natural's not as popular as it used to be," Sharlinda cut in.

"So?"

"So, some people say the Afro's on its way out."

"Stevie, you're welcome to use my straightening comb and curling iron if you want to be on the safe side," Today offered.

I stared in the round mirror above the dresser. I was proud of my recently sculpted 'fro. Too bad if they didn't like it. I had no intention of straightening my hair just to please some man I'd never even met.

"No thanks. I'll take my chances."

"You're brave. Most women aren't willing to sacrifice style just to make a political statement anymore," Today said.

"Maybe I'm just not *most* women," I said as the phone rang. "Besides, I don't feel like I'm sacrificing anything."

"Today, it's for you," Sharlinda announced.

"Who is it?"

"Who may I tell her is calling?" Sharlinda sounded like a secretary.

"Oh, hi, Brian this is Sharlinda," she said in a breathy voice.

"Give me the phone, Miss Thing," Today said, grabbing the telephone.

Sharlinda headed toward the bathroom. She began rubbing acne medication on her face. I would just wait and put my eye shadow and lipstick on when she was finished. I wasn't big on makeup. I didn't wear much and I didn't wear it often. And I could apply it in two minutes flat.

I opened a drawer and pulled out my blue and white striped top. I decided to wear it with my new white pants.

"Bad news," Today reported, hanging up the phone.

I turned away from the dresser, and Sharlinda walked into the bedroom with zit medication all over her face.

"What is it?" she asked.

Today plopped down on the bed. "Brian's friend Rodney can't make it."

"That's too bad. Wasn't he the one you said would be perfect for Stevie?" Sharlinda asked.

"I said, we'd just see who naturally gravitated to who."

"Yeah," I agreed. "We said we'd just let the chips fall where they may."

"Well, my mistake. So, what are we going to do now?"

"I don't know," Today sighed. "I mean we could all go and just see what happens. See which one of you my cousin falls for. Of course, I've got first dibs on Kyle. I mean you two can fight over Brian."

"Well, Stevie, you want to flip a coin or draw straws?"

Suddenly, I remembered the stewardess. Maybe it was time to put myself in a situation where I could check out my feelings toward women. With a few phone calls, I could probably find a women's bar. This was my chance. I was away from home and no one would ever have to know. My heart raced at the thought of entering such a forbidden world.

"No, Sharlinda, you and Today go 'head on."

"Stevie, we wouldn't feel right about us going out to dinner and partying while you're cooped up in this room. Right, Sharlinda?"

"Well, I would feel better if she at least had a view."

"Who says I'll be cooped up anywhere?"

"Well, where would you go?"

"She could take the Chinatown at Night tour," Sharlinda suggested.

"Look, I have the tour guide. I'll figure something out. Don't worry about me."

"Stevie, are you sure? I mean, won't you be lonely?"

"Or scared?" Today cut in.

"I'll be fine. It will be an adventure."

"But won't you be scared out there alone?"

"Look, Today, you're forgetting that I'm a sistah from the South Side of Chicago. Now, if I can't handle San Francisco, then I oughta quit. Don't you think?"

"Hey, I heard that," Today agreed.

" 'Miss Thing,' I owe you one," Sharlinda winked.

"That's fine by me. You can start by taking my turn on the cot tonight."

Sharlinda and Today had finally gone. I could hear my heart beating fast. I felt relieved to be alone with my plan. I thumbed through the *People's Yellow Pages*, a progressive, nationwide reference book I'd had sense enough to bring along with me. The San Francisco Women's Switchboard . . . hmmmm . . . the book said that they dealt with lesbian issues. What should I do, just call and ask where the women's bars were? I supposed that would qualify as a lesbian issue. A bar—I wished there was some alternative to a bar. I wasn't much of a drinker, although I'd probably need a few drinks in a lesbian bar.

I really wanted to talk to somebody, not just sit around some dive. Maybe I should go to a shrink instead. But why should I have to go seek psychiatric help? I was one of the sanest people I knew, sort of. And besides, talk was cheap. No, it wasn't, not that kind of talk. Anyway, I was ready for some action, sort of. I reached for the phone and dialed the number of the San Francisco Women's Switchboard.

"What kind of scene are you into?" The woman who'd answered the phone asked cheerfully.

I hesitated. How did I know? I'd never even been inside of a lesbian bar before.

"There are several women's bars here in the city."

"Oh, well, I guess I'd like to go to the best one, then."

"That's probably a matter of opinion. You see, it depends on what you're looking for. Some women like Maude's in the Haight, 'cause it's a friendly neighborhood place. But, if you wanna dance, you might prefer Peg's Place or A Little More."

"This is my first time. You see, I'm just visiting San Francisco. I've never been to one of those kinds of places before, anywhere. So, I'd like to go where I'd feel the most comfortable."

"I see. Well, it's not all that easy going into any bar alone. But it's a lot easier than in a straight bar. Actually, I'm straight," the woman whispered.

"Oh, wow, you could've fooled me."

"Well, I wasn't trying to fool you."

"I just meant that you sounded like you had a lot of firsthand experience, that's all."

"Well, most of my friends are lesbians, and I do go to women's bars and dances. You see, I love to dance and I hate being hassled by men."

"Oh," I said, feeling relieved that you could go to a lesbian bar and not necessarily be a lesbian.

"In fact," the woman continued, "I'm going to a women's dance tonight."

"Oh, is it open to the public?"

"Sure. I didn't mention it before because it's in Berkeley."

"Berkeley, is that far?"

"Not really, I live in Berkeley. I take BART and it's not a bad commute. It's only about a half-hour ride."

"That's nothing. It takes longer than that for me to get from my house to downtown Chicago."

"Sounds like you might be game, then."

"Yeah, actually a dance sounds better than a bar."

"I can give you directions. But you have to remember to get into the BART system by the stroke of midnight."

"Or I'll turn into a pumpkin?"

"Or you'll have to take a cab back, which costs about twenty-five bucks. Unless of course you get lucky and meet someone tonight and get picked up by her."

"I'll manage to get into the BART system on time or else spring for a cab. I don't think I'm ready to go home with anyone just yet. It'll be a big deal for me even to get up enough nerve to go inside the place, believe me."

"Well, good luck, here are the directions."

Taking BART was an experience in itself. I'd read in the newspaper last year about the Bay Area's new transit system. Yet I was startled when the shiny silver train with blue trim sneaked up on me. Its sleek design reminded me more of something out of *The Jetsons* than Chicago's creaky old el trains. BART even put the newer trains that ran along the Dan Ryan Expressway to shame. BART was computerized; machines gave you your ticket to get in and out of the system. The ride was amazingly quiet; the cars spacious and almost squeaky clean.

I liked what I saw as I walked along the streets of Berkeley: Comfortable-looking houses, quaint shops, harmless-looking hippies. If I got lost, it wouldn't be hard to walk up to one of the several smiling people strolling with backpacks and ask them for directions.

Even though the night air caused me to fasten my sweater, I marveled at the number of people wearing down jackets in June. After eating dinner at Kentucky Fried Chicken, I wiped my mouth good and sucked on a peppermint Life Saver. I didn't want to look greasy or blow chicken breath in anybody's face.

It still tripped me out that a lesbian dance was being held

at a church. But that's what the woman at the switchboard had said. Maybe the parishoners envisioned prim and proper ladies waltzing with one another or something.

The closer I got to the dance, the more nervous I felt. What kind of women would be there? I wondered. The few known lesbians I remembered observing during my childhood were never anyone I'd aspired to be like. Take Lois and Gwen from my 'hood, for example. Lois walked and dressed like a man. Gwen was just as feminine as Lois was masculine. And Lois referred to Gwen as "my woman." Melody, a girlhood friend, had lived upstairs from the couple. She told me that her mother had to call the police on Lois and Gwen more than once. Judging by Gwen's bruises, Melody concluded that Lois also hit like a man. I never saw any advantage in Gwen's being a lesbian. She had two children from a failed marriage. And it baffled me that she would substitute a woman for a man without gaining any ground. What was the point of kissing some woman's behind who hit you whenever she got ready? Not to mention that you got ostracized by society on top of it. I decided that if it was my lot in life to be a lesbian, I wouldn't be *that* kind of lesbian. I would be the kind who'd heard about Women's Liberation.

I turned up the street that the church was supposed to be on. I spied a group of women milling around in the distance. I was shocked to see two women in flannel shirts all hugged up against the church's CALL TO WORSHIP sign. I could hear Mama now. "What if the trumpet were to blow at this instant? If God brought an end to the world, you'd be surrounded by the daughters of Satan!"

I breathed in the pungent odor of marijuana and the fragrance of flowers as I hurried past three happy-looking women smoking outside the church. I was greeted by the sound of sweet soul music as I hit the doorway. I tried to act as cool as the music, but I was nervous. My hand shook as I gave the small, wiry woman at the door a dollar bill.

My ears were filled with the sounds of Martha Reeves and the Vandellas. My eyes searched the dark, crowded room for a place to buy a drink. This is an experiment, I reminded myself. If you don't like it, you don't have to stay. I made a beeline for a table with a jug of wine on it after checking my sweater.

I dug out fifty cents from my pants pocket and handed it to the big woman behind the table. I clutched the Styrofoam cup like it was my security blanket.

I slouched against the wall in a corner where I could observe the action. Occasionally I peered over my wine to watch the room full of white women dressed like farmhands, bouncing up and down.

"Are you into rolls?"

"Huh?" I asked, suddenly looking into the face of a cinnamon-colored stranger. I stood up straight. I was almost as tall as this woman, although she was about ten pounds heavier. She was wearing a vest, jeans, and cowboy boots.

I was intrigued by her style.

"I asked you, are you into rolls?" The woman repeated with just a hint of irritation in her voice.

I glanced over at the table in the far corner of the dimly lit room. Perhaps they served egg rolls at dances here. Maybe they were some sort of San Francisco treat. But I wasn't in the mood for a roll, not right after eating one of Kentucky Fried Chicken's good-ass biscuits.

"No, thank you," I answered politely. "I ate before I came."

The woman's full lips broke into a grin. She had a devilish look on her face that showed off her twinkling eyes. "I ate before I came," she laughed, running her fingers through her short natural. My Afro was big compared to hers.

What was so funny? I wondered. This woman had some kind of nerve to be laughing at me. I was glad to see a sistah, but I wasn't in the mood for any mess. Nobody told her to walk her behind over here. I didn't want to have to "read" her.

"What's so funny?" I asked nervously.

"I saw that on a T-shirt in the Haight, once," she explained.

"What?"

"I ate before I came."

It dawned on me that this sistah wasn't talking about food. And she must've meant roles as in butch/femme. I'd read about them in my social psychology book. They talked about butch/femme roles in the chapter on Deviance.

"You mean butch/femme roles?"

The woman nodded.

"Sorry, I was distracted by the music."

"So, are you into roles or not? You still haven't answered my question," the woman pointed out.

So what if I haven't? Who are you, the roving reporter? And who says I want to be interviewed?

But her large dark eyes were soft like hush puppies and she was boyishly cute, without looking hard enough to bite nails. So I decided to be nice.

"I'm just visiting."

"From where? Another planet? They got roles everywhere."

"Chicago. Look, I just got here this week. Gimme a break."

"Chicago, the Windy City. Chi town, that's a place I wouldn't mind visiting. Well, what brings you out here?"

"Celebration. I just graduated from college a few weeks ago."

"G'on with your educated self," the woman said, slapping my back. "I'm still trying to get my A.A. degree."

She extended her hand. "I'm Traci."

I gave Traci the black handshake, just to let her know that I was cool. I liked the feel of her firm grip.

"I'm Stevie."

"So, Miss Stevie, what's the women's scene like back in Chicago?" Traci asked, popping her fingers.

I liked the way Traci's voice sounded. It was smooth like molasses. I'd always been into nice voices.

"I've been away at school for four years."

"Didn't you check it out on weekends and holidays?"

"Not really. I'm sort of new to all of this."

"Well, welcome to 'the Life.' "

"Hey, like I said, I'm just visiting. I'm not ready to sign on the dotted line or anything."

"So, do you call yourself experimenting or what?"

I shrugged my shoulders. "Do you have a problem with experimenters?"

"No, hey, my lab is open."

I didn't know what to say, so I gulped the last of my wine and glanced around the room. It was full of women dancing up a storm.

"You look like you're in culture shock. Or was it something I said?"

"I'm more shocked that a church would allow lesbians to hold a dance in their building. I don't care if they are Unitarians. This would never happen in Chicago, even on the North Side, and certainly not downstate. Although the women here do remind me of farmhands."

"We're feminists, you know how we are."

"I didn't mean any offense. I'm used to hippies from my college days. But hippies are about played out, where I'm from." I looked down at my powder-blue-and-white-striped top with see-through sleeves. "I guess people look at me and think I'm dressed weird."

Traci flashed her white teeth. I could feel the warmth of her smile. "I didn't think you were from around here. San Franciscans tend to wear dark colors. And we wouldn't be caught dead in white shoes."

I glanced at my pants and sandals.

"Not even in the summertime?"

Traci shook her head. "We don't have a traditional summer."

"Yeah, I've noticed. I like to have frozen out at Fisherman's Wharf Thursday."

"Hey, we laugh at the fools shivering in their shorts, waiting for the cable cars."

"Well, tonight I wore long pants and a sweater."

"I heard that. You say you might've been a fool a couple days back. But you ain't gonna be the same fool twice."

"You got it."

"Let me throw that away for you." Traci tossed my cup and pulled me onto the dance floor toward a soulful beat. For some reason, I felt comfortable with her.

I'd be lying if I said I wasn't having fun dancing to the Motown oldies with Traci. And I'd be lying if I said she wasn't cute. I'd danced with girlfriends before, when we were learning a new dance, but this felt different. Different from dancing with a man, different from anything that I'd ever experienced.

A wild dancer accidently bumped into me. She apologized while I held my breath to block out her sour odor.

"There are some real stompers in here, huh," I commented to Traci.

"You know they tend to overdo it when it comes to dancing."

"They're not so big on deodorant, though, huh?"

"Stevie, we're into being natural. We'd rather smell funk than perfume."

"Different strokes for different folks." I shrugged. I know they say when in Rome, do as the Romans do. But that's easier said than done, I thought. 'Cause I can't get into funk. I take a bath or shower every day and yes, I do wish everybody did.

"Stevie, let's say we blow this pop stand. I'll give you a ride back to the City, OK? You are staying in the city, aren't you?"

Wait just a sardine-eating minute. What did Traci mean? I hoped she didn't call herself picking me up. Although it was an exciting thought. But I hated to have to rain on her parade. Call me a prude, but I knew I wasn't ready to get down with a woman.

"The city? I'm staying in a hotel in downtown San Francisco."

"San Francisco *is* the City. That's what everybody calls it. This is the East Bay."

"Oh, well, I don't want you to drive all the way across the bridge on my account." I figured Traci wasn't offering to drive me back to San Francisco for her health. It wasn't like I could invite her up for tea and crumpets. "It would help if you just gave me a ride to BART."

"Look, I stay in the City. I've got to go back over to that side anyway."

"OK, well, in that case, thanks." I went and got my sweater.

As we left the church, my mind was a ball of confusion. This might be the perfect opportunity to get next to a woman. I was on vacation, in a strange city, and no one would ever have to know. If I didn't like it, I could forget it ever happened.

But the thought of me being sexual with a woman made my legs turn into Jell-O.

We walked down the street toward Traci's car. There was an unmistakable charge in the air, and we were definitely creating it.

I would've thought twice about climbing into some man's car I'd just met, but it was different with a woman. I felt completely safe with Traci in her little red Volkswagen bug. Well, maybe not completely safe; that would have been boring. Traci shifted gears.

"Isn't it hard to have a stick in a place with so many hills?" I asked.

"There is such a thing as an emergency brake," she reminded me.

"I know that." I shook my head. "But all that stopping and starting, especially on the hills."

"I wouldn't drive anything else. You have more control over the car."

"That's what the last dude I dated used to say. But I wonder if having more control over the car isn't overrated."

"I don't know whether your squeeze overrated his joystick, or not."

"No pun intended, I'm sure."

Traci smiled. "But as far as I'm concerned, if you ain't shifting and dealing with the clutch, you ain't driving. You just steering, that's all."

"I can barely drive an automatic. I just got my license a couple of months ago."

"Well, I've been driving ever since God was a corporal."

"How long is that?"

"Almost ten years."

I made a mental note. That would make her around twenty-five. Traci was an older woman.

"Changing the subject here, I'm just curious. I finally saw an Asian woman and a Latina woman, but where were all the sistahs tonight? I mean, Oakland has a pretty large black population, doesn't it? And it's right next to Berkeley. Where do they go?"

"Stevie, a lot of black women are into roles. This wasn't their scene tonight. This was a political scene."

"Where *is* their scene?"

"They got a club in East Oakland called the Jubilee. Saturday nights the joint be jumpin'."

"I'd like to see it. Can we check it out?"

"I'm sorry, Stevie. But I can't take those 'Negroes' tonight. I'm in the mood to kick back."

I wondered why Traci didn't want to be around the sistahs. And if she planned to kick back by herself or if she was hoping to have some company.

"I had to work today," Traci explained. "Let's say we go back to my place for a glass of wine and conversation before dropping you off at your hotel?"

There's your answer, I thought. She's hoping to have some company. It had been my experience that when a man suggested going back to his place, he expected more than wine and conversation. But Traci wasn't a man; maybe it would be different. Maybe she wouldn't push.

After a long pause, I said, "All right." Traci smiled. She was so cute with her bunny rabbit nose and pretty lips. What would Sharlinda and Today think if they could see me now, I wondered? It would blow their little minds.

Traci said that her neighborhood was called Noe Valley. Even at night, I could tell that it was nice, with its colorful

Victorians and quaint-looking shops. Traci parked the car on a hill, curbed her wheels, and put on her emergency brake. You didn't have to worry about runaway cars back home.

I paused to catch my breath as we headed uphill toward Traci's building.

"How can they call this a valley, with all these hills?" I groaned.

"We're on the outskirts. It's pretty flat in the center."

"You sure had to park far away."

Traci shrugged. "Only a block and a half. You call that far?"

"Definitely."

"In San Francisco, we call that lucky."

"On the South Side of Chicago, if people have to park two houses away, they have a fit. In the winter time they put out chairs and brooms to hold their spots all day."

"Brooms and chairs, huh?"

"Yeah, when you've cleared away ice and snow in front of your house, you figure you own it. Some people will shoot you over a parking space."

"I've heard that they're more rigid back there."

"Yeah, Chicagoans are big on routine. We're not lounging in cafés during the day like you see people doing here. We're somewhere busting our butts trying to make a living. During the week, Chicagoans basically go to work, come home, park in the same spot, eat dinner, watch TV, and get some z's. It's easy to get in a rut back there."

"That's why I left Sacramento."

I huffed and puffed at the top of the hill. I hoped we were almost there.

"Chicago has a reputation for being tough," Traci added.

"Yeah," I agreed. "People in France told my old roommate Celeste, who's French, that she'd better be careful because of all the gangsters." I wondered how Celeste was doing back in France. I wondered which she missed more, me or San Francisco.

"I guess they think Al Capone and Dillinger still live there." Traci laughed as we walked up the steps of a purple and white Victorian.

I panted as Traci swung the door open. "You mean there's another set of stairs inside?"

"Yep, keeps me in shape."

The steps led to a long, tan-colored hallway. "I was expecting to see a living room."

"This is called a railroad flat. They're common in San Francisco. Actually the living room is my bedroom."

"Oh," I said, afraid of going stepping into Traci's bedroom. Even though I liked Traci, I wasn't ready to be in a reclining position.

"Don't you miss having a living room? You know, for entertaining."

"It's cheaper, rentwise. I have two roommates. And my room has a view and a fireplace. So it's worth it."

"What about your kitchen?"

"What about it?"

"Can we go in there?"

"Sure, follow me. There's a view from in there too."

We sat down across from each other in the old-fashioned blue and white kitchen, sipping wine and munching on corn chips. Traci was busy rolling a joint. I hoped she didn't plan on seducing me. I was in a quandary. I liked to get high because grass relaxed me, but sometimes it also made me as horny as a toad. I knew I was attracted to Traci, but I was still scared. And I didn't want to lose control behind a joint.

Traci licked the ends of the fat joint with her sexy tongue. I hoped Traci would be able to drive me to my hotel after smoking that sucker. I figured if worse came to worst, I could always call a cab.

"This is an interesting dip."

"It's got cilantro in it," Traci informed me.

"Cilantro, what's that? I've never heard of it."

Traci took a hit off of the joint. "It's an herb. I got it today from Loving Foods, where I work."

Traci offered me the joint. I shook my head. "No thanks, I think the wine is enough."

Traci looked disappointed. Why was I being such a prude? Wasn't this trip supposed to be a celebration? Wasn't it about time for me to kick up my heels a little bit? Maybe so, but I was still too afraid.

Traci made a pitiful face. "Don't tell me you're gonna make me smoke all by my lonesome?"

I was tempted, but I knew I had to be strong.

"I don't ever mix wine and weed," I lied.

"No problem, I want you to be comfortable."

"Thanks. So far, I am."

Traci looked at me like she wasn't sure how to take that.

"So, what do you do at Loving Foods?" I asked after sipping my wine. "Are you a manager?"

"We're all managers, baggers, checkers, everything. It's a collective."

"A collective? That's interesting," I said, sucking the tangy sauce off of a corn chip.

"Yep, there are no bosses at Loving Foods. We're all workers."

"Right on!"

"So tell me about yourself. I know you just graduated from college. What was your major?"

"Journalism. I was on the school newspaper. In fact I just got offered a job on a paper in Monmouth, Illinois. My practical side says I better take it. But after four years in the Heartland, I'm ready to cut loose."

"Well, San Francisco is the perfect place for that." Traci smiled, revealing a cute dimple underneath her chin.

"I don't doubt it. Our tour bus went down Broadway in North Beach. I couldn't believe it. Talk about a red-light district!

"I was thinking more of the Castro."

"I don't believe we went there."

"You can't go back to Chicago without seeing the Castro. The Castro is becoming the gay capital of the world. It's like a Moslem not going to Mecca." Traci laughed.

I shuddered a little when Traci insinuated that I was gay. I couldn't think of anything to say that wouldn't make me sound defensive or even possibly offensive. So I just sipped some more wine and said, "Maybe I'll be able to work it in."

Traci sucked on the joint. "So, what kind of stuff did you write about on the school newspaper? Political shit?"

I shook my head. "Mostly features. I did an article on streakers last year."

"What did you say in the story?"

"Why they did it. You know, how people reacted to them. What their mothers would say, etc. I actually interviewed a black streaker."

Traci really seemed interested in getting to know me. It was refreshing not to have a man trying to get into my pants for a change.

Traci nibbled on a corn chip. "I suppose a black man running buck naked through the cornfields might qualify as a political statement."

"A couple of the brothas saw him. Everybody was talking about it at the 'black table' at dinner for days. We couldn't believe it, a black streaker!"

"They probably would've arrested his behind or worse if he'd done it in town instead of on campus," I continued. "The funny thing about it was the brothas who saw the dude said he was short on equipment, was a disgrace to black men everywhere." I laughed, clapping my hands. I could tell I was feeling the effects of the wine.

"I hope I'm not disturbing anybody," I said, covering my mouth.

"You're not," Traci assured me. "Jawea is at her lover's down in Santa Cruz, and Kate is in India studying to be a yoga teacher."

"Yoga, I've wanted to learn yoga for a long time."

"Kate's pretty good. She's taught me some stuff."

"Could you show me?" I was surprised that I felt comfortable enough to suggest that we do something that might require us to leave the kitchen. But I'd been curious about yoga ever since I'd heard about it, back when I was in high school. I was feeling mellow from the wine, and I was comfortable in Traci's company. I doubted that she would come out of a bag that I couldn't handle.

"Sure, why don't we go into my room and sit on the rug. I'll put on some Joan Armatrading and show you a few postures, OK?"

"Who's Joan Armatrading?"

"A dynamite West Indian sistah from England. You'll love her."

I followed Traci down the long hallway into her room.

Traci turned on the box and disappeared into the closet. She reappeared wearing drawstring pants and a T-shirt. She hit the lights and played with the dimmer switch.

"That's good," I said when the room was not too dark, but not too light.

We sat down on the blue and turquoise braided rug in front of the empty fireplace listening to Joan's deep, rich, jazzy voice. The sole of my right foot was resting on the inside of my left thigh as Traci had instructed. I glanced around her crowded room in the soft light. I admired the large Boston fern that hung in front of the middle window. A poster that read "A woman needs a man like a fish needs a bicycle" made me chuckle. The furniture was mostly crates, cinder blocks, and pieces of plywood, except for a foam mattress and rocking chair.

"Just a little more," Traci said, gently pressing my right knee toward the floor.

"Whoa, I don't know if I'm in shape for this."

"Just go with the flow. You're doing pretty well, although you really shouldn't exercise in these tight pants."

"I guess it would be a little easier without them," I agreed.

"Take them off, then."

The thought of sitting around in my panties with somebody that I barely knew was a little strange. But like I said, I was feeling kind of mellow after the wine. Besides, what was there to be afraid of? And I was wearing my good panties. So, I unzipped my pants and pulled them off. Traci took them and threw them over the bentwood rocking chair.

"Cool, now let's try the other side." Traci knelt in front of me and began pressing my left knee toward the floor.

"Good, all right, now sit cross-legged and let's try both knees."

"Are you sure I'll ever be able to walk again?"

Traci ignored my concern and squatted in front of me and started pressing my knees down.

"Mmmmmm, mmmmm," she giggled.

"What's so funny?" I asked.

"Nothing," Traci said, but she continued laughing at me.

I straightened my legs out. "Why are you laughing then?"

Traci sat back on the rug and sighed. "It's not something I can tell you."

"Why not? I want to know." Maybe she was laughing because I was in lousy shape, I thought. What kind of a hostess was she, making fun of somebody? Traci knew I'd never done yoga before.

I frowned. "It's not polite to laugh at somebody and then not tell them why."

"Stevie, I wasn't laughing at you."

"Traci, I'm the only person here. We've already established that."

"Look, Stevie, I'm just a little high. You know things are funnier when you're high."

"Yeah, but what was funny in the first place?" I asked. I was beginning to feel paranoid, even though I hadn't smoked any of the joint.

"All right, Stevie, I was laughing because," Traci giggled and covered her mouth.

"Tell me," I demanded, feeling more and more irritated by the minute.

"OK, I was laughing because . . . I could smell you, OK?"

My throat felt tight. "You could smell me?"

Traci nodded.

"What do you mean, my perfume?" I asked, knowing full well that I wasn't wearing any.

Traci shook her head.

I held my breath. Was Traci trying to say that I needed deodorant?

"I'm not funky, am I?" I smelled under each arm to be sure.

"No, you don't understand. I could smell your pussy."

I stared at Traci in horror. It felt like the room was caving in on me. I wanted to throw on my pants and run home. But home was two thousand miles away. Besides, I was too shocked to move. Had I heard this woman right?

"I beg your pardon?" I mumbled hoarsely.

Traci had the nerve to repeat. "I said I could smell your pussy."

I cleared my throat. "Maybe you smelled something in the rug. Has it ever been cleaned?"

"It wasn't the rug, Stevie."

"Do you all have a cat?"

"Yes, but Stevie, this was you," Traci insisted. "I know this kind of pussy when I smell it."

My face was on fire, my breathing had stopped. I couldn't feel my legs. I was torn between homicide and suicide. Somehow, I managed to stand up and grab my pants.

Traci stood up and stared at me in silence.

"I take a shower or bath every day and I'm not even on my period!" I blurted out.

But didn't those women in the magazine ads for feminine-hygiene sprays and douches claim they showered or bathed every day too? And didn't the ads make it clear that washing with soap and water simply wasn't enough? What if other people smelled me, and Traci was the only one who had the guts to say anything? A chill ran down my spine. What if the feminists were wrong? What if women did need to douche after all?

"Traci, you have a lot of nerve. As far as I'm concerned,

you're worse than a man! I refuse to stay here any longer and be insulted."

"Worse than a man!" Traci shouted, folding her arms. "What the fuck does that mean?"

"A man would've shown me more respect. You don't know me from Adam. You had no right to talk to me like that."

"Like what? What are you talking about?" Traci asked, looking surprised.

"Don't play dumb with me. Hey, I'm sorry for offending you. If I can use your phone, I'll call a cab and get the hell out of your apartment."

Traci walked toward me while I zipped up my pants.

"Whoa, wait a minute, Stevie, I wasn't offended in the least. I like the way you smell."

"You mean you weren't trying to say that I stunk?" I gulped as I reached for my shoes. I jammed my feet into my sandals.

Traci shook her head. "Quite the contrary, I think you smell wonderful. It has nothing to do with being dirty. I wish women would appreciate themselves more." She sighed. "Don't you ever smell yourself sometimes and like it?"

I hunched my shoulders. "Not really. I guess I never thought about it one way or another."

"Stevie, it wasn't like I could smell you from across the room. I practically had my nose between your legs," Traci reminded me.

I felt myself relax a little. "It's just that it's so personal, that's all." Maybe I had made too much of it. But I still couldn't believe that I was talking about something so intimate with somebody I barely knew.

"Stevie, the last thing I want to do is make you feel uncomfortable." Traci's dark eyes looked as soft as melted chocolate.

I felt my stomach quiver. On one hand I was a little tipsy from the wine and feeling attracted to Traci, but on the other hand I still couldn't accept the idea of getting it on with a woman.

"Traci, this has been educational, but it's late and I'd better go."

"Stevie, why don't you extend your visit and stick around for a *real* education?"

"Look, this isn't my *real* life. This is a vacation. I've got to go back to Chicago and job hunt."

"And then what?"

I wasn't sure what Traci meant. "I don't know, I guess once I find a job, I'll get an apartment."

"And then what?"

"Who knows, eventually I'll probably get married and have kids." I was surprised at how high my voice had gotten.

"Stevie, you can run, but you can't hide."

"Who says I'm trying to hide?"

Traci picked up a plastic bottle and began spraying her Boston fern.

"It may not be tonight or next week or even next year," she insisted between squirts. "But sooner or later you're gonna have to face who you are."

Traci's words shot through me like a cannon. I stiffened my body in an attempt to deaden their effect. But I couldn't help imagining myself running through a dark tunnel, being chased by a monster. And I could see no escape.

"I know who I am," I insisted, folding my arms defiantly.

"Sure, that's why you were hanging out at a lesbian dance. And that's why you let a lesbian bring you home."

"It was a women's dance."

"Whatever you say."

"And you brought me home, but now I'm leaving." I might not be able to control my attractions, I thought, but I could damn sure control my feet. Besides, who's to say that my attractions were sexual anyway? When a paper clip is attracted to a magnet, it has nothing to do with sex.

But I still felt scared inside. What if Traci was right? How would I ever know for sure what I was if I was too afraid to find out? Maybe if I faced my fears they wouldn't be able to haunt me anymore. But I didn't want to get high and get it over with. I'd tried that with a couple of men, and it hadn't worked.

"Look, Traci, I admit that I'm confused," I said, sitting in the rocker. She plopped down on her foam mattress across from me. "I've had a few schoolgirl crushes," I continued. "And I do notice attractive women, but I don't hate men."

"Stevie, it ain't about hating men, it's about loving women," Traci explained.

"Well, I've also been attracted to men," I continued. "I don't know what that makes me. Besides, I'm not so sure I want to slap a label on myself. I guess I would really like to be free to explore."

Traci nodded as a long-haired, gray-striped cat sauntered into the room.

"Meet Artemis, Jawea's fur child."

I smiled. "Hi, Artemis, you're so pretty." Artemis rubbed up against my legs.

"Plenty of women are exploring, so why don't you hang out here and explore then?" Traci asked as I rocked back and forth.

I petted Artemis. "Hang out here in this apartment?"

Traci nodded.

"Thanks, but I can't hang out here. I have a hotel room. And I have to consider my friends. I'm here on vacation, remember."

"Stevie, I think it would be easier to blow your friends off than to go back to being a tourist and pretending like none of this ever happened. And by the way, you won't be in a hotel room, you'll be in the closet."

My mind was a blur. I hoped I wasn't on the brink of a nervous breakdown. I needed to think. So, maybe I couldn't just walk away like nothing had happened. But I couldn't tell Sharlinda and Today about my feelings toward women without risking our friendship. When Traci suggested that I hang out here, what did she mean? Where did she expect me to sleep? I decided to ask her.

"Let's say I were to take you up on your offer. Where would I sleep?" I asked nervously.

"You can stay in Kate's room. The rent is paid through the month. And we haven't found anyone to sublet it yet."

I breathed a sigh of relief. At least Traci wasn't pushing herself on me.

"You picked one of the best times to be in San Francisco. This is Gay Pride week, coming up."

"Oh," I swallowed. Maybe it was fate.

"There's a big women's dance next Saturday night, not to mention the parade on Sunday," Traci continued. "If you want to find out if you're really a lesbian, this is a golden opportunity."

Sharlinda and Today would probably be understanding if I told them I'd met a man and wanted to spend the week with him. It's not like they wouldn't go off with some dude if either of them had half the chance, I thought. The hardest part would be dealing with their curiosity rather than their disappointment.

How could I afford to pass up an opportunity like this? Especially one that had fallen into my lap. Tell me it just happened to be Gay Pride week. Tell me that wasn't a sign. But the question was, a sign from who? The forces of good or the forces of evil? Well, didn't I owe it to myself to find out?

"OK, I admit, I'm curious. I'd be lying if I said hanging out with you doesn't appeal to my sense of adventure. Especially when I consider the alternative. But how much difference can a week really make?"

"Haven't you heard that song, 'What a Difference a Day Makes?' "

I nodded. "I've also heard that a little knowledge can be a dangerous thing. I just hope I'm not opening a Pandora's box. I'd hate to end up more confused than ever."

"Free your mind and your behind will follow. Personally, I think you should consider subletting Kate's room and staying out here and finding yourself. I mean, Chicago is a nice place to be *from*."

"Wait a minute, I have a plane to catch tomorrow. I can't just drop out like some white hippie. I wasn't born with a silver spoon in my mouth. I just spent four years in college so I could get a decent job."

"What's that got to do with anything? A decent job don't mean jack shit if you ain't happy!"

Artemis hopped onto my lap.

"It's hard to be happy if you can't make a living," I pointed out as I stroked the cat's soft fur.

"Stevie, you're coming from a survival place."

"Hey, sounds reasonable to me."

"Fuck reasonable! Stevie, you're not here to survive," Traci shouted, standing up.

"I'm not *where* to survive?"

"You're not on this planet to survive. That is not your purpose. Do you understand?"

"What *is* my purpose? This should be interesting, especially since you've only known me for a few hours," I said, rocking harder. Artemis jumped off my lap.

"I could've told you after ten minutes that your purpose wasn't to survive."

"Fine, so what is my purpose then?"

Traci hesitated, "Your purpose is to learn," she said.

"To learn what?"

"Just to learn what you're supposed to learn. That's what you have to find out."

"Can't I learn what I'm supposed to find out in Chicago? Can't Chicago be my learning tree?"

Traci shook her head. "Chicago would be a step backward for you. If you get on that plane tomorrow, you're destined to go through life with the emergency brake on."

"Sounds tragic, but like I said I can't afford just to hang out. I'm on a pretty tight budget."

"Look, you got a place to crash, rent free, until the first of July. And if you take the sublet, the rent on Kate's room is only sixty dollars a month."

That's not too bad, I thought. It wasn't like I didn't have savings. I could probably find a job out here in a month. Then I told myself, I must be crazy. This woman is almost a complete stranger. Maybe she put a stupid pill in my drink.

"Like I said, my money is funny and my change is strange. Even if I could swing the rent, I can't eat the paint off of the side of a building."

"We've got enough tofu burgers in the freezer to last till we put a black woman in the White House."

"What are tofu burgers?" I asked as Artemis stretched and yawned on the windowsill.

"Bean curd."

"What the hell is bean curd?"

"The curd of the bean," Traci answered matter-of-factly.

"Traci, I'm from Chicago, city of broad shoulders, hog butcher to the world. Do you expect me to survive on bean burgers?"

Traci smiled. "Your purpose is not to survive, remember?"

"That's right, I forgot." Artemis suddenly flopped down and walked over toward Traci. Traci reached out and petted her with her long fingers.

"So, Artemis, you finally decided to give me the time of day. I guess you remembered who feeds you when Jawea's gone."

"I must say you've certainly given *me* some food for thought."

Traci stood up, scooping Artemis into her arms. "Stevie, the chances of us meeting were one in a million. And therefore, we crossed paths for a reason. Who knows, I may be your spiritual guide."

"Really?" I asked, tempted to laugh in Traci's face.

Traci nodded as Artemis jumped out of her arms and headed for the door.

"Yeah, only time will tell," Traci answered mysteriously. "Like I said before, you'd be a fool to go back to Chicago tomorrow."

I remembered my cramped, non-air-conditioned bedroom in ninety-degree heat. Summer in San Francisco was awfully tempting. And I did want to find myself. I was twenty-one years old. If not now, when? It was exciting to think that I could turn my world upside down, just like that. But I knew that I wouldn't actually follow through with it in a million years. Sure, it would make sense to sleep here tonight in Kate's room, and yeah, I'd have brunch in the Castro in the morning. But my butt would be getting on that plane tomorrow as scheduled and returning to Chicago. Next week I might see snatches of the Gay Pride parade on the TV news or read about it later in the newspaper. But that would be the end of it. Soon I'd find a job in the media and get an apartment in Hyde Park and date men and learn to count my blessings.

"Traci, I'll stay here just for the night and go to brunch with you in the Castro tomorrow. I'll call the hotel and leave a message for my friends."

Traci patted my shoulder when I hung up the phone. "Come on, let's get us some shut-eye."

Get us some shut-eye. I hoped Traci didn't think that we were shutting our eyes together in the same bed or even in the same room, for that matter. She'd said I could sleep in Kate's room, hadn't she?

I hoped Traci wouldn't come into Kate's room in the night and try to seduce me. I wondered if I should sleep with one eye open.

I bit my bottom lip. "Traci, you're not going to try anything tonight, are you?"

Traci rolled her eyes. "Try anything? Stevie, what do you take me for?"

I felt embarrassed. "I'm sorry. I didn't mean to insult you."

"Do you think that I can only deal on one level?" Traci asked, raising her arms. "Is that what you think?"

"To tell you the truth, I don't know what to think."

"Well, I can operate on many levels. I can tune into your energy. I don't just want a piece of ass."

It wasn't like Traci had met me in the church choir. It wouldn't be so shocking if all she wanted was sex, now, would it? "Well, what *do* you want?"

"I want to participate in your personal growth. I want to be a catalyst for change. That's what I want."

I couldn't help but be impressed. If a man were saying this stuff, he would probably be full of shit. No "probably" to it; he *would* be full of shit. But it sounded beautiful coming from a woman. I had to admit that I was attracted to Traci's mystical style.

"I've never met anyone who wanted to do all that before."

Traci smiled and reached her hands out and grasped my cold fingers. Our faces moved closer to each other as if by osmosis. My knees buckled as I sank my mouth into Traci's soft lips. I felt my heart swell; I was scared by the intensity.

"That was nice," Traci breathed after our lips parted.

"Yeah," I agreed. "Well, I'd better turn in now," I said, afraid that Traci might get ideas. The kiss was nice, but it was enough for one night.

"I'll get you some sheets for the bed."

I breathed a sigh of relief.

"Stevie, just wait until you see how the morning light shines on the stained glass hanging in Kate's window."

5

I was still half-asleep when I felt something heavy against my thigh. I stiffened. Traci had promised that she wouldn't try anything.

I opened my eyes and stared into the face of Artemis, sitting on top of me.

"How did you get in here?" I yawned.

I sat up on Kate's firm mattress and opened my arms to the cat. I could hear loud music with a strong beat. I glanced around the room in the sunlight. The floor was covered with a straw mat. There were a lot of books, big pillows on the floor, candles, and a poster of a yogi with his legs crossed, wearing swimming trunks. I got a good laugh out of the poster of Prime Minister Indira Gandhi that asked, "But Can She Type?"

I was sitting up in the bed petting Artemis when Traci stuck her fuzzy head in the door. "You up?"

I nodded, pulling down on the big T-shirt she'd given me to sleep in.

Traci walked in the room wearing a faded blue terry cloth bathrobe. I'd always been a sucker for terry cloth.

"You could wake the dead with that loud music," I said smiling.

"Don't you like reggae music, mon?" Traci asked, dancing and popping her fingers.

"I s'pose, but I'm not that familiar with it."

"That's Jimmy Cliff, mon. Did you catch the flick *The Harder They Come?* Well, this is the sound track."

I shook my head. "I've been in the boonies for the last four years. We had to drive to Peoria just to see *The Exorcist.*"

"Well, you'll just have to make up for lost time."

"Can I take a shower first?"

"Sure, I'll get you a towel."

"Thanks, mon."

Traci had been right, I thought, staring at the stained glass image of a lotus with the sun shining through it. It gave me a warm feeling. And so did she. I decided to stay the week.

The airlines had let me change my flight, and Today and Sharlinda had bought my story, lock, stock, and barrel about staying an extra week to be with Mr. Goodbar. It had been easy getting my brother Kevin to tell my parents that I was extending my vacation to check out graduate schools. All he was interested in was an autographed Oakland A's baseball cap for his eighteenth birthday.

The Castro had really been a trip. I'd never seen so many good-looking men who didn't want women before. Traci informed me that the slim, alligator-shirt and jean-clad replicas were called Castro Street clones. A T-shirt in a store window had said it best: "San Francisco, my favorite city, where the women are strong and the men are pretty."

After a brunch of quiche and fruit in the Castro, Traci

dropped me off near the hotel. She would return in an hour, after my homies were gone.

Today and Sharlinda sat on the beds with their mouths open. I slumped down across from them in the boxy chair.

"Some people just have all the luck. I hate you." Today pretended to be angry, but her striking features made her look pretty, no matter what. Today and Sharlinda said their dates had been all right, but neither of them had heard bells or anything.

"You two are going to freeze in those halter tops," I teased.

"Yeah, this is no town for a tan." Sharlinda sighed.

"Don't worry, it's burning up back home. In another week, Sharlinda, you'll look like the rest of us," Today said, laughing.

"Hey, maybe if we show some skin, one of the only two straight men in San Francisco will finally notice us," Sharlinda joked.

I was about to share my impressions of the Castro with Sharlinda and Today, but then decided against it. No point in drawing unnecessary attention to the subject of homosexuality.

"Come on you all, it's not that bad," I said, leaning back in the chair and resting my arms on the sides.

"It's not that bad? Easy for you to say, you've got yourself a man."

"Yeah," Today agreed. "What's his name, Stevie?"

"Mr. Goodbar, honey."

"Stevie, what *is* the brotha's name?" Sharlinda demanded.

"Traci," I mumbled.

"And where is he, with his fine self?"

"He just dropped me off. He had to go pick his mother up from church," I lied.

"Tracy?" Sharlinda asked, a little puzzled.

"Yeah, Spencer Tracy."

"Spencer Tracy?" she repeated.

"Yeah, Spencer Tracy Washington," I rattled off.

"Go 'head, check her out, Miss Thing knows all three of his names. Doesn't sound like a one-night stand to me," Today chuckled.

"Well, what happened with you and Mr. Spencer Tracy Washington Goodbar last night?" Sharlinda wanted to know.

"Did y'all go straight to the groove?" Today asked.

"No, we did not go straight to the groove. We're getting to know each other gradually. And it's nice."

"Did you hear that, Today? A quality brotha."

"By the way, has he got a brother?"

"Today, I told you we're taking it slow. I haven't examined his family tree."

"Why not?" Sharlinda demanded, playfully throwing a pillow at me. "Honey, inquiring minds want to know." She laughed as the pillow landed on my face.

"All I ask is that I be maid of honor at your wedding. And that you name your first daughter after me," Today giggled.

"You better take your crazy butt on back to Maywood. Nobody's thinking about marriage, yet."

"You heard her say, 'yet,' Sharlinda."

"Honey, Stevie has picked out everything, including the silverware by now."

I threw the pillow and got Sharlinda upside her head, real good.

We'd checked out of our room. And it was time to say goodbye in the hotel lobby. Suddenly, I felt emotional.

"Stevie, what's wrong? You've got tears in your eyes, girl," Sharlinda said, puffing on a cigarette.

"It's like the end of an era for the three of us."

"Girl, why you say that? You'll be back in Chicago in another week."

"Yeah, but you'll be out in the burbs, and Sharlinda might get that job in Milwaukee. It won't be the same. Remember all the Thursday nights we ordered pizza together?"

"Yeah, and how we used to borrow each other's clothes before Today gained weight from all that pizza?" Sharlinda laughed, exhaling.

"Stevie, you better hold me back before I hurt her."

Today pretended to punch Sharlinda. It had been a cold thing to say, but it wasn't like Today was fat. She could just stand to lose twenty pounds, that was all.

"Stevie smoked her first joint with me," Sharlinda reminisced. "I taught her how to inhale."

"You didn't teach me nothing," I lied. "You practically choked on it yourself. It was more like the blind leading the blind."

"Well, I taught both of y'all the difference between cashmere and cotton, when it came to men," Today sniffed.

"It will never be like old times again," I swallowed.

"Y'all nursed me back from bronchitis." Today sighed.

I saw the shuttle bus pull up outside the thick glass door. I pointed. "Well, I guess it's time."

"Don't forget to call us when you get back to Chi-town and tell us all the intimate details." Sharlinda winked and mashed her cigarette in an ashtray.

"Hey, how's about a three-way hug?" Today suggested.

I was sort of glad when the hug was over and Today and Sharlinda had disappeared into the airline shuttle bus. It was a relief not to have to pretend anymore. I felt sad that I couldn't be myself with somebody who'd taught me how to inhale my first joint, and someone I'd nursed back from bronchitis.

summer 1975

6

The next day Traci drove me across the Golden Gate Bridge to Mount Tamalpais in Marin County. We hiked for several hours. I complained every step of the way, but when we reached the top and looked out over the Bay Area, it took my breath away. Traci and I kissed and held hands. It was nice; I was really getting into her. I still wasn't quite ready to take that big leap, so I planned on sleeping in Kate's bed. But I'd be dreaming about being with Traci.

On Wednesday night, Traci made us a delicious catfish dinner. She and I sat in her room in front of a toasty fire. I couldn't believe that it was cold enough to need heat in June. But it was cool and windy out there tonight.

Traci wondered aloud if the roommate interviewee they were expecting was a no show. Then Jawea stuck her head in the door and announced, "She's here."

Traci told me that I could learn a lot from Jawea because she was on a spiritual path. But I had my doubts about the slightly chubby white woman whom I imagined would be pretty if she ever combed her long, tangled hair, or ironed her rumpled clothes.

"I think this one is a separatist," Jawea whispered.

"How could you tell already?" Traci asked, leaving the blazing fire.

"She asked me if Artemis was male or female. I told her female."

"What did she say?"

" 'Good, because I want to live in a woman-only space. I don't want to put my energy into anything male.' "

"Tell her you're not sure about the turtle," I joked as Traci and Jawea headed toward the kitchen.

I felt sorry for the two of them, and yet it must be interesting to interview prospective roomates; especially in San Francisco. Last night a woman had shown up with a black eye, explaining that she was into S-M. Another claimed to be an ex-Weatherwoman. She meant as in terrorist, as opposed to meteorologist. And a nice woman who did macramé said she had to consult her four children and three teenagers about the space. She nonchalantly explained that all seven beings lived inside of her body. So far, Jawea was leaning toward her, and Traci was partial to the masochist.

Traci reappeared in the room, rolling her eyes.

"I can't understand why somebody named George with a beard and tattoos up and down her arms can be so down on men!"

"Yeah, she does have a funny way of showing it," I agreed.

"George says she was a part of a collective in Mendocino County. They gave away their boy children. She's a stone separatist."

"Gave away their boys! That's terrible!"

"Well, look at it this way," Traci said, standing close to the crackling fire. "The kids were probably better off."

"Yeah," I agreed, watching the embers burn.

Traci sat down next to me. "I don't know why Jawea is still farting around with her. Why not just come out and tell the woman this is not a separatist household."

"Why didn't you tell her?"

"I tried, but Jawea is going on about how she supports women-only space. Hey, I support women-only space too. But I want a male friend or relative to be able to visit. George said she didn't want to deal with a man unless the house is on fire."

"Wow, she actually said that?" I asked.

Traci nodded. "Maybe she's been abused by men. In all fairness, women who hate men, hate them for a reason."

I nodded as we heard the front door close. Traci called out to Jawea.

"We both concluded that this wasn't the right space for her," Jawea said, walking into the room.

"It took your pea brain all that time to figure that out?" Traci joked.

"Fuck you, Traci," Jawea pouted.

"I hate looking for a roommate," Traci groaned.

"Stevie, why don't you be our roommate?" Jawea asked, arching her eyebrows. "Then I can get to be a minority."

"Sacajawea, you've always been a minority in this household."

"How so?"

"You're the only white girl who thinks she's an Indian."

"Fuck you, again, Traci."

"Jawea, you're all talk and no action."

"Traci, you're bad, you're sooo bad," Jawea smiled, shaking her head.

I wasn't crazy about them flirting in front of me, but I could tell there was nothing behind it.

"Stevie, you should really think seriously about being our

roommate," Jawea whined. "My consciousness-raising group would be so jealous if you provided me with yet another opportunity to struggle with my racism."

Traci and I had just finished washing the dishes. We'd known each other a whole week now. I was still sleeping in Kate's room. We'd only hugged and kissed, but Traci had made my love come down. I had a feeling that things would heat up soon. I was going back to Chicago on Monday night, so the next couple of days were critical.

"This is gonna be a big dance, huh?" I asked, washing out the wok. I had to remember to tell my family that I'd eaten vegetables stir-fried in a wok.

"Yeah," Traci nodded. "Anybody who's anybody will be there. Too bad Jawea's down in Santa Cruz. Women of Power are playing; it's gonna be hot." Traci walked over to the refrigerator and took out a can of beer.

"Then we gotta jump clean," I said.

"Huh?" Traci asked, popping open the can.

"That's a term we used back at college. It just means you gotta look nice, you know, wear your best threads."

"Hmm, you learn something every day."

"I'm not sure what I should wear," I said, drying the wok. "I have a skirt that I brought."

"Hold it, you don't need to get all fancy," Traci said, sipping her beer.

"I didn't bring anything fancy. It's just a simple rayon skirt. Besides, I thought you said this is a big dance."

"It is, that's why it's gonna be at the Women's Skills Center. That's a big place."

"Well, what's wrong with my wearing a skirt then?" I asked, heading toward Kate's room.

"Stevie, are you crazy? Nobody would be caught dead in a skirt at this dance," Traci insisted, following me into the bedroom. "Besides, it would look like we were into roles."

I opened my suitcase and rummaged through it. "Well, you can wear a skirt too, then nobody will think we're into roles."

Traci sat on the edge of the bed, holding her chin.

"Stevie, I don't even own a skirt."

"What about a dress?" I asked sitting down in the rattan chair. I preferred pants in general, but for special occasions, I just automatically wore a skirt or a dress. It was ingrained in me. But there was something bold and exciting about a woman who dared not even to own a skirt.

Traci sipped her beer. "I have a dress for funerals, you dig?"

"Don't you ever go to church?"

"Not to a church where I need to wear a dress."

"So, the women are going to be dressed pretty much the way they were the other night?" I sighed.

"Yeah, pretty much; maybe a few more vests."

I frowned.

"Hey, that's one of the things that's so great about being a member of the women's community. You don't ever have to dress up."

"Yeah, but sometimes it's fun to get all dressed up. And wearing a dress makes me feel feminine."

Traci wrinkled her forehead. "You sound like a drag queen, I swear."

"Traci, aren't you ever in the mood to feel feminine?"

Traci shook her head. "Look, Stevie, just be patient, you'll get over these feelings. Now, throw on a pair of jeans and a T-shirt and call it a day."

"Can I at least iron my T-shirt?"

"We don't have an iron. Nobody I know has an iron, Stevie."

I sat soaking in a hot bubble bath. I rubbed on some sandalwood soap. I decided to wear my Caribbean shirt to the dance tonight. It was colorful and roomy, so it'd be good for dancing. I wasn't jumping clean, and yet I wouldn't be looking bummy.

Actually I was glad that I'd entered a world where you never had to sit like a lady. I could uncross my legs all I wanted to. Who the hell needed to feel feminine when she could feel comfortable?

I remembered how relieved I felt as a little girl when I'd taken off my Sunday clothes. The stiff patent-leather shoes, that always had to be broken in. The cutesy dress, the scratchy petticoat, the lacy socks, the little white gloves. It all used to be part of being a girl. We weren't allowed to wear pants to school unless it was freezing cold, and then we wore them under our skirts. We used to have to take them off in the coatroom. I was in high school before we stopped being forced to wear a stupid dress or skirt to school everyday. It made me mad just thinking about it.

I rested my head against the inflated bath pillow and soaked in the warm, soapy water. A part of me was nervous about going to the dance tonight. It was like I was making my debut in "the Life." Unlike last week, this time I'd be "with a woman." I wasn't just a curiosity-seeker any more. Now I fantasized about holding Traci's body close to mine, without any clothes on.

· · ·

The freckled-face woman who stamped our hands at the dance took one look at us and said to Traci, "Don't tell me this is the new link in your chain. I thought you liked vanilla."

"Fuck you, Nancy," Traci mumbled.

"What chain?" I asked.

"Her chain of fools," the woman replied.

"She's just mad 'cause I didn't want her ass," Traci insisted, walking away.

"Sounds like a bad case of sour grapes," I agreed.

The big, dark warehouse was packed with women decked out in cotton, flannel, and denim. A racially mixed women's band outfitted in vests played a bluesy tune onstage.

"The sistah on harmonica is Pauline Trump," Traci informed me.

"She's good," I nodded. "Is she a friend of yours?"

Traci leaned up against the wall. "We're cool, but I wouldn't say we were friends. I know a lot of people. But I'm basically a loner, except for a few associates."

"You wanna dance?" I asked Traci. "This song has a nice beat."

Traci nodded. "This tune is called, 'Sister, Woman, Lover.' "

We danced to three songs in a row and worked up a sweat. Unlike some people, we'd remembered our deodorant. The place was becoming hot and stuffy.

Two women approached us as we headed toward a bench to rest our legs.

Traci introduced the bald, black woman as Pat, and the serious-looking blonde as Gretchen. I'd never seen a bald woman before, but I had to admit that Pat was attractive, despite her Issac Hayes–looking head.

"We were on our way outside to get some air and to fire up a joint," Pat shouted above the music.

"I could use some air," I sighed.

"I could use a joint," Traci added.

"Sounds like a plan," Pat said, leading the way.

The four of us positioned ourselves on the steps of the building. It was refreshing to be out in the cool, foggy night.

"You all marching tomorrow?" Gretchen asked after sucking on the joint.

I looked at Traci. It suddenly occured to me that she might be expecting me to march. I could just see my family watching the evening news and seeing me stepping in the gay and lesbian parade. It wasn't a pretty picture.

"We could join the 'Lesbians of Color' contingent."

"That would be cool," Pat said, passing me the joint.

"We're marching with Maude's Bar. We're both on the soft-ball team," Gretchen said. "Stevie, are you excited about marching?"

I almost choked on my inhale, partly because the reefer was a little harsh.

"Are you all right?" Traci asked.

I nodded. "I guess I sort of assumed that we would just watch the parade."

"Don't you want to be able to say you marched?" Gretchen asked, reaching for the joint. "The one in Chicago is nothing compared to this."

No, I didn't want to be able to say I marched. I mean, who would I want to say it to, back in Chicago? On the other hand, I didn't want to rain on Traci's parade.

"I think I'd rather watch. I don't want to miss anything. But Traci, don't let me stop you from participating."

"Hey, if that's the space you're in, that's cool. Let's stick together. I don't mind cheering from the sidelines."

I breathed a sigh of relief. A red-faced man walked toward us carrying a can covered by a brown paper bag.

"Is this the Women's Skills, whatever?"

Before I could nod, Gretchen asked, "What's it to you?"

"My wife is in there." The man spat on the ground near us. "That's what it is to me, bitch."

Pat stood up. She turned out to be taller and heavier than the dude. "You see a bitch, you knock her down. So, I can kick your mothafuckin' ass."

The man sized up Pat. He probably concluded that she covered all the ground she stood on and wasn't to be tested. He took a step back but continued to face her.

"Hey, if your wife is in there, she must be where she wants to be at," Gretchen said, raising her eyebrows.

"Yeah, they ain't put a gun to nobody's head up in there," Traci added.

"Well, I'm gonna get her outta there. Move out of my way, you bunch of bull dykes!"

I felt my stomach tighten. None of us moved.

The man kept his distance. "I know what you are. I know what kind of place this is. You're not fooling anybody."

Pat mashed the joint against the banister. "We ain't trying to fool nobody."

"Cathy! Cathy!" the man bellowed. "Cathy, come out here!" The man sipped from his beer. "You mean to tell me that you can satisfy a woman?" he asked nobody in particular. "How the hell can any of you satisfy a woman?" He turned his can up and emptied it into his mouth. "You ain't got the equipment to satisfy no woman!"

Pat groaned. "Obviously, your rusty dick ain't satisfied no-body, or you wouldn't be here."

"Fuck you, bitch."

"Yeah, you would like to," Gretchen cut in.

"I'm gonna pretend like I didn't hear that," Pat said.

The voices had gotten loud, a group of onlookers had gath-ered in the doorway.

"Cathy! Cathy!" the man bellowed. "Cathy, come out here!" He still had sense enough not to try to get past us.

To my surprise, a dark-haired woman who looked like a young Mary Tyler Moore appeared in the doorway. "Rusty, it's over between us," she shouted.

We couldn't help but laugh because she'd called him "Rusty."

"Cathy, please, we can work it out!" he pleaded.

"Go home, Rusty. It's too late. I've discovered women!"

Rusty lunged toward Cathy as she turned to go back inside.

Two big, tough-looking women closed ranks with us. They announced that they were security, and if Rusty didn't turn around and leave, they would throw him off the property. The women had plenty of backup. Rusty looked at all of us blocking the doorway and turned around. He threw his beer can on the ground and muttered, "Dykes are destroying this country."

"There will be no littering!" one of the security women bel-lowed. "Now pick up that can!"

Rusty hesitated and then stooped down and retrieved his can. "Goddamn commie cunts," he muttered.

"Prick," several women shouted. But the mood was upbeat. There was a sense of triumph in the air. There was even a full moon. People seemed ready to party hardy when we got back inside.

"Party over here!" I clapped my hands in the air and shouted across from Traci on the dance floor.

"Party over here!" Pat chimed in nearby.

"We having a funky good time!" Traci yelled.

After we'd finished getting down on the dance floor, Traci and I headed for home. Did I call her apartment home? I realized that it had begun to feel familiar.

Traci drove up to the top of Twin Peaks and parked. There were only a few other cars up there. The fog hovering above the skyline gave San Francisco a magical quality.

"San Francisco is a beautiful city," I said.

Traci put her arm around my shoulder. "It's the most beautiful city in America."

"Chicago has its beauty too, with its downtown and lakefront and great architecture. But it's beautiful in a different way."

"I imagine Chicago to have a masculine feel to it. San Francisco is like a beautiful woman."

"Yeah," I agreed. "I think that's true."

"Which do you prefer?"

I shrugged. "They're like apples and oranges."

"So, you can still have a preference. Which do you prefer, apples or oranges?"

"Right now, I prefer being here with you."

"Hey, I can't argue with that." Traci leaned over and sank her soft lips into mine. It was a long kiss. I had to come up for air.

"Traci, you know, I still don't know that much about you."

"What do you want to know?"

"How you grew up, what your family's like. I guess anything you wanna tell me."

"Let's see, I was raised by wolves."

"Be for real."

"You really want my life story?"

"Yeah."

"Sure you wouldn't just rather live in the moment?"

"For me, conversation can be a great aphrodisiac."

Traci perked up. "My parents are divorced. My father had a roving eye. He owns a little fish market in Sacramento with his girlfriend. My mother's an administrative assistant at the State Department of Education. My brother is in the California Conservation Corps. My sister is a single mother with a little boy. She's a cashier at a grocery store. I'm the oldest. I was raised a good Catholic, went to confession, and the whole bit. I always thought I'd grow up to be a nun."

"Are you serious?"

"As serious as gangrene. Lots of little dykes aspired to be nuns. It was one way of being in a community of women and still being socially accepted."

"Did you know when you were little that you were a lesbian?"

"I'd say so. I mean, I didn't have a word for it. But I knew I was different. I knew I wasn't going for the okeydoke. I was four years old and I was playing one day and I realized I wanted to be the one who got the girl. I mean it was fucked-up enough to be colored in this society. But to be female on top of it. That was like adding insult to injury. When I thought of Negro women, I thought of suffering. I didn't want 'Good Morning, Heartache' to be my theme song. I knew that at an early age."

I arched my eyebrows, "So, you wanted to become a nun?"

"At least I wouldn't have to put up with the bullshit I'd seen my mother and aunts go through. And no matter what they'd been through, it was like you were nothing without a man. Damn if I was gonna honor and obey some mothascratcher. I wanted to be independent, so I ended up being one of the first girls with a paper route. I met these two women who lived together. And everybody said they were funny. They were into roles. Seems like everybody was, back in the early sixties. Of course I was fascinated. I was nosy and I always tried to prolong my paper collection duties. One day I just blurted out, 'I think I'm like y'all.' "

"What did they say?"

"They were cool. They told me that they suspected as much. But that it wasn't easy being in 'the Life.' You were forced to live in secrecy and shame. Your family members might turn their backs on you. The church saw you as a sinner, and the shrinks were convinced you were crazy. I told them that I was still drawn to it. It still seemed like more fun than being cooped up in a convent. They showed me the ropes, got me into a bar when I was only sixteen. And hey, the rest is herstory."

"Were you ever with a man?"

"Yeah, but only one, and he turned out to be gay. Michael and I are still tight. He lives in Guerneville on the Russian River. He works at a bed-and-breakfast."

"Is Michael black?"

"Yeah, very much so."

"How did your family react? Did you ever come out to them?"

"Not in so many words. But they all know the real deal. Like I said, my parents are divorced. Neither of them are into the Catholic church anymore. They were never all that deep into it. They mainly wanted us to go to Catholic school."

"It's cool with them that you're a lesbian?"

"My old man is cool with it. He said to me, 'Why should you let some man rule you? You better go for what you know, baby girl. You always did have your own mind.' My father encouraged me to be a tomboy, pissed my Mama off. We used to fish together and shit. He used to tell me, 'Always have your own money. Traci, always have your own shit. Find a man who loves you and that you like.' Daddy always said I had too much 'get up' to be a girl. Daddy says, 'I ain't worried about you, 'cause I know you can take care of yourself. I'm worried about your sister, 'cause she all the time hooking up with trifling-ass men.' "

"How does your mother feel about you being gay?"

"She says I'm all crossed up. Going against my nature and shit."

"Sounds like my mother."

"I mean she wants the best for me, don't get me wrong. But she's from the old school. Thinks every woman should act like a lady, find a good husband, and raise a family. I'm a renegade."

"Stevie, when did you first think that you were a lesbian?"

"I'm still not sure I'm a lesbian."

Traci smiled. "When did you first question your sexuality?"

"I got a crush on the school nurse back in high school. We never got involved sexually, though. Looking back, it was more affection than anything else. She was single and had a nice ride and stayed near the University of Chicago."

"What did she drive?"

"A Ford Mustang."

"They were superbad."

"Last time I saw Nurse Horn, she told me she was going back to graduate school to get a master's degree in public health. I went away to school and we sort of lost touch. But I'll never forget her."

"Was she white?"

"Yeah, but that's not why she was unforgettable. She was open-minded. She thought I was special. She could've been any color. I was put down by my friends because I was up in a white woman's face. I lost my best friend because she suspected me of being funny. Although Carla eventually did come back around. But by then, I'd outgrown her. She got pregnant senior year and went to East St. Louis to stay with her grandmother. I never kept up with her. I heard she had twins, a boy and a girl."

Traci sighed. "I lost touch with my high-school friends after I moved to the Bay Area. But I don't have any regrets. Stevie, there's no community like the women's community. You remember how the black community was, folks looking out for each other and shit?"

"Yeah, nosey as all get out, but they cared. You felt like you belonged. If somebody dies, they're still there with food in my old neighborhood. And it's still a crime not to speak."

"Speaking of crime, that's the problem with living in the 'hood. You get a sense of community, but you also gotta watch your back. And of course it's hard to be an 'out' gay person. In the women's community you really get the support, plus a sense of security. I mean they will trash you and analyze you to death. So, I'm not saying the women's community is perfect. But when I broke my ankle playing softball last summer, plenty of women where there for me. I had so many visitors, till it wasn't funny. The nurse said she'd seen cancer patients get less attention than I did. Nobody supports each other like the gay and lesbian community. A lot of folks are ostracized by their families. So, friends and lovers become our families."

"That's nice."

"A lot of lesbians have been lovers with most of their friends."

"Really?"

"It's different with men and women. They're seldom friends with their exes. I mean let's face it, men and women are seldom close friends, period. With dykes, if we break up, unless your lover was like Bette Davis in *What Ever Happened to Baby Jane*, you usually stay connected. I mean sometimes, you wait about three months. But some folks don't even have a cooling-off period. They go straight from being lovers to being friends. I know a woman who isn't even a lesbian, but she sleeps with dykes because we make such good friends."

"Come again?"

"Rita's a straight feminist, but she's committed to being part of the lesbian community. She swears that the best way to make intimate friends is to sleep with them. Her sexual relationships never last more than two months, but then they always end up being great friends."

"What about her sexual desires?"

"I know this woman who's a sex therapist, and she says with women, desire isn't that important."

"What is then?"

"Willingness. It's her theory that you just have to start out being willing to make love. Desire may follow, but you don't have to start with desire. You just have to be willing to open the door."

Maybe tomorrow night I will, I thought.

7

I was amazed by the sheer number of people marching and the hundreds more lining the parade route. There were men dressed up as nuns, women with their breasts exposed, drag queens galore, and a naked man. There was even a drag queen who couldn't decide what to wear and brought a closet on wheels along. And bunches of folks shook their half-naked bodies to blaring music atop an array of colorful floats.

But there were moments during the parade when my mood matched the cool, overcast skies: When I reflected on the teenager that I'd heard about who was thrown into a river back East and drowned because he was gay; and also when a mental-health group's placards reminded us of the high suicide rate among young gays and lesbians; and, of course, reading the signs of teachers who'd lost their jobs, teenagers who'd been kicked out of their homes, and mothers who'd lost custody of their children, simply because they were gay, was all quite sobering.

A short, black man wore big signs, back and front, that read AMERICA COME BACK TO GOD. Traci said the dark-skinned brotha was a permanent fixture at the cable car turnaround at Market and Powell, rain or shine.

I was shocked to see a mayoral candidate and elected officials riding in the parade. I had major trouble imagining Mayor Daley doing such a thing.

Traci had suggested a hot tub as the perfect way to unwind after the parade.

"Are you sure this is cool?" I whispered to her as she opened the creaky wooden gate of a dark backyard.

"Positive," Traci assured me.

"And are you sure Sunday nights are 'Women Only'?" I asked as I followed her through the tall grass.

"Stop tripping, Stevie."

I'd never heard of such before. Rank strangers just coming in off the street to use somebody's hot tub. Then again, I'd never even seen a hot tub, let alone soaked in one. According to Traci, the deal was you put a dollar in the plastic jar and took a shower before you hopped in. Of course you had to bring your own towel. There were certain nights for women only, and tonight was one of them.

"Nobody steals the money?" I'd asked Traci.

"No, this is a mellow scene, people aren't into ripping this place off. It doesn't attract that kind of energy. Besides, it's a word-of-mouth thing. Not every Tom, Dick, and Harry knows about it."

"You sure men won't crash it on Women's Night?" I'd wanted to know.

"Why would they?" Traci shrugged her shoulders. "For over half the week, it's coed. They can wait till then to see a naked woman. Besides, the people that use this place have pretty good vibes. They're not tripping on nudity."

I couldn't believe that I was standing buck-naked under an outdoor shower with Traci.

"More hot water," I shivered.

Traci adjusted the faucet.

"Now it's too hot," I squealed, reaching out and tinkering with the knobs myself.

I paused to admire Traci's wet, well-toned body in the moonlight. Her firm breasts with big "come suck me" nipples and the curly bush between her legs made me want to reach out and touch her. But instead, I followed Traci's plump, bouncing behind toward the big wooden tub. I was glad that I had gotten up the nerve to do this, I thought, stepping into the bubbling hot water. It felt good. Chicago seemed a world away.

I smiled shyly and made brief eye contact with the three strangers inside the tub. Two of the women were white and one was Latina. They were passing a joint among them.

"Happy Gay Day!" The Latina woman greeted us. She had large, bobbing breasts, despite her boyish haircut. "Happy Gay Day," Traci and I responded.

I couldn't help but notice that the brunette had ample breasts too. The blonde was flat enough to be mistaken for a boy. But I appreciated glimpsing the rest of her slender body when she sat on the edge of the tub. I imagined she could be a dancer.

"We were discussing orgasms," the curly brunette said casually.

"Oh," I said, somewhat taken aback.

"If it bothers you, we can talk about something else." The Latina woman with a crew cut smiled.

"I'm cool with it, but she's visiting from the Midwest. It might be too much of a culture shock for her," Traci added.

"I'm not from the Midwest," I protested. "I'm from Chicago."

"Last time I looked at a map, Chicago was in the Midwest," Traci insisted.

"Well, technically, Chicago is in the Midwest," I acknowledged. "But it's different. Traci, you make it sound like I'm from Nebraska or some damn where."

"Like I said, we can talk about something else."

"Yeah," the Latina woman agreed, "*Chica*, this is as much your space as anyone else's."

"Yeah, you're a child of the universe. And you have a right to be here, same as the trees and the stars," the blonde chimed in. She made a little splash hopping back into the tub. When she passed me the joint, I noticed that she had a ring in her nose.

"Look, feel free to talk about orgasms all you want to," I insisted, and sucked on the reefer. "Knock yourselves out."

"Lisa, you were saying that if you can't have a beautiful orgasm, you'd rather not have one at all."

"It's not that I don't value them," Curly explained to the blonde. "It's just that if it isn't special, why bother?"

"What do you mean by a beautiful orgasm?" The Latina woman wanted to know.

"I think I know what you mean. Otherwise, it's just a release," the blonde explained.

"Exactly," Lisa agreed.

I wouldn't mind just a release, I thought.

"I want to feel music between my legs, ride a roller-coaster ride," Lisa sighed.

The Latina woman exhaled. "Why not just go to the Santa Cruz boardwalk, if you want to ride a roller-coaster?"

"It's not the same," Lisa groaned.

"Sounds like you wanna be speaking in tongues and shit," Traci smiled, joining in the conversation.

Lisa looked confused. "What's 'speaking in tongues'?"

"You have to get the Holy Ghost," I explained.

"The thought of Lisa getting the Holy Ghost and speaking in tongues is funny," the Latina woman said, cracking up.

Everyone whooped, including Lisa. It was like none of us could stop laughing.

"Having fun, Stevie?" Traci asked.

I nodded. Although I worried that we were being sacrilegious.

"Girl, you ain't in Kansas no more," she teased.

I had a good feeling about tonight as we walked back to the house. It was like the stars and the planets and the moon were all in the right place. In the right place for love.

"Traci, I feel so relaxed from being in that hot tub. It's amazing."

"A hot tub allows you to lay your burdens down, all right. People make fun of us Californians and our hot tubs, but that's because they don't know how to relax."

"Hey, I'm sold. Don't you wish you had one of your very own?"

"Sure, but having one a few blocks away ain't too shabby, either."

"I'm hipped. Well, tomorrow night, Cinderella will be back to her ashes, with no hot tub," I sighed.

"Cinderella, huh? So, you feel like Cinderella?"

"A little," I admitted, pausing to appreciate the Victorian houses that looked good enough to eat. "I mean, it's been wonderful and exciting. Soon, I'll be back at home, cramped in my little non-air-conditioned room in ninety-degree heat. I'll probably end up taking some job on a newspaper in a small market. The town will be too small to turn around in."

"Didn't you tell me that practically everybody has to start out in a small market?"

I nodded and motioned for Traci to stop. I put my arm around her shoulder as we gazed at the panoramic view of San Francisco from above Dolores Park.

"I used to think that all I wanted was a job in the media, period," I continued as we admired the view. "Any job, anywhere. But you know, after spending this past week with you and being in San Francisco, I'm not so sure."

"What do you mean?"

"I mean, I'm beginning to ask myself, 'What is really important? What do I really want out of life?' "

"And what's the answer?"

"Happiness. I suppose I'd rather be happy on a bicycle than crying in a Rolls-Royce."

Traci pulled me close to her. "I can dig it," she agreed.

I can dig her, I thought as my knees weakened. Our lips touched, and then our tongues.

"I'm willing," I whispered.

We were on Traci's foam mattress. She'd promised me the total Traci treatment. So far, I had no complaints. We'd drunk some Blue Nun wine out of her good glasses. And she'd brought the vase of fresh-cut flowers from the kitchen table and put them on the wooden crate near the bed. Traci had even lit a bunch of white candles inside little glass jars. The candlelight had transformed the room into a romantic hideaway.

"I almost forgot the music," Traci said, breaking away from

my embrace. "Roberta Flack? Phoebe Snow? Chris Williamson? What is your pleasure tonight?"

"I love Roberta Flack, and 'Poetry Man' is one of my favorite jams. I've never heard of Chris Williamson before."

"Not everybody can get into women's music. Even I can only take so much." Traci smiled. "But Chris Williamson is exceptional. Her album *The Changer and the Changed* is beautiful. I think you'll dig it."

Traci and I sat on the bed in the candlelight. She pressed her finger against my lips. I licked it with my tongue and sucked it inside my mouth. I felt more excited than scared. It wasn't like I was a virgin. It wasn't like Traci had anything to hurt me with. It might be different being with a woman, but I could hang with different, I told myself. I was ready to get it on.

I gathered Traci in my arms and she kissed me long and hard. I rubbed my fingers against her soft face. "It's nice being with you."

"You ain't seen nothing yet."

Suddenly, I felt shy. It was put up or shut up time.

Traci drew circles with her thumb around my nipples through my T-shirt. They felt hot and hard. I wanted to unfasten my bra. I wanted to feel her bare hands on my breasts.

"Let me help you," I offered, raising my T-shirt. Soon Traci's lips were sucking my breasts and I was running my hands up and down her back.

"Let me relieve you of your threads. I promised you the total Traci treatment, remember?"

"Yeah, and I'm ready for it," I answered bravely.

Traci slowly unsnapped and pulled off my jeans. She planted kisses on my bare thighs. By the time she tugged at my panties, my love had come down. But despite my wetness I obeyed her request to lie on my stomach so that she could rub vanilla-scented massage oil all over my body.

"You sure know how to rub me the right way. I feel so relaxed," I moaned, stretching my well-oiled body.

"I just aim to please."

"Traci, you're so sweet. No one has ever done all this before."

"Baby, I just want you to be happy."

"Well, I'm very happy."

"Hey, we've only just begun," Traci promised. She undressed and laid down next to me. I shivered with excitement as our naked bodies touched. It was strange feeling a woman's soft breasts and stomach against me. But it felt strange in a good way. It was like an adventure. Traci rubbed her hands up and down my thighs. I was glad that she was taking the lead, but I still couldn't help feeling nervous. After all, it was my first time being with a woman.

We kissed and wrapped our bodies around each other.

Feeling her breasts against mine made my heart beat faster. And holding her warm, woman's body reminded me of the gentle rocking of the boat that took you into the tunnel of love at Riverview Amusement Park back when I was a child. I sighed. Traci ran her fingers up and down my thighs. I felt my vagina muscles open and shut. I wanted Traci as much as I'd ever wanted anyone.

She made circles with her finger around my clitoris. I reminded myself to breathe. Traci's finger found my spot. She rubbed it gently. I grabbed her and kissed her as she stuck her finger inside of me. I was wet.

"Stevie, you're beautiful inside and out!" Traci breathed. "You deserve to feel good. You deserve to feel good," she repeated like a mantra as she stroked me.

Traci's voice trailed off. I closed my eyes, turning inward, paying attention to my own sensations. I was losing touch with the world. I couldn't believe it, it *was* like I was climbing a roller-coaster ride! It was thrilling and exciting.

"I don't care what anybody thinks! I don't care what anybody thinks!" I shouted as I reached the top. There were fireworks between my legs.

"You came, didn't you?" Traci asked.

"Yeah," I marveled.

Traci hugged me.

"It *was* like a roller-coaster ride. And then it was just like Chris Williamson sang in that song, 'about an endless waterfall!' " I exclaimed.

"Well, congratulations. You not only came, you came with a bang."

I sat up. "Traci, I can't imagine ever feeling any better than I just did!"

"It's not always that good," Traci said smiling. "In fact, it doesn't sound like it gets any better than you described."

"Thank you so much. I never came before. I can't believe it!" I said, giving her a big hug.

"What can I say? Traci is my name, and love is my game."

I swallowed. "I can't believe this is our last night together."

"Yeah, it's a damn shame," Traci sighed, and twisted her face like she'd bitten into something rotten.

"I'm not going." I was surprised to hear the words come out of my mouth.

"You're not going back to Chicago?"

"No, I'm not going." I said clearly. "I'll just use the rest of my savings until I find a job. I've made up my mind."

Traci's face lit up. "You won't regret it."

"It's cool with you?"

"Hey, I'm all for it!" We hugged and kissed. I felt so excited. I'd be lying if I said I wasn't scared too. But it felt good taking a risk. It felt right stepping out on faith.

"Traci, you want me to make love to you now? I think I can figure out what goes where. I'll do my best to please you."

"Hey, I'm already pleased."

After breakfast, I called home to deliver the news. Mama answered the phone. I took a deep breath. "Mama, I've made some new friends and I'm gonna stay in San Francisco and look for a job."

For a minute Mama was speechless. Then she shouted, "Jean Eloise, have you lost your mind? None of us can rest with you all the way out there alone."

I tried to reassure her. "San Francisco is safer than Chicago."

"I don't care about crime statistics. The only safety is in the Lord. I need you to be nearby, so I'll know what you're up to."

"What about what I need?" I asked.

"You're not ready to be out there in the world all by yourself."

"I read that mother birds kick the baby birds out of the nests when it's time for them to fly. Well, it's time for me to test my wings."

"Ray, come to the phone. She says she's going to stay in San Francisco! She's talking some foolishness about needing to fly. See if you can bring her down to earth. I have to take something to calm my nerves."

"Jean, what's going on?" My father sounded concerned. "You've worried your mother half to death. She had to take a blood-pressure pill and lie down."

"I'm sorry, Daddy, but I've gotta do what's right for me. I have to live my own life."

"You ain't into something out there are you?" My father asked, lowering his voice.

"Of course not," I answered. He made it sound like I was part of a drug-smuggling ring. "I'm not stupid. I've got sense enough not to get involved in any mess."

"I thought so. But you know your mother has bad nerves." Daddy paused. "We're so proud of you, Jeannie, we don't know what to do. We'd hate to have you so far away." I could hear the emotion in my father's voice. And I was touched.

"I still love you all. I'm just checking out the possibilities. If things don't work out, I'll be back. But I'll never know if I don't try."

"You gotta point there. You know, I was younger than you when I struck out on my own," Daddy admitted. "But, I guess you're just more protective of a girl."

"Some women have a sense of adventure too, you know."

"I suppose you get that from me," Daddy bragged. "Well, if you're doggedly determined then go'n out there with your bad self. Remember, you can't hit any higher than you aim. So, reach for the sky. And while you're trying out your wings, don't forget your roots."

"I won't, Daddy."

8

I 'm a San Franciscan now," I announced to Traci over a burrito in the Mission District. "I've got a job interview with KPIX tomorrow. I even hopped a cable car in the middle of Powell Street yesterday and went to Fisherman's Wharf. I can't believe that all those dumb tourists line up at the foot of Powell and Market streets waiting. And to think two weeks ago, I was one of them."

"A true San Franciscan doesn't even ride the cable cars," Traci said between swallows of Mexican beer. "And we wouldn't be caught dead at Fisherman's Wharf. Unless it was in the middle of winter when the place is deserted."

"I'm not going to lie to you, Junior. Riding the cable cars up and down these steep hills and listening to the clanging of the bells does peel my paint. Maybe I'll have to get that out of my system before I can become a true San Franciscan."

"Well, you might not be a true San Franciscan, but you're sure full of beans," Traci teased.

"Can't I be excited? I'm in this beautiful city with a beautiful woman. Of course I'm feeling my oats."

She laughed. "Can you keep a secret?"

I nodded.

"Even us jaded folks like to hop a cable car every once in a while for old-time's sake. We just tend to get the urge in January."

I sat across from the interviewer, who insisted I call her Vickie rather than Ms. Hauser. It was only my first interview. I'd just opened the job-hunting book *What Color Is Your Parachute?*, and I didn't even know the answer yet. I got to face the window that looked out on the bay. Everybody seemed to have a view in this town. I reminded myself not to get too distracted.

I was thankful that I'd packed my beige skirt and white blouse, although I could've gotten away with my pantsuit. Vickie was wearing a navy one. I still had to adjust to these dark colors in the middle of summer.

"Jean, I must say that I'm really impressed," Vickie said, looking up from an open folder.

"Thank you," I mumbled, briefly making contact with Vickie's green eyes. Maybe in San Francisco, a blonde had to compensate by having short hair, and not wearing makeup. Probably you wouldn't get any respect otherwise. If you were blonde, slim, wore a dress, and had hair down your back people would probably think you lacked leadership qualities. Vickie was a tough blonde, I decided.

"I believe that you're perfect for the Minority Outreach Training Program."

"Well, thank you." I wondered why I was perfect for a training program. I was already trained. Hadn't Vickie seen my résumé? I decided to hip her to the facts. "As my résumé indicates," I said sounding like a job-hunting manual, "I worked at a

TV station in Evanston the summer before last, and at a radio station in Normal last summer."

"Yes, I see, station WILD, Normal, Illinois." Vickie smiled and winked.

"I think it was pretty tame by San Francisco standards."

"You know, they say, 'You get an interview because you're qualified, but you get a job because someone likes you.' Jean, what can I say, I like you."

"Thanks," I said, not knowing what to say after the interviewer says "I like you." It would sound silly to answer "I like you too." Although I'd be willing to say it if it meant getting the gig. "Does that mean that you're offering me the job?"

There was a moment that seemed like an eternity and then Vickie nodded and said, "Yes, welcome aboard."

"Thank you," I said letting out a breath. It was too good to be true.

"Vickie, I'm really excited by the opportunity of making a contribution to KPIX." You don't have to sound so damn formal. You've already got the gig, I criticized myself.

"Well, Jean, we're excited about having you, regardless of where you end up being assigned."

"Assigned?"

"Yes, KPIX is hosting the two-week training program, but after that you could end up anywhere. Maybe even Normal, Illinois."

Ha, ha, very funny, I thought. "So I might not be working in San Francisco?" I tried to mask my concern.

"Chances are, you wouldn't, since your interest is in news reporting. Right now the only need here is for minority account executives."

"Maybe I'd be open to sales."

"There's still no guarantee that you would be placed in San Francisco. A prerequisite for the Minority Outreach Training Program is that you be willing to relocate."

"Well, I'd really love to be a reporter, and I would love to work in San Francisco, too."

"You and everybody else," Vickie groaned. She opened the drawer and took out a pack of cigarettes. She pulled out one and offered me the pack.

"No thanks," I said, watching a ship gliding across the water.

"Jean, the only entry-level jobs in the media here are clerical and production-assistant positions." Vickie puffed furiously on her cigarette. I felt like I must have driven her to smoke.

"I'm willing to start on the ground floor."

"Those jobs are often part-time, and they pay less than four dollars an hour." Vickie exhaled.

"Money isn't everything. An opportunity is all I want."

"Are you sure that you want to turn down *this* opportunity just to hold out for something that may end up being a dead end? Is it *that* important to stay in San Francisco?"

"I love this city and I've met people here. I don't want to relocate. I just located."

"Well, there must be something in the fog," Vickie declared, and blew smoke practically in my face. "Sorry," she said, waving the air. "I know people with master's degrees waiting tables on Union Street, and Ph.D.'s driving taxicabs. They'll take any job just for the privilege of living in San Francisco. Personally, I need a certain amount of comfort."

"Maybe when I'm older, I'll feel that way, too."

Vickie almost choked on her cigarette.

"I'm sorry, I didn't mean to imply that you were old. I mean you're not old."

Vickie shrugged her shoulders, but her finger wiped at a

wrinkle under her eye. "I just hope that you're not making a big mistake."

"I hope not either. But I feel like San Francisco is where I can really blossom."

"Spoken like a true dreamer."

"Working in the media in San Francisco would be a dream come true."

"Well, if we get an opening that you would be suited for, I will give you a call."

"Thanks a lot. I really appreciate that." I stood up to go.

Vickie hesitated. "Jean, let me be frank. Dreams die hard in this town." She mashed out her cigarette. "San Francisco has the highest suicide rate in the country."

I swallowed. "I'm sure it won't come to that. I'd head back to Chicago before I'd head for the Golden Gate Bridge."

"Well, I've tried to level with you."

"I think you have."

"It's just that an opportunity like this doesn't come across my desk every day. They're not like BART trains. If you miss one, you can't just catch the next one."

"I know."

Vickie lit another cigarette and inhaled. "Jean, a smart flea knows when to hop."

I leaned toward the door. I wanted to hop on out of here.

Vickie suddenly mashed her cigarette out. "Save yourself some shoe leather. Accept this slot in the Minority Training Program!" she insisted.

"I'm just not willing to relocate at this point." I sighed. "But thank you very much for considering me."

Vickie stood up and extended her hand. "Jean, good luck, then. And have a nice day."

"Thanks."

"Jawea, the mail's here," I called down to her in the small yard below. "Your *Sojourner* newspaper and your *Ms.* magazine came."

Jawea continued to sway with her hands and feet. It looked like she was dancing in slow motion. It looked weird.

"Jawea, did you hear me?"

"Yes, I heard you, but maybe I don't give a shit!"

I was taken aback. Just last night Jawea had said I had a tall spirit. And that I projected beautiful energy. We didn't see each other that much, but when we did, everything seemed cool. I thought that Jawea liked me, that she was glad I was living here.

"Jawea, I don't appreciate you talking to me like that."

"Well, I don't appreciate your interrupting me when I'm practicing Tai Chi."

"Well, you didn't have to get funky. I didn't know what that was. I've never heard of Tai Chi before."

"Ok, Stevie, just try and tune in to the vibes a person is putting out before you insert your energy into their space, from now on, all right?"

I sighed and walked away, rather than telling Jawea that she could tune in to kissing my ass.

I went back into the pad and found Traci in the kitchen. She was getting stuff together to make a salad for Pat's birthday party.

"I just told Jawea the mail's here, and she went off on me."

"Is she doing Tai Chi?"

"Yeah, that's what she called it."

Traci set a big pottery bowl on the table. "Don't go to Hollywood. She just didn't want anybody to break her concentration."

"Well, I didn't know. Jawea's the one who went to Hollywood."

"Don't take it personally. It wasn't about you. Jawea is studying to be a master."

"At the rate my job hunt is going, maybe I should join her."

Traci kissed me on the cheek. "Don't worry, baby, you'll find something. But maybe you need to forget about the glamour jobs. There's way too much competition. Everybody can't be Barbara Walters."

"Hey, I'm just trying to use my skills." I watched Traci cut up vegetables.

"Maybe you should consider working with your hands, doing manual labor."

I shrugged. "Not intellectual enough." I crunched on a carrot. "How come it's potluck? Are they that poor?"

Traci shook her head as she sprinkled sunflower seeds on the salad in the big pottery bowl that Jawea had made. "No, 'course not. I mean, they're downwardly mobile like everybody else. Gretchen actually comes from money. She's in a land-surveyor apprenticeship. And Pat goes to the People's Law College. Her parents own a dry-cleaning business back in Philly. I'm pretty sure Pat grew up middle-class."

"I just never heard of a birthday party being potluck before, that's all."

"Everything out here is potluck, you'll see."

Traci began stirring together her secret herb dressing.

"Are you sure they wouldn't rather have some fried chicken?"

Traci sighed. "Most of them will be vegetarians."

"Even the sistahs?" I imagined they'd be glad to get their mitts on some of my fried chicken.

"There won't be that many sistahs there."

"Why not? It's Pat's party, isn't it?"

"That doesn't mean anything. Pat is a feminist first, black second."

"Really?"

"Yes. Remember, this is San Francisco."

My baby had been right; I'd never seen folks get so excited over a salad before. Me, I wouldn't mind sucking on a bone right now, I thought, surveying the table full of breads, quiche, dips, vegetable dishes, and this cheese that reminded me of cement. They even had the nerve to have that nasty Perrier water that Traci insisted I'd get used to. That's what people had said about sexual intercourse with men, too—that I'd get used to it. Maybe, if Myron had believed in longer foreplay, it wouldn't have hurt. And if Skylar had lasted more than two minutes, I could've gotten used to it. Just when it started getting good, it was over.

There were about ten women, mostly dressed in denim or flannel shirts and jeans, in the homey living room furnished with crates and comfortable old furniture.

"You can hardly hear the music," I complained to Traci as we headed for a spot on the couch with our drinks and little plates of food.

"Yeah, and it's Sweet Honey in the Rock, too. They're a dynamite a cappella group. Their music has a powerful message."

"The sistahs sound good. Pump up the volume."

"Somebody turned it down, said they were trying to have a conversation," Traci explained between sips of wine.

"You don't go to a party to talk, you go to a party to party," I whispered.

"Stevie, later on we'll pump it up and turn it out, don't worry," Traci assured me.

"Give me some couch, I'm gonna get over here in the sistah corner."

It was Pat, dressed no differently than if she were going camping. I dug myself into the corner to make room for her sturdy frame.

"So, you decided to become a native?"

"How can you *become* a native?" Traci challenged her.

"You know what I mean. You know what I mean, right, Stevie?"

I nodded. Two of the white women who'd introduced themselves as Tamar and Miriam edged closer, drawn to us like bees to honey.

"Hey, I told Stevie, you only go around once in life, so you gotta grab for all the gusto you can," Traci said, gulping her wine.

"Sounds like a slogan from a beer commercial." Pat laughed. "You made the right decision, 'cause it ain't happening back in Chicago, if you know what I mean," she added.

Traci nodded, although she'd never been to Chicago.

A knot of white women had drawn close to us. It was obvious that their attention was focused on our little corner.

"In Chicago, the Mafia runs all the bars," Pat informed us. "Same with Boston," she added. " 'The Man' ain't getting up off of nothing there."

Tamar whispered to Miriam, "Who's 'the Man?' " Miriam pointed to her white arm. It was obvious from the puzzled expression on Tamar's face that she still didn't get it.

"Chicago and Boston are racist as hell." Pat continued to hold court.

"You see how fucked up they acted in Boston around bus-ing," Traci reminded us.

"Didn't Dr. King say that Chicago was worse than the South?" Miriam cut in, straightening her glasses. She was the librarian type, with her dark hair pulled back, and her forgetta-ble features.

"Yeah, he did say that," I confirmed. I remembered the time Grandma and I had marched with Dr. King through a white Chicago neighborhood, and how vicious the taunts had been.

"San Francisco is the only place to be. Can I get a witness?" Pat asked.

Traci raised her glass in agreement.

"What about Seattle?" Tamar asked respectfully.

Traci shook her head. "Rains so much, you'll rust."

"Seattle's like being lovers with a beautiful woman who's sick all the time," Pat added.

"I heard that!" Traci smiled, giving Pat five.

"What about New York?" Miriam asked, sounding like a game show contestant.

Pat hesitated. "New York is cool for a visit, but I don't want to smell piss three hundred and sixty-five days a year."

"New York smells like piss?" I asked.

"Their subways stank," Traci explained.

"They got too many roaches for me," Pat added. "I bet even Jackie O's got roaches. Now, you know that's a damn shame."

"When I visited my cousins, I swear, there was roaches at every meal," Traci cut in. "I lost ten pounds in two weeks."

"Stop lying," Pat laughed.

The white women in the room were now gazing at us like an audience watching a play. I felt a little uncomfortable being onstage, and yet I enjoyed being the center of attention.

"If I'm lying, I'm flying," Traci insisted between gulps of wine. "You open the refrigerator and ten roaches come out. They up in the bed with you and shit. The killer was when I went to brush my teeth and the mothafuckas was crawling on the toothbrush."

"Stop!" Pat yelled. "People will lose their appetites."

"I heard that," I said. But I realized that I'd lost some of my appetite for visiting New York.

"Not to change the subject," Pat said lowering her voice considerably, "but, Traci, I can't believe you finally got up with a sistah." Pat had slurred her words so that most of the white women couldn't understand what she'd said.

"Traci usually likes to play in the snow," Pat added for my ears only.

"You got your nerve," Traci whispered, "blonde as Gretchen is. Besides, we integrating your damn party. So, you need to shut your ass up."

"Hey, y'all look good together," Pat smiled. "I was just making an observation, that's all."

I didn't want to stick to Traci like glue, so when Gretchen asked if anyone wanted to go with her on a beer run, I volunteered.

"Coors," I exclaimed happily, pointing to a case of beer behind the glass door. I remembered how my white dorm-mates had packed their car trunks full of Coors beer after a Colorado ski trip. Everybody put Coors beer on a pedestal. You couldn't get it east of the Rockies.

"Not Coors!" Gretchen shouted as color rushed to her normally pale face.

"Why not? Is it too expensive?" I asked sheepishly.

Gretchen shook her head, her face relaxed, and she sighed as though she'd suddenly remembered something.

"I forgot, you're new. You see, we're boycotting Coors."

I knew about not eating grapes, I supposed the whole country knew about that. But I had never heard of boycotting beer.

"How come we're boycotting Coors?" I asked, anxious to be considered a part of the "we."

"Because they're racist, homophobic, classist, sexist, and otherwise oppressive," Gretchen recited as calmly as a teacher explaining a math problem to a third-grader.

"Oh, I didn't know," I said. "Here I was thinking that Coors beer was the cat's meow. Thanks for hipping me to the fact."

"I realize that you didn't know, Stevie. Well, now you've learned something," Gretchen said in a patronizing voice that made me want to scream.

Gretchen and I walked up the hill, each carrying a six-pack of Miller's. A couple wearing down jackets walked toward us, a man and a woman.

"It's my sister, Susan," Gretchen muttered. Susan looked like a slightly younger version of Gretchen, except her hair was a darker shade of blond.

"We couldn't get in," she moaned. The man, a good-looking Asian, stood by nervously.

"Susan, you should've known better than to bring a man."

Gretchen made the word *man* sound as welcome as a rattlesnake. "You remember what happened last time."

"I know," Susan whined. She hung her head like a child being blessed out. "But this is different. Donald was a rich, white stockbroker. Roger is an artist and he's Chinese."

Gretchen glanced at Roger as if she hadn't noticed his ethnicity before.

"He even grew up in Chinatown," Susan added proudly.

Gretchen hesitated and then sighed. "He's still a man, Susan, and this *is* a women's party."

"Too bad, 'cause there's no way Roger and I can snort all that coke by ourselves."

Gretchen's eyebrows arched with interest. "All what coke?"

Roger's large dark eyes twinkled, and his thin lips looked like they might break out into a smile.

"The coke Roger's got on him."

"Does Pat know Roger's got coke?"

Susan shook her head. "We didn't even see Pat. This diesel dyke who answered the door didn't give us a chance. She just said that I was violating a women-only space. And I'm thinking, Who the fuck are you to keep me out of my own sister's house?"

"I'll get you in," Gretchen assured them. Susan and Roger grinned like they'd just been accepted into the college of their choice. I never would've thought that straight people would kiss somebody's behind just to get into a lesbian party. And as expensive as cocaine was, too. I'd never been around people doing coke, but I'd read about it in my social psychology book. Maybe there was a place in the world more unusual than San Francisco. But I had never been there.

I stared down at the thin line of white powder on the plastic cutting-board, hoping I wouldn't sneeze. I couldn't afford for my sinuses to act up at a time like this.

"Hold one nostril and just inhale it in with the other," Traci said gently. "It's her first time," she explained to the group huddled around the dining room table.

My nostril was working like a vacuum cleaner as it sucked up the cocaine. It smelled good, but I couldn't think of anything it reminded me of. Didn't people say that cocaine was in a class by itself? I wondered how it would feel once it got into my system. I looked around the room at the people who were already high. They were talkative, energetic, and smiling.

Susan and Roger were in the corner blowing bubbles.

"I want to blow bubbles too," I shouted. I went over and grabbed the bottle.

"Far fucking out," Susan exclaimed, admiring my huge bubble.

"So, Stevie, how do you feel?" Traci's eyes looked brighter than usual.

"I feel pretty."

"You feel pretty?"

I nodded.

"Sounds like *West Side Story*," Traci said.

"Sounds like a nice high," Pat said, nibbling on a piece of her carrot birthday cake.

"Roger, give me your number before you leave," Traci winked. "You're a good connection."

Things were looking up. KPIX had called me about a production-assistant opening, and I'd interviewed with Vickie again. It had gone well, and I was pretty sure that I would get the job. She hadn't actually come out and offered it to me, so I didn't want to count my chickens before they hatched. But I couldn't help feeling hopeful as I rushed into the apartment looking for Traci.

"I think I might have a job as a production assistant at KPIX! The interview went well. She all but offered it to me."

"That's good," Traci mumbled without looking up. She continued to pore over some figures at the kitchen table.

"Are you balancing your checkbook?"

Traci shook her head. "Stevie, how is your money situation?"

"Tight, my savings are really dwindling. But if I get this job at KPIX, my money problems will be over."

"We're trying to put some money together to buy a gram."

"A gram of coke?"

"Of course. How much can I hit you up for?"

I sat down next to Traci at the kitchen table. There was no money in my budget for drugs. "I barely have enough bus fare to go on job interviews. Even if I get this production-assistant job, it won't start for two weeks. No telling how long it will be before I see my first paycheck. And the refrigerator is practically empty."

"We've got food," Traci sounded defensive. "Ain't nobody here going hungry."

"I didn't say I wasn't dirtying a plate on a regular basis. It's just that I get tired of eating beans and rice and tortillas every daggone day."

"We eat healthy. We got all kind of vegetables in there. I don't know what you're talking about."

"I'm talking about variety."

"I suppose next you're gonna tell me that you miss the smell of frying bacon."

"Don't remind me. Look, Traci, I can live without bacon and steak and pork chops, but I would like to be able to buy some chicken or fish each week. I can't see spending food money on drugs when we can't afford certain groceries."

"Look, just give us what you can. I'll get you some fish. I get paid next Friday. Jawea gets her SSI check soon."

"SSI check, what's that?"

"Social Security Insurance. Jawea's on for a mental disability," Traci explained as she drew a glass of spring water from the cooler.

I stood up. "Is Jawea crazy? Am I living with a mental patient?"

"Jawea's not crazy. She's just sensitive, that's all. She's an artist."

"How come she qualifies for SSI then? Do you just have to be an artist to get it?"

"Jawea told them that she was a lesbian."

"So?"

"It was back before the Psychiatric Association dropped homosexuality from its list of mental disorders."

"Are you trying to tell me that you could just go down to Social Security and tell them that you were gay, and they would start sending you checks?"

"Pretty much. If you were on that list, you were as good as crazy. And up until a couple of years ago, homosexuality was on that list. What could SSI do? Their hands were tied."

"Well, when the APA dropped homosexuality from its list, how come SSI didn't stop sending Jawea money?"

"I guess it wasn't retroactive. Once you've been certified crazy, you're crazy."

"Incredible!"

"Anyway, Stevie, how much money can you contribute to our cause?"

"What cause?"

"The coke cause."

"OK, ten dollars," I answered reluctantly.

"Cocaine will soon be blowin' through my brain," Traci sang.

I reached into my pocket and handed Traci my last ten-dollar bill. She clutched it so tight, I swear, she made the eagle holler.

"These are the best of times," Traci declared. "I'm even gonna be on TV."

"For real?" I asked, filling up the teapot.

"Yeah, KPIX is doing a segment about people stealing milk crates from the grocery stores. It's to raise awareness to let folks know that crates cost money and taking them is hurting the stores. I was chosen by the collective to speak for Loving Foods."

"Where did you get your crates from?"

"I liberated them from a large supermarket chain, nowhere like Loving Foods."

I didn't trip. Stealing crates was hardly a federal offense.

"I can't wait to see you on TV!"

Traci sang, "Kate, thank you for buying us a 'colored' TV." She made her voice sound like Janis Joplin's. I smiled, but underneath I was tripping about the drugs. I mean, my family had such high hopes for me. What would they think if they knew I was spending my last ducats on cocaine? After they'd worked so hard and made so many sacrifices. It was a high price to pay just to put something up my nose.

I watched as the husky reporter with long sideburns shoved the microphone in front of Traci.

"Bring back the crates, y'all," Traci pleaded, wearing her "Sappho Was a Right On Woman" T-shirt.

"Well, I think that pretty much sums up the sentiments of everyone here. Bring back the crates, y'all," the reporter repeated solemnly. "This is Mark Mitchell reporting from San Francisco. Back to you, Bob."

"Yea, Traci." I clapped the loudest among the group of workers and customers gathered in front of her checkout stand.

The cameraman and the reporter were off to the side talking and pointing. They'd probably never seen a store like Loving Foods. Besides food, you could buy all kinds of health products: herbs, lotions, incense, candles, vibrators, backpacks, you name it. And there were posters on the wall like "When God Made Man She Was Only Joking," "Legalize Marijuana," and "Free Huey Newton."

"Didn't you interview at the station?"

I was headed for Traci, but I turned my attention toward a tall, slim, cocoa-complected man. He looked familiar, but I couldn't quite place him.

"You're from Chicago, aren't you?" he asked.

I nodded. "How'd you know?"

"I was on the desk while the receptionist was on break."

"Oh, I remember. You're from Chicago too. At first I didn't realize that you were with KPIX."

"Yeah, I'm a production assistant. Sterling Grant."

"Jean Stevenson, but call me Stevie."

"I'm just waiting to run the film back to the studio. I heard they offered you the job, but you turned it down."

"Turned it down!" I exclaimed. "I've been waiting to hear from them."

"If I'm not mistaken, Vickie said your roommate or somebody told her you couldn't drive a stick. That you could barely drive an automatic. So, they went with their second choice. Vickie said she'd forgotten to ask you at the interview."

Traci walked over toward me, smiling.

"I done good, huh."

I frowned. "This man says they offered me the job at KPIX, and my roommate told them I couldn't drive a stick."

Traci looked blank.

"I think it was Tuesday, I'm pretty sure Vickie called you on Tuesday," Sterling cut in.

"You were home on Tuesday," I said to Traci. "I was down at Media Alliance checking their job listings. And Jawea was still in Santa Cruz."

"Tuesday . . . Tuesday . . . oh yeah, somebody did call."

"I'll let you two deal with this, they need me. Check with you on my way out."

"Thanks." I turned to Traci. "What do you mean *somebody did call!*" I shouted. "Why didn't you tell me about it?"

"Sorry, I guess I forgot. Look, I gotta go back to work."

"You cost me a job!" I said angrily.

"We can talk about it later."

"I want to talk about it now!"

"Now, don't act colored."

"Don't act colored! I'll act any way I want!"

"Stevie, be cool, don't make a scene. Look, I've got a break in fifteen minutes. We can talk then."

It was all I could do not to grab the back of her T-shirt and smash a tomato in her face.

Sterling walked toward me, carrying the film.

"Sounds like a real drag."

"I could've learned to drive a stick if I'd known."

"I've gotta book. Follow me to the car. Give me your number, and I'll keep an eye out for you. In this business, it's a lot about who you know."

"I really appreciate that, Sterling."

"Hey, I'll do whatever I can to help a sistah from the Southside."

I found Traci in the break room. I'd charged around the block a few times, but still hadn't completely cooled off. She had the nerve to have one of the other collective members rubbing her bare feet.

"I forgot that Hope said that she would give me a foot massage this afternoon," Traci said.

"What's wrong with your feet? I asked irritably.

"Nothing, I'm ovulating."

"Ovulating?"

"Yeah, I get a twinge of pain some months. Hope does reflexology. She can rub places on your feet that correspond with different parts of your body, including your ovaries."

"Really?" Hope bobbed her head of long, auburn curls up and down. She turned and gave me a silly smile with her dizzy-looking self.

"Well, I didn't come here to discuss reflexology. And if you want an audience, it's OK with me. But I'm not gonna bite my tongue. You had no right to tell those people that I couldn't drive a stick. First of all, it was none of your damn business."

"I'm really having trouble creating a healing space with your energy," Hope complained.

"I could've *learned* how to drive a stick in two weeks," I said, ignoring Hope's stupid ass.

"Look, Stevie, it's no point in me bullshitting you. I was high when they called. I had just smoked me a joint. I'm sorry, but when you're high, you're more likely to tell the truth. The woman said she forgot to ask you if you could drive a stick. You'd be picking up and delivering stuff all over the Bay Area. I told her that you could barely drive an automatic, which is the truth."

"You shouldn't have told her anything. You should've stayed out of it and let me handle it."

"Why would you want to work for the media anyway?" Hope asked, staring over Traci's foot. "Except for the alternative media, all they do is promote lies and propaganda."

"I'm not interested in debating the merits of the media with you right now. This is between me and Traci, so why don't you just butt out of it!"

Hope sighed but otherwise turned her attention back to Traci's foot.

"Stevie, you ain't got to get funky with nobody."

"I wasn't getting funky, I was just making myself clear."

"OK, like I said, I was high. Besides, that job might sound glamorous, but wait till you have to drive up and down these hills not knowing where the hell you're going at breakneck speed. You'd just be a glorified messenger, that's all. Actually, I did you a favor."

"Do me another favor."

"What?"

"Don't do me any more favors," I said, turning on my heels and walking out.

I slept in Kate's room that night and was able to avoid Traci in the morning altogether. I was still fit to be tied, but I was also plain hurt. I wondered why Traci had come between me and a job. If the media wasn't right for me, I had the right to find that out for myself. So what if I was just a glorified messenger? Traci was just a glorified grocery clerk. She probably just wanted to keep me dependent on her. Deep down, maybe she was afraid that if I got involved in a career, she'd lose me. I was still mad when she called at lunchtime to invite me out to a crab dinner at a restaurant out by the beach. I reluctantly agreed, partly because I couldn't take beans another night. Traci showed up with a dozen red roses and waving a white handkerchief. I had no choice but to forgive her.

We sat in the cozy restaurant wearing large bibs and sipping wine. It was quite romantic, despite our messy mouths and hands. And I still had to admit that Traci was the cutest person in here. Her reddish-brown skin and silver hoop earrings shone in the candlelight. Her puffy Afro framed her face, and her colorful Guatemalan vest contributed to her artistic persona.

"I believe this is the best crab I've ever eaten."

"How much crab have you eaten?" Traci looked like she immediately regretted her question. I suppose she realized that this was no time to be sarcastic; there wasn't enough water under the bridge yet.

"I had crab when I was in Boston with the debate team last year," I snapped.

"I think this is the best crab I've ever eaten too," Traci smiled. "Maybe because it's roasted."

"It has a nice garlic flavor."

"That too," Traci agreed.

We walked along the beach after dinner. San Francisco was in the middle of a heat wave, so it was delightfully cool along the water tonight, instead of the usual plain cold. We held hands and had fun running from the tide.

"Goddamn dykes," a voice shouted in the moonlight. I glanced over at the hostile group of teenage boys passing us. One of them grabbed his crotch crudely as he walked by.

The teenagers had gone about their business. But their vibe was still in the air. Traci kicked sand in their direction.

"I bet a couple of those boys are worried about their own

sexuality," I said. "Sometimes, they're the worst ones. People hate what they fear."

"Fuck all of 'em," Traci muttered.

"Don't trip, they're not worth it," I said. I didn't want trouble. But I was angry too. We had a right to be here just like anybody else. And yet a part of me felt embarrassed about being called a dyke. It was like they were saying I was a freak. And I didn't want to be seen as a freak just because I was in a relationship with a woman.

"Does it bother you to be called a dyke?" I asked.

Traci shook her head. "I'm proud of it."

I marveled at her ability not to feel ashamed.

"But it does bother me when people use it as a put-down," she continued. "And I don't appreciate folks invading my space. You never know if they're gonna back it up with violence."

"It's so unfair. The world smiles on straight people. Every institution is against us, and people still wanna give us a hard time." I was proud of myself for saying "us."

"People are control freaks, that's the bottom line."

I stopped and cut my eyes at Traci.

"Why are you looking at me like that?"

"If the shoe fits, wear it," I answered playfully.

"What do you mean?"

"Just remember that the next time I get a call about a job."

"I'm willing to grow, Stevie. I realize now I have to step back and let you make your own mistakes."

"Maybe they won't all be mistakes."

"To change the subject, you know one of those bastards tonight could've easily been my brother."

"What do you mean? They weren't black."

"I know, but Dwayne's got the same attitude."

"That's a shame."

"He wants to be free to hate and discriminate against gays, but then he wants to holler about how he's being mistreated as a black man."

"Yeah, we're the perfect scapegoats these days." I was proud of myself for saying "we."

"You wanna sit down on this log for a while?" I asked.

"Cool," Traci nodded as we faced the ocean. There were a number of people out strolling. So, actually I felt pretty safe. Traci put her arm around me, and I didn't trip. Most folks in San Francisco were more tolerant than those jokers we'd encountered earlier. I leaned against Traci. The wind was beginning to kick up.

"That's why my brother can kiss my ass," Traci continued. "He's always crying about the black man this and the black man that. As if black women don't have to deal with racism too. Not to mention sexism."

"I'm hipped to what you're saying. We've been dogged royally and so have they."

"Yeah, and they never let you forget it either. I just can't get behind this 'stand by your man' shit. My mother's into that 'put the man first' bullshit. Hell, that's masochistic. I'll be damned if I'm gonna be in collusion with my own oppression."

"They're not all dogs. There are some good men out there."

"That doesn't negate what I just said. Why are you arguing with me?"

I realized that I was afraid that being with Traci and living in the women's community, I was becoming too cut off from men. That worried me because I wanted to have men in my life outside of my family.

"I don't wanna hate men," I said, smelling the breeze.

"Look, I don't hate men. I just believe in calling them on their shit. When a woman refuses to be in collusion with her own oppression they call her uppity, then they call her a dyke. The only choice in this world a woman has is to be a feminist or to be a victim. And black women are only fooling themselves if they think that racism is their only problem. They wanna act like feminism is a dirty word."

"They see it as a white thing, and so they're skeptical," I said. "You know we've always wanted the privileges we saw white women enjoy. When we were women, they were ladies. Now they wanna be women. But some black women still haven't gotten the desire to be treated like ladies out of their systems. And a lot of sistahs are also afraid of driving a wedge between them and brothas, which I can understand."

Traci sighed. "Like if racism ended tomorrow, black men would suddenly start treating them like queens. They have to see the white woman as their enemy because the truth is too painful."

"Look, they haven't always been in our corner. White women can be racists too, you know."

"Obviously, but I've also seen righteous white women be there for black women who are victims of rape and domestic violence. And I've heard sistahs say, 'She asked for it.'"

"That's why in the end, you have to see people as people," I said gazing up at the stars.

"And that's why I'm willing to struggle with men. I've even demonstrated with straight white men against nuclear power at Lawrence Livermore Lab. And of course I will struggle with brothas, I just won't give them a pass. If they're not willing to confront the destructiveness of patriarchal oppression, they're not my allies. I'm waiting for black men to confront those issues."

"And, they should," I agreed, watching the tide roll in and out again.

"But they won't, 'cause men are raised to care about themselves and women are raised to care about everyone else."

"You're right. This is a sexist society."

Traci glanced up at the sky. "Hey, it's a full moon," she pointed. "You wanna go home and make love?"

"Sure. I'm surprised you're in the mood after all that ranting and raving you just did."

"Hey, when women hold back their anger, they also hold back their sexuality. When women release their anger, they free up their sexual energy."

"I didn't know there was a connection."

"Yeah, I heard about it at a barbecue last summer, from a feminist therapist. It's all about energy."

"Well"—I winked—"let's go home and fire up those sheets, then." It struck me how comfortable I'd grown being with a woman sexually. What could be more natural?

9

I got a letter from Today. She got hired with Model Cities. Sharlinda had a second interview with Head Start in Milwaukee. According to Today's letter, they were each dating somebody fine. "How are things with Mr. Goodbar? Are you coming back home?" Today was on a waiting list for a co-op apartment in Chatham Village. Chatham was a black, middle-class neighborhood on the Southside with manicured yards and well-maintained brick houses and apartment buildings. My old friend Linda lived in "the village" now. I'd been impressed by the wide lawns with flowers and ornate benches. The residents appeared to be friendly "about-something" black folks. Maybe that's where I belonged. No, the grass is always greener on the other side, I reminded myself. Remember, you're having an adventure. There's no way anybody back home is experiencing anything like this.

But it was getting old not having a job. I wasn't a soap-opera fan, but lately I'd been tempted. It was hard watching everybody, including the cat, beat it outta here on a regular basis. Jawea was always going to some meeting or class or therapy session. She just happened to be home today. It was a wonder she wasn't getting Rolfed or hypnotized or doing Primal Scream therapy.

Sometimes, when I got bored at home, I walked to the Full Moon Coffeehouse in the Castro to drink tea and read. It was run by a women's collective, and they even had a bookstore on the premises. At night I'd gone there with Traci to hear music or just to hang out.

I was getting frustrated with job hunting. Traci said I was too picky. But I just didn't want to settle for something dead-end. After four years of college, why should I? Traci said it wasn't so important what I was doing, just so long as I was doing it in San Francisco. I loved this beautiful, naturally air-conditioned city, and I loved Traci. But I would have also loved to have a great job. Was that asking too much?

The telephone interrupted my thoughts. I answered it.

"Jawea, telephone, it's Raven."

"Thanks," Jawea mumbled, turning away from her weeding. I decided to help her by pulling some weeds. It wouldn't hurt to be on good terms with her, I thought. I knew how much people hated weeding.

I was working up a sweat in the afternoon sun. I'd forgotten how boring and unpleasant weeding could be. But it felt good to be accomplishing something. I could see my progress.

"You're a space invader!" Jawea shouted over me.

I looked up and shaded my eyes. Jawea looked tense and angry.

"What are you talking about?" I asked surprised.

"You've invaded my space!"

"Invaded your space? What do you mean? I'm helping you." I pointed to the pile on the ground. "Look how many weeds I've pulled."

"I don't need your help!" Jawea shouted, kicking the pile, scattering the weeds into the dirt. "Pulling weeds is part of my therapy."

"Pulling weeds is part of your therapy?"

"Yes, and you're interfering with my therapeutic process!"

I stood up. "Look, I'm sorry, Jawea. I was just trying to be nice."

"Stevie, don't try to be nice, OK? Just be yourself."

"But, I *am* a nice person."

"I hate nice! Ugh, that word makes my skin crawl."

I folded my arms, "Jawea, would you rather I just leave you alone, not say anything to you?"

Jawea looked me directly in the eye. "Stevie, I would *rather* you be the custodian of my solitude. That's what I would *rather*." Her voice sounded more dreamy than angry.

"The custodian of your what?"

"The custodian of my solitude."

I couldn't decide if Jawea was super-deep or super-crazy.

"I think I need an ice cream cone," I sighed as I walked away.

I minored in psychology, but that probably wasn't enough to tackle Jawea's neurotic ass. Actually, Jawea and I usually got along, even though she was . . . different. She let me borrow *Sisterhood Is Powerful* and her magazines. And we'd gotten high a few times together on her dope. When I smoked weed, I usually got talkative and laughed a lot. But when Jawea was high she got real quiet and spaced out. Those were the only times I'd seen her watch TV. But she insisted on watching it with no sound. Just Joan Baez singing on the stereo in the background. People do that shit when they're high.

So, anyway, just when I thought Jawea and I were cool, she

came outta a bag on me. Last week, she went off just because she saw me drinking a Coca-Cola. She said by supporting a mega corporation, I was contributing to my own and other folk's oppression. Traci wouldn't back me up, either. She said I should be drinking a natural juice or mineral water. Traci said that as a member of the Loving Foods Collective, she could never condone my behavior.

Most of the time harmony prevailed in our household. We ate together when we were all there. And it worked out well. Whoever felt like cooking did. Jawea was good at fixing stuff with beans in it. Traci made big pots of vegetable stews with tofu and brown rice. I'd learned to make vegetarian dishes like eggplant Parmesan sesame and spinach quiche, since we hardly ever had any meat. I couldn't complain because most of the time, I ain't buying, I'm crying.

If I knew a job was around the corner, I could enjoy walking down Twenty-Fourth Street more, I thought. There were so many interesting shops in this neighborhood. My family had never even tasted quiche, and there was a store called Quiche and Carry that made them fresh. It looked like something out of France. And the coffee shop next door sold croissants. There was no such thing as a plain cup of coffee over there either. It was all about cappuccinos, lattes, and mochas. The health-food store down the block was as big as a supermarket. And a folksy shop nearby sold batiks, stained glass, macramé, candles, and pottery made by local artists. There was even a bookstore that sold crystals, incense, and self-improvement tapes. And the Noe Valley Ministry around the corner offered belly-dancing classes, concerts, and political meetings, in addition to Sunday services.

Noe Valley was definitely a "live-and-let-live" type of neighborhood. It wasn't unusual to see two women holding hands on the street. The mostly gay male Castro was only a stone's throw away. I felt more or less accepted by the bohemian crowd that favored backpacks, Birkenstock sandals, Tai Chi slippers, drawstring pants, heavy Mexican sweaters, and down jackets. Us folks·who lived on the J Church streetcar line were indeed living in one of the most desirably hip parts of the city. Yet I missed the.lack of color in the laid-back faces. I was a bit home-sick for my family and even that black, South Side of Chicago drawl.

But how could I complain, when I was about to join the line outside Bud's Ice Cream? Soon, I'd be wrapping my tongue around a double scoop.

"Can I help the next person?" the tall, thin clerk asked. I paused for a moment to ponder how he could work in an ice cream parlor and be so skinny. Before I could say "vanilla cara-mel fudge on an old-fashioned cone" a man in a denim jacket elbowed his way ahead of me.

"I'll have two hot fudge sundaes."

"I believe I was next," I snapped. After Jawea, I wasn't in the mood for any shit.

The clerk stood holding his metal scoop in midair.

"One for me and one for her," the man grinned.

It was Gretchen's sister's boyfriend, who'd brought the co-caine to the party a month ago. "Roger, I didn't even recog-nize you."

"I saw you through the window. I just happened to be pass-ing by."

After thanking Roger, I plunged my tongue into a big spoonful of soft, cold ice cream with hot fudge, whipped cream, and walnuts.

We settled on a nearby bench. Roger's black hair shone in the warm sunshine. He took off his jacket. I noticed that his T-shirt read "Women Hold Up Half the Sky."

"It doesn't get any better than this," Roger smiled.

"Uhmmm hmm, this is pure ecstasy," I agreed, glancing into his oval face, with its broad features.

"They use real whipped cream."

"I've never felt so rich and been so poor."

"You still job hunting?"

I nodded. "I've started to look outside my field. But I did get offered a job at KSOL a couple of days ago."

"The radio station?"

"Yeah, but I turned it down."

"Why?"

"It's in San Mateo. It would be an impossible commute without a car. It took me all day to get out there and back on the Greyhound."

"Maybe you should've bought a car."

"I can't afford to. And Traci won't teach me to drive hers 'cause she just put in a new clutch."

"That's too bad."

"The job really wasn't worth it. It was just a three-fifty-an-hour job in traffic."

"I thought you said it was in a radio station."

"It was; traffic is scheduling airtime. It's detailed and tedious."

"At least you'd have your foot in the door. Jobs in the media are hard to come by."

"Yeah, but traffic is just a clerical job in a glamorous field. And they usually don't lead to anything."

"The immigrant in me says, 'You better take what you can get, until you can do better.' "

"You're an immigrant?"

"I was born in China. My family came here when I was ten.

My parents took any work they could find. Now they own a house in Pacifica and two stores in Chinatown."

"Traci says she'd rather see me on welfare for a while rather than doing something that's not going to be right for me."

"Well, the artist in me can understand that philosophy. But the immigrant in me says, 'Next time they offer you a job, you better take it.' "

"Next time, I probably will. I hope there will be a next time. It's been over a month. I'm getting desperate."

We finished our ice cream and said good-bye.

When I got back to the pad, I decided to call Grandma. I still needed some down-home understanding after dealing with Jawea. The ice cream hadn't been enough.

"Grandma sometimes I feel like I have to walk on eggshells around Jawea. You never know what's going to set her off."

"They're like that," Grandma said.

I cradled the phone under my chin and continued petting the cat. "Grandma, I hate to stereotype people."

"Baby, I know the white man and I know the black man and I know the white woman and I know the black woman."

"You sound like there are only four people in the world. What about the Asians, the Latinos, and the Native Americans?"

"I haven't studied them. But I know Mr. Charlie and Sam and Miss Ann and Mathilda."

"Grandma, I don't see how you can know white folks so well, when you're never around them."

"I don't need to be around them. I got my education early. I worked for them. I was right in the house with them. I've studied their ways."

The cat put her head up right to the phone. Even she knew

that there was a story coming on. She looked toward the window and back, as if deciding whether she wanted to hear it.

"The first white woman I worked for, I was nothing but about fourteen. I remember once there was a storm and part of the road was washed out. The water was too deep to make it out on foot. Anyway, I was stuck at their house. So Miss Ethel says to me, 'Sadie Mae, why don't you sleep up in the attic with A.C. tonight.' "

"Who was A.C.?"

"He was an older man that did work for them. But it didn't matter who he was. He was a man and I was a fourteen-year-old girl. There was no way in the world I would've closed my eyes in the same room with some man."

"So, what did you say?"

"I said, 'Miss Ethel I can't sleep up there in the attic with some man who isn't even any kin to me.' "

"What did she say?"

"She said, 'I don't see what the problem is; you're both colored.' "

"That's pathetic, Grandma."

"It's worse than pathetic. Now, she would've never expected her daughter to sleep in the room with some old peckawood."

"Of course not. Her daughter was a person; you were just another nigga."

"You got it, baby. And they will never see you as anything other than that. 'Cause the bottom line is, you don't deserve the same dignity they do, as far as they're concerned."

"I know what you're saying. But it's hard, because I know that there are different kinds of white people. They can't all think alike."

"Yeah, there are different kinds of beans too, but they all wind up giving you gas."

"That's cold, Grandma."

"The truth ain't hate. Jean, I don't know why you even fool with 'em. Getting back to Miss Ann, everybody knows how fragile the white woman is. You gotta all the time handle her with kid gloves. But *you're* not supposed to have any feelings. Just so long as she can stay on her pedestal. Anyway, you don't need to run up your bill talking about Miss Ann. She gets enough attention. So, how's the job hunt?"

Artemis rose up and yawned. She was ready to move on.

"So-so, mostly clerical stuff. They still expect you to type."

"I'm going to send you some money for this call."

"Thanks, Grandma."

"Jean, can't you type?"

"Yeah, twenty-five words a minute."

"Maybe you should brush up, take a course."

"I don't want to. They don't expect male college graduates to be able to type."

"Chile, it's a man's world."

"Well, I'm working to change that."

"You need to be working at something that pays."

"I talked to a counselor at the Women's Career Center and she said that most women who take clerical jobs never move up. Often they've even trained the men who are their supervisors. It's a trick bag that I refuse to step into."

"Well, remember, pride goeth before a fall."

"What's that supposed to mean?"

"It means you can get as hungry as the next person, so it's no point in you acting like you're rich and white. Chile, you know you weren't born with a silver spoon in your mouth."

"Grandma, I know that, but I also know that my purpose here is not to survive."

"Your purpose where?"

"My purpose on this planet. My purpose is to grow."

"Grow? You're twenty-one years of age; you're already grown. I swear you sound as nutty as that roommate of yours. You sure she's not beginning to rub off on you?"

I sighed. It was unfair to make Grandma pay for me to raise her consciousness level, long-distance.

Maybe I had been too hard on Jawea, I thought as I held the pottery mug she'd just given me.

"Thanks, Jawea, this is beautiful. But my birthday isn't until September."

"Stevie, I'm not into birthdays. I was just working on this and it reminded me of your energy."

I ran my hands over the rough tan bottom and the smooth jade-colored glaze dripping over the sides. I didn't know what Jawea meant, but I was crazy about this mug, so I had no inclination to challenge her.

"Well, I love it, thanks," I said. The telephone rang in the hallway, and Jawea ran off to answer it.

I was drinking a cup of tea in my new mug when Jawea returned to the kitchen.

She appeared agitated; her mouth was pretty poked out for a white person.

"My mother just pushes all of my fucking buttons," Jawea groaned.

"I understand. I have a mother who doesn't know when to quit sometimes, too."

"She's picking me up in about an hour. My sister's got a bad cold, so it's just going to be me and Donna this afternoon."

"You call your mother Donna?"

"Yeah, that's her name."

"I guess I would feel funny calling my mother Evelyn, unless I was joking or something."

"So, what *do* you call your mother?"

"Mama."

"Mama," Jawea repeated. "It sounds so warm and cozy and earthy. I could never call Donna 'Mama.' It wouldn't fit. She's just not a 'Mama.'" Jawea ran her thumb over the old oak kitchen table and stared out at the view of Bernal Heights.

"I never had a Mama," she continued. "Donna and I have always been more like friends. Sometimes I wonder what it would've been like if I had."

"You'd be a different person. Just like I'd be a different person if I'd been raised by Donna."

"Yeah. Too bad my sister's sick. Tricia's this straight housewife on the Peninsula, but at least she would've been somewhat of a buffer."

"What are you two planning to do today?"

"We're going to the beach, and we'll probably have dinner at this Mexican restaraunt in Tiburon."

"Where's Tiburon?"

"Over in Marin. Sort of like Sausalito, but minus some of the tourists."

"I liked Sausalito. Sharlinda and Today and I took the ferry over there."

"Want to come with us?"

"You sure you don't want your mother all to yourself?"

"Positive."

I filled the old teakettle with water. "What about her? You don't think your mother will mind if I come along?"

"Donna will be totally psyched."

I swallowed. "It won't matter that I'm black?" After all, I'd heard of white people in Chicago who wouldn't even allow a black person in their house.

"Are you for real? Donna will think it's far fucking out that you're black. She'll be able to brag to all of her friends in Big Sur about having a black friend, now."

I sat back down at the table. "I don't want to be a novelty. I just thought it would be a good chance to see another part of the Bay Area."

"Look, Stevie, don't worry; my mother is really harmless to the outside world. Plus, it's a beautiful day and the beaches over in Marin County are spectacular. The Mexican restaurant that we're going to has far-out food, dynamite margaritas, a great view. And Donna will insist on paying for everything."

"OK, Jawea, you talked me into it," I said as the kettle whistle blew.

Donna's blue eyes sparkled, complementing her purple batik shirt, and her long red hair made her look like a folksinger instead of a grown person's mother. When Jawea told her I was coming along, she'd smiled, showing her perfect teeth. As we headed toward her car I tried to imagine my mother in drawstring pants and Indian-style sandals.

Jawea and her mother were able to agree on at least one thing: I should ride in the front seat of the Saab. I figured that they would probably be embarrassed to have a black person in back, looking like I was riding Jim Crow or something.

"Stevie, I couldn't help noticing how regal you are," Donna said, tossing her head back, but keeping her eyes on the road.

"Regal?" I asked, a little surprised.

"Yes, you carry yourself like an African queen."

"Really?"

"Yes."

"Well, I've never been to Africa."

"Donna has, and of course she'll never let anyone forget it," Jawea mumbled from the backseat.

"African women are some of the most beautiful women in the world. Are you familiar with the Maasai?"

"No, I don't believe so."

"Well, they are just absolutely stunning. You look like you could be one of them."

"Thank you." I ignored Jawea's grumbling. I was happy to alter my self-image from "down-and-out job seeker" to "absolutely stunning."

"Seeing you reminds me of how much I miss Africa," Donna sighed.

"Oh fuck, this is too much," Jawea moaned. If I'd ever said that to my mother, I'd be dead. But Donna continued to drive across the Golden Gate Bridge as if nothing had happened.

Growing up in Chicago, I'd associated beaches with crowds of people, burning sand, and hot sun. And for the most part, I'd avoided them. But this beach was pleasant rather than oppressive. The temperature was only up in the seventies and there was actually a nice breeze. I liked that the sun wasn't beating down on you like you were in the cotton fields. And, of course, looking at the Pacific Ocean was a mind-blowing experience.

Donna and I had stripped down to our bathing suits. Hers was black and mine was purple. Jawea had just plain stripped.

"Jawea, you're naked," I blurted out, unable to contain my shock.

Jawea just smiled with her chubby, flat-chested self. It wasn't like I hadn't occasionally seen her naked before. But it was one thing in your own home, another out in public!

I looked to Donna for support, but to my surprise she seemed as unfazed as the rest of the people on the almost deserted stretch of beach.

"It feels great," Jawea said, stretching herself out like a cat. "My body never gets enough sun in San Francisco."

"Aren't you afraid that you might get arrested?"

"The ranger might give me a warning, at worst a citation. It's like a parking ticket."

I still couldn't get over Jawea, but mostly I couldn't get over Donna. What kind of a mother was she? Mama would threaten a murder/suicide if I pulled a stunt like this. As far as I was concerned, Jawea had it made. So what if her mother tried too hard, said dumb things. Of course she could get on your nerves. But it didn't take an Einstein to figure out that Jawea had her mother wrapped around her little finger.

"I know someone who has a birthday next week," Donna said in a singsong voice as we strolled along the beach.

"Who could that be?" Jawea groaned.

"You. What do you want for your birthday?"

"What day is your birthday on?" I asked, concerned that I couldn't afford to give Jawea anything after she'd given me the mug.

"I don't want anything for my birthday, OK?"

"Judy, you must want something. Come on, give me a hint."

"Don't call me fucking Judy!"

"I'm sorry, honey, I forgot."

"And I don't want any shit from you or anybody else. I am a child of the universe. I have everything that I need."

"I know, but are you sure that you don't want some new clothes, or maybe a bicycle?"

"I don't need clothes, I got some great stuff out of the free box last month. My bike just needs new tires and it will be fine."

"Would you rather just have money?"

"I don't want your goddamn money!" Jawea shouted so that half the people on the beach could hear her. This outburst aroused more stares than her nakedness.

It was all that I could do to keep from saying, I'll take your money. I wondered if I was too old to be adopted.

"Would you prefer to go out to dinner or a play? We've got to do *something* to celebrate your twenty-fifth birthday, dear."

Jawea shook her fists. She reminded me of a two-year-old throwing a tantrum. "I don't want anything! I don't want to go anywhere! Can't you get that through your thick skull?"

Instead of slapping Jawea, Donna sighed and nodded. "I just want the day to unfold," Jawea explained. "I just want to experience it for whatever it's meant to be, naturally. Anything else would feel like a burden," she insisted, shrugging her shoulders.

"Miss, I'm going to have to ask you to replace your clothing."

We stared at the tall, curly blond ranger who seemed to have come out of nowhere all of a sudden.

My last contact with law enforcement had been just after Christmas in Chicago. Linda and Melody, two old friends from the Southside, and I had just left a blues club on North Halsted Street, when we saw a flashing light. Melody was driving. Unlike the ranger, the officer hadn't been polite. He'd snarled that Melody hadn't stopped long enough at a stop sign. To our surprise, he informed us that there was a warrant out for her arrest due to outstanding parking tickets, and carted her off to jail. Linda and I were frantic. Neither of us had a driver's license, so we were stuck at a police station, way over on the North Side, at three in the morning in subzero weather. We didn't know who to call at that ungodly hour. Before we could coordinate a plan, the police, who are sworn to serve and protect, gave us a choice between a holding cell and the cold, deserted streets.

"Ms., not Miss," Jawea corrected the ranger.

"Mizz, will you please replace your clothing."

"Did someone complain?" Donna wanted to know.

"No, ma'am, but someone might. This is not a clothing-optional beach."

"Well, it should be," Jawea insisted.

"That's not up to me. I'm just doing my job. And you're in violation of code 106472."

"It's dangerous when someone says he's just doing his job. It smacks of fascism," Donna interrupted.

"Look, he's even wearing a brown shirt," Jawea pointed out.

The ranger's face turned red. "I'm just warning you; if you don't comply, you could be cited." He sighed and walked away.

I remembered that night in the Chicago police station. A young black man leaving the jail had shouted, "Suck my dick!" To Linda's and my horror, several burly white policeman had rushed toward the man, pushing him into a corner and beating him, ignoring our pleas. We felt completely helpless. Then they finally called for an ambulance. I'd never forgotten how powerless I felt witnessing that.

"Isn't my daughter beautiful?" Donna asked, interrupting my thoughts. I saw the pride in her eyes and nodded. I watched her admire Jawea, dancing like a schoolgirl, showing her flat white butt to the world. Nothing that Jawea ever did would reflect upon an entire race of people. She was an individual. She was white.

It struck me that I'd never been inside a nice Mexican restaurant before. It was not only spacious but almost downright plush. Of course, the only Mexicans were the waiters. The weekday crowd was up-to-date white folks. After all, this was Marin. Our outside table allowed Jawea and I to face the ferryboat dock.

Jawea had been right about the food. My chicken breast was broiled to perfection in a wonderful brown sauce; the black beans were spicy; the corn tortillas, warm and fresh; and the margaritas made you want to slap the judge.

"Did Jawea ever mention to you that I was actually at the March on Washington?"

"Wow, that must've really been something! I'd never met anyone who was actually there."

"It must have slipped my mind," Jawea answered sarcastically.

"I watched it on TV. I was only nine, but I'll never forget it as long as I live."

"It was a defining moment in my life," Donna said solemnly.

I sipped my strawberry margarita, but my mind was back in 1963.

"I knew Dr. King," Donna continued.

I turned toward Donna with interest. "You knew Dr. King?"

"Yeah, we had him over for dinner all the time," Jawea cut in, rolling her eyes.

Donna cleared her throat. "Well, we weren't really friends. I mean I spoke with him once."

"Oh," I said, somewhat disappointed.

"I marched with him in Selma," Donna continued.

"My grandmother and I marched with Dr. King in Chicago. And my parents took us to hear him speak at Soldier Field. It was very powerful."

"I also worked with the Black Panthers," Donna announced.

"And she knows where Patty Hearst is, too."

"I didn't say that. However, I do know Bill and Emily Harris from my political work."

"Donna, maybe we could try something a little different."

"Sure, dear, what?"

"Maybe we could ask Stevie something about herself, or the waiter, or that woman over there. Maybe we could have a conversation that doesn't revolve around you for a change."

"I haven't minded listening," I said diplomatically. Donna looked embarrassed. She picked at her tostada.

"How was the movie that you and Traci saw last night?" Jawea asked me.

"*Alice Doesn't Live Here Anymore.* It was good; it was about a woman whose husband dies. He was a jerk anyway."

"That doesn't surprise me," Donna cut in. Jawea had told me that her parents were divorced.

"Well, anyway, Alice sells everything and strikes out with her son and pursues a singing career. She gets involved with another jerk and works in Mel's Diner."

"That movie got a good review in *The New York Times* and *The Bay Guardian.* I also noticed your reviewer in Sunday's pink section liked it."

"Donna, I don't give a shit what *The New York Times* or *The Bay Guardian* said, or whether the little man in the pink section was jumping out of his seat or not."

"I was just simply showing that there was a consensus. Those sources represent a diverse sampling of opinions."

"I don't give a shit about a diverse sampling of opinions.

What I care about is what Stevie thought, felt, and experienced. Not what some critics who I don't give a shit about thought."

"Well, didn't Stevie already say that she liked it?"

"That's right, I did, so now let's drop it," I commanded. "Just watch the people getting off the ferryboat or something," I suggested. "I don't want to hear any more mess."

We were walking toward the parking lot, having actually managed to finish our meal in peace. I wondered if the three of us could get back to San Francisco without another argument.

"Look out, Jawea," Donna said pointing to the ground.

"I don't need for you to tell me to look out. I've been capable of avoiding dog shit for all these years without your help."

"I wasn't sure that you saw it."

"Well, if I didn't, then I would learn to be more observant in the future. And besides, if it's my karma to step in dog shit today, who are you to interfere with it?"

"I really don't care, except that we're all riding in the car together and I would have to smell it," Donna snapped.

After Donna dropped us off, Jawea said, "That's the first time she's ever stood up to me like that. Stevie, I think you brought out the 'Mama' in her."

10

I'd decided to come out to Mama, if I could work it into the telephone conversation. Maybe seeing that there was hope for Jawea and her mother had given me courage. Artemis was in my lap. I wasn't sure if she was sticking around to give me moral support or if she was just being nosy.

"Today called, wanted to know if you were still out there with that man," Mama said, sounding resentful.

"Oh," I gulped. As far as Mama was concerned, I was out here checking into graduate schools and trying to find work.

"I just sent Today a postcard." But I'd kept it short and sweet. I hadn't given her the "411" on me.

"Jean, what man is this? I hope that you're not letting some man use you. You're not out there shacking up are you?"

"Mama, whatever I'm doing, I'm over twenty-one."

"Everybody feels like they have the right to do their own thing these days," Mama continued. "David announced that he's moving out of the dorm next semester, and Kevin has jumped up and joined the army."

"And I'm gay," I said, trying to casually complete Mama's sentence.

"What do you mean, you're gay?"

"I'm a lesbian."

"Jean, don't be ridiculous! There's no way that you're a homosexual. That doesn't run in our family."

"You make it sound like it's a disease."

"I read enough to know it's not a disease. It's a mental disorder."

"No, it's not, Mama, the American Psychological Association dropped homosexuality from its list of mental disorders two years ago."

"Why would they go and do a thing like that for?"

"Because it's not a sickness, that's why."

Mama sucked her teeth in. "They probably just couldn't come up with a cure. So they threw in the towel. They took the easy way out."

"There's nothing to cure."

"Hold on while I take a pressure pill." I felt my stomach tighten and I took a deep breath. At least we were talking about it. That was better than having to keep it all a big secret. But it was hard; I'd driven Mama to take a blood pressure pill. I tried not to feel guilty.

Mama had returned to the phone, but Artemis had jumped out of my lap. I guess she didn't want to be bothered with this conversation anymore. I was on my own.

"Well, Jean Eloise, you might be able to outwit the psychiatrists, but you can't outwit the Master. You can't go against God and Nature without paying the consequences."

"God made gay people too."

"God made everybody, including rapists and murderers."

"Mama, are you equating gays and lesbians with rapists and murderers?"

"I'm just saying that people make choices. And you can't blame God for your actions."

"What if people are born gay?"

"They still don't have to act on it."

"But straight people get to act on their feelings."

"Sin is wrong no matter who commits it.

"But we're not allowed to get married."

"Don't give me this 'we' stuff. You're not one of *them*. And I know for a fact that *you* weren't born gay."

"How do you know that?"

"Because I carried you for nine months, that's how. I knew you before you knew yourself. There has never been anything abnormal about you. You weren't even a decent tomboy. If you had some boy in you, I would've picked it up a long time ago."

"Mama, not all lesbians are diesel dykes."

"Well, I know that you're not a lesbian. You need to get your behind out of that crazy place and away from those sick people. That's why California is sliding into the ocean now."

"Why is California sliding into the ocean?"

"Because San Francisco is dripping with sin, that's why. I saw a piece on that 'Gay Parade' they had out there. It was just like Sodom and Gomorrah."

"It had nothing to do with Sodom and Gomorrah. The parade had to do with people standing up for their rights and celebrating themselves."

"Half-naked men dancing with each other, bare-breasted women kissing on one another. God could send an earthquake there anytime. We're in our final days. You need to read Revelations."

"We've been in our final days ever since I've known you."

"Jean, the signs are everywhere now."

"Hold on, there's somebody at the door, I don't know who it could be. I'm not expecting anybody. I'll be right back."

I returned to the phone.

"Who was it, Satan?" Mama asked with a touch of humor in her voice.

I had to laugh. "No, it was somebody dropping off something for my roommate. Anyway, it really bothers me that you won't accept me for who I am."

"That's not true."

"How can it not be true?"

"Because, I accept you just fine. It's you who doesn't accept yourself. You're the one who's going against your own nature."

"Mama, loving another woman *is* my nature."

"No it's not. You think rubbing your body up against another woman makes you a lesbian. Well, you're wrong. You're just going through a phase right now, that's all."

"A phase?"

"Yes, and all I ask is that you keep this mess to yourself. It would break your father's and your brothers' hearts if they knew. They might take this as a rejection of them."

"Mama, this is not about hating men. This is about loving women."

"And you certainly don't need to upset your grandmother," she continued. "Her blood pressure is higher than mine. You don't want to cause her to have a stroke, do you?"

"So I'm just supposed to pretend to everyone, live a lie?"

"I'm trying to protect you."

"Protect me?"

"Yes, because when you grow out of this mess, you'll look back at this time and thank me for not letting you make a complete fool of yourself with everybody."

"Mama, I am not going through a phase. I'll be twenty-two years old next month. I'm old enough to know what I want."

"Talk to me again when you're pushing thirty-five. Then I'll give what you say more weight."

Pushing thirty-five! "Mama, I'm no virgin!" I blurted out. "I was never satisfied by a man."

"How many men have you been with? You sound like a streetwalker."

"I've had a few experiences, OK?"

"Jean, there's more to a relationship than just sex. And most of these young dudes out here don't know what they're doing anyway. You just haven't met the right man yet, that's all."

"Mama, there might not be a *right* man."

"When your father and I were newlyweds, I had problems."

"You and Daddy had problems?" I shouldn't have been surprised, since I'd never remembered them showing any affection for each other.

"I had trouble relaxing," Mama whispered, even though I was sure that she was alone. "The doctor told me to drink a glass of wine beforehand. It worked, and I have three children to prove it. That's what you need to do. Find you a good husband and drink a glass of wine beforehand."

"Mama, it's not that simple."

"Jean Eloise," Mama lowered her voice even more, "you're not doing anything oral, are you?"

"What's this about Kevin joining the army? Is he crazy? I know the Vietnam War is over, but still."

"Never mind about Kevin, I'm gonna say an extra prayer for you, just in case."

.   .   .

That night Traci and I rolled around naked on clean-smelling sheets. The Isley Brothers album was playing on the box. We held each other and kissed. "You wanna do 69?" Traci murmured.

"What's 69?"

"We both eat each other at the same time. We're head to toe and toe to head."

I tensed up. I'd never done oral sex before. Except for the time a college boyfriend forced me to go down on him. When Myron initially asked me to give him some head, I refused, saying I wasn't ready for that. I was still pretty green, sexually.

To my surprise, Myron became angry and pushed my head on top of his dick. I was afraid not to go along with it, because we were already in the middle of having sex. I knew Myron was stronger than me and I was afraid of getting hurt. So, I sucked Myron's dick like he ordered me too. But I went numb, and I didn't feel much of anything. After that incident, I broke up with Myron. He apologized later, saying he only wanted to make me an all-the-way lover. But I was too through with him. Grandma used to say, "Don't never stay with a man you're afraid of." And Daddy used to say, "If you ain't got respect, you ain't got anything."

Traci and I had taken a hot bubble bath together earlier. And even though I'd washed her pussy myself, the thought of tasting genitals didn't appeal to me.

"I . . . I . . . I . . . d-don't think I'm ready for that."

"Well, I don't want you to do anything before you're ready."

"I'm sorry," I said.

"You don't have to be sorry. You just have to be comfortable."

"You're so sweet." I kissed Traci. "I love you."

"I love you too."

I felt a warm glow. It was the first time that Traci and I had said we loved each other.

"If you like, I could just go down on you," Traci offered.

"No, that wouldn't be fair."

"Haven't you heard all's fair in love and war?"

"I don't believe everything I hear."

"Well, let's just rub our chocolate pussies together and see what we come up with then."

I got on top of Traci and mashed myself into her. We giggled when our vaginas made mushy sounds. Our clitorises touched and we both moaned. I imagined myself wallowing naked in warm sand, waiting for the tide to come in.

I became aware of my own saliva and my tongue pressing against the roof of my mouth, tasting my teeth. The walls of my jaw trembled. Suddenly my mouth felt the urge to merge with Traci's pussy. I slid down her hot, sweet, cinnamon skin. Traci writhed with pleasure when my tongue sampled the salty, gumbo flavor between her legs.

I was sitting at the kitchen table staring out at the overcast sky when Jawea walked in with the mail and handed me an envelope. It turned out to be a rejection letter from a public relations firm I'd interviewed with. I felt disappointed, even though the people in the office had been uptight.

"This woman named Bear came by and dropped off a bunch of fliers. Over there on the counter."

"Far out," Jawea said, picking up the stack of papers. "These will help Inez Garcia's defense."

"Who's Inez Garcia?"

"She's a Latina sister on trial for killing some asshole who raped her."

"Sounds like self-defense."

"Damn straight, but they're trying to nail her cause she killed him some time afterward. Like big fucking deal."

"Yeah, women are just supposed to be victims."

"Inez is a righteous woman who struck a blow for all of us. I'm going to go over to the East Bay and put these up."

"Oakland and Berkeley?" I asked with interest.

"Yeah, you wanna come?"

I hesitated, but then I remembered that Jawea's mother wouldn't be joining us.

"It beats moping around here on a Saturday afternoon," I said.

"Sistah!" A black woman in army fatigues and dreadlocks called out in the Berkeley Women's Center. It was like she'd just found her lost kin.

I figured that she was talking to me, since I was the only other black woman in the reception area.

"Hey," I greeted the woman with a smile. Mama would dis-own me if I wore my hair like that, I thought. Mama needed to count her blessings.

"Nice to see you in here."

"This is my first time. Interesting board. I'm job hunting."

"Any luck?"

"I wrote down a couple of things. One is a receptionist job at the Personal Change Center in the city. The other one is at a TV station, KTVU in Oakland."

"Channel Two, down by Jack London Square."

"Where is Jack London Square?"

"It's near downtown; Oakland's version of Fisherman's Wharf."

"Oh."

"By the way, my name is Brenda."

"I'm Stevie."

"Stevie, be sure and tell other sistahs about this place. I just joined the collective, and I want to get more women of color involved. We've got to make our voices heard."

"Well, I'm living in San Francisco. I'm sort of new in town."

"Welcome. Now, don't get over in the city and get lost and we never see you again. You know where we are now."

"Don't worry, I shall return."

"You don't know, trying to get folks who stay in the city to cross the bridge is like pulling teeth. They think they're living in Camelot over there. They turn their noses up at us. They really look down on Oakland."

"Well, I don't have that attitude. I think Oakland has its good points," I said, recalling the beauty of Lake Merritt and the hills perched above.

"Hey, Brenda," Jawea said, walking over to us.

"What's happenin', Jawea?"

"Putting up fliers to help Inez."

"Right on!"

"So, you met my new roommate?"

"Y'all are roomates?"

"Yeah, Stevie is subletting Kate's room while she's in India studying yoga."

"Traci still your roommate too?"

"Yeah."

"Tell Traci I said to bring her butt over to the sistah side of the bay, sometimes. Didn't she get my flier?"

I shrugged my shoulders.

"We had a racism workshop a month ago and Traci was nowhere to be seen. Probably was somewhere seducing some white woman stead'a being over here taking care of business."

I gulped. I didn't appreciate Brenda talking about my Traci like that, especially in front of a white person.

"Traci's been busy with Loving Foods, they were short-staffed for a while. She has to work on Saturdays," I said in her defense.

"Whatever," Brenda said.

Jawea cleared her throat. "By the way, Stevie and Trace are lovers now."

"You and Traci?"

I nodded, I felt a little embarrassed about having it put so bluntly. It wasn't like all we did was have sex. Quite the contrary these days; Traci was often either tired because of her long collective meetings, or only interested in getting high on coke. But I knew that it was the way gays and lesbians usually referred to their relationships. I supposed I'd get used to it.

"Well, wonders never cease. Never say never. Tell Traci I'm glad to see her up with a sistah for a change. Seems like a together sister, too."

"Thank you."

Jawea turned toward me. "Well, we gotta head over to the Women's Health Collective, KPFA, and La Peña."

We nodded our good-byes.

"That woman sure takes up a lot of space," Jawea sighed when we were out of earshot.

"She's average size."

"I mean her energy."

"Oh."

"Brenda doesn't usually give me the time of day. She's never asked me 'what's happenin' before. Probably did it because I was with you."

"Really?"

"Yeah, you count. I'm just another white girl as far as she's concerned."

"Brenda was kind of downing Traci, don't you think?"

"Yeah, and Traci's got good politics. She helped start a shelter for battered women. She's volunteered with Bay Area Women Against Rape. She's fighting to keep them from tearing down the International Hotel. And she contributed money to the Justice for Joann Little Committee. It pisses me off when somebody whose political work can't hold a candle to Trace's puts her down."

"I hear you," I mumbled as we walked up Shattuck Avenue, Berkeley's main drag. But I was still bothered by Brenda's comment about Traci and white women. What did she think Traci thought I was, chopped liver?

Traci and I were sitting on the countertop, watching our clothes spin dry.

"Traci, am I the first black woman that you've ever been with?"

I'd waited till the laundromat was empty, except for two old women speaking Spanish, to start this conversation.

"Been with how?"

"You know, lovers with."

"Why do you ask me that?"

"I'm just curious. People seem so surprised that we're together. Like Pat and Brenda, for example."

"Pat's just talking. She's living in a glass house. Pat knows what side her bread is buttered on. And Brenda is too hung up on this black thang. Hey, I'm black and I'm proud too. But, I've got sense enough to rub the cat the way the fur lies. Stevie, I don't know about you, but I refuse to let my color limit me. I've got places I can stay all over the world, counta I'm open."

"Sorry to interrupt you, but one of the dryers stopped." I pointed. I hopped down and felt the damp clothes and fed the dryer.

"Can't none of us go home again," Traci continued. "Brenda wants to put me down, but the black community doesn't want her bulldagger ass. They ridicule her hair and her clothes on the streets of Oakland. But yet she's so black. She's always tripping on racism. Hell, if her ass was on fire, plenty of black folks wouldn't even piss on her. Hey, all kinds of white women would be bringing me pails of water."

"It's hard to be black and gay," I said defending Brenda. "I mean racism is still a reality and yet you're right; a lot of black people are anti-gay."

"Yeah, racism is a reality," Traci agreed. "But people don't have to be all the time dwelling on it. This is 1975, it's time to reap some of the benefits of the struggle. Like Werner Erhard says," Traci continued, "most people are afraid to take responsibility for their own lives."

"Are you into est?"

"No, but I slept with a woman who was into it, once. Some of it makes sense. Like the whole thing about not letting folks go to the bathroom."

I shook my head. "Sounds contradictory: 'Take responsibility for your own life; but let me tell you when to pee.'"

"They don't actually *stop* you from going to the bathroom. They just refuse to give you permission. The whole point is to get people to draw their own boundaries," Traci explained. "Only wimps pee on themselves in the process," she added.

"I get it now," I said. "But it still sounds like a cult."

I hoisted myself back up on the countertop next to Traci.

"When you were with white women, didn't you feel cut off, you know, isolated sometimes?" I asked, swinging my feet.

Traci shrugged her shoulders. "I can go anyplace and never forget where I came from. And I can be with anybody and still know who I am."

"Are you out to your whole family?"

"Yeah, they know. They'd have to be stupid not to know. They're right up there in Sacramento."

"Does your sister accept you?" I knew that Traci's father was cool with her sexuality, but her mother and brother weren't.

"Yeah," Traci answered. "Just as long as it's never mentioned. You know how some black folks are. They can accept anything so long as it's hidden."

"Yeah, I know what you mean." I'd told Traci about my conversation with my mother. "Look, another dryer has stopped," I pointed. "You deal with this one."

"What it is?" David greeted me.

"I just called to see what's happenin' with you all. Thought I'd catch up with you before you went back to school."

"So, what's the nigga's name?" David joked.

"Who are you talking about?" I asked, cradling the phone.

"Don't play dumb with me, Jean. I was born at night, but I wasn't born last night. The word on the street is, you out there laid up with some nigga."

I got quiet. I felt like I was in a bind. I wanted to be able to be honest with David. I'd always gotten along with my brothers. "Look, I was with somebody for a minute, but that's dead. Right now I've got some roommates and I'm trying to find a job. So it's not even about a man. Hey, I just fell in love with San Francisco, that's all."

"You just fell in love with San Francisco, and that's why you're staying out there?"

"Yeah."

"You not grinning up in some man's face?

"No, I'm not."

"So, that's the real deal, huh."

"You got it, brothaman."

"Well, if you say so." David sounded like he was torn between disappointment and skepticism. "So, how do you like those A's? You think they'll wind up in the series?"

I reminded David that for the most part I didn't follow sports.

David yelled upstairs for Mama to pick up the other phone before saying good-bye.

"Kevin flunked his physical, on account of his asthma," Mama reported matter-of-factly.

"I wasn't so gung ho about him going in the army, anyway," I reminded her.

"Well, I wasn't knocking it. At least it would keep him off the streets. Thank goodness, David is headed back to Iowa soon. He and Kevin both can rattle off the names of boys who have been shot or are in jail or who are selling pot. There's a lot worse out here than the military."

"Is Kevin taking it hard?"

"Not too hard to keep him from going out partying with his friends. He said to thank you for the baseball cap."

"Tell him he's welcome."

"But like I told Kevin, he better try to get his behind in somebody's college. That little piece of job he has at the record store isn't hitting on anything. Education is something that nobody can take away from you. Everybody can't play football or basketball or cut a hit record. That's why it's really sad to see you out there wasting your potential."

"Me, wasting my potential? What do you mean?"

"I mean you could be back here really doing something with your life. You refused to follow through on that newspaper job offer in Monmouth."

"I have no desire to be stuck in Monmouth, Illinois. I'm sorry."

"No, you'd rather spend your time standing around in some bar, picking up women. You're sorry all right."

"Mama, I'm out here pounding the pavement. I am not standing around some bar all of the time. And for your information, I'm in a relationship."

"The other women at church used to say to me, 'Mrs. Stevenson, what did you feed your children, for them to turn out so well? You have to let us in on your secret.' " It was obvious that Mama didn't want to hear about my relationship. "There was a time I could hold my head up high," she continued, "but now . . ."

"But now, what?"

"Never mind, your father just walked in. Say 'hello' to him."

"Hi, Jeannie." I could tell my father missed me, because Jeannie was his pet name for me. "It's hot here in Chicago! Is it hot out there?"

"No, Daddy, it's cool and foggy. You need a serious coat here, some nights."

"You're wearing a coat in August?"

"Yeah, I had to borrow my roommate's."

"I can't believe that, we're burning up out here."

"San Francisco has different weather."

"I'll say. It sounds like a strange place. Your mother and I were talking and we both agreed. If you can't find anything out there, you should just pack up and come on home."

"The job market is pretty tight, but I'm not ready to throw in the towel yet."

"If you need anything, don't be too proud to ask. We don't want you out there doing without."

"Thanks, but I know you all are trying to make ends meet with David in college and Kevin maybe going."

"David's on a basketball scholarship. We can't afford to support you out there, but we can at least scrape up enough money to send you a one-way ticket back. And if you live here at home, you can count on three hots and a cot."

"I know, but I like San Francisco. It's an adventure."

"Well, I'm just reminding you that you got a home that you can always come back to."

"Thanks, Daddy, that means a lot."

"Your mother wants to talk to you again."

"Jean, have you found a church yet?"

I hadn't ever said that I was looking for a church. But I just simply answered no.

"Well, nothing in your life is going to be right until you get right with God." Of course we both knew she was talking about my sexuality. But I didn't want to get into it with her so I just said, "Good-bye, Mama." Besides, Daddy might be in earshot.

"A penny for your thoughts."

Traci made me jump. I'd been sitting and staring out of the kitchen window ever since I'd hung up the phone.

Traci wrapped her arms around me. I turned and kissed her on the mouth. "I didn't even hear you come in. My mind was somewhere else. I just finished talking to my mother about a half-hour ago."

"Is she still praying for you?"

I nodded. "She says nothing will be right in my life until I get right with God."

"Yeah, hint, hint," Traci sighed. "I bet if your Mama kicked back with a joint, everything would be cool."

"Traci, drugs aren't the answer."

"Don't tell me you're crusading against a little weed. Hey, coffee is a drug and cigarettes are drugs. Alcohol is a drug."

"I don't smoke cigarettes and I hardly ever drink coffee. And I'm far from being an alcoholic."

"You took some aspirin for your cramps the other day."

"So, there's a big difference in taking aspirin for pain and taking drugs to get high."

Traci filled up the teakettle. "There's different kinds of pain, Stevie. People get high to take them away from their pain. Just 'cause you like a drug, doesn't make you a drug addict. I like coke, but I'm not addicted to it."

"You seek it out."

"So? You seek out ice cream, but does that make you addicted to it?"

"I only eat ice cream about once a week, big deal."

"That's about how often I do coke."

"Yeah, well that's still more often than we make love." My stomach churned. I was surprised that I'd come out with that. But I wasn't ready to take it back, because it was true. Our sheets hadn't smelled like french fries in a long time.

Traci's face looked hard as she filled the strainer with tea leaves. "So, this is what this is really about, sex."

"It's just that we hardly do it anymore. It's been almost two weeks now."

"So, you've been keeping a record?"

"No, I mean I've read that lesbian couples have less sex than anybody else. But I didn't expect it to decline in the first two months."

"It takes two to tango, Stevie. I mean if you've wanted to have sex, why haven't you said anything?"

"I guess you just haven't seemed in the mood and I didn't want to push the issue."

"Stevie, right now I'm in the mood to get high. If you've got the time, I've got the coke."

"OK, Traci," I sighed. Maybe cocaine would change her mood.

I'd be lying if I said I wasn't intoxicated by the sweet smell of cocaine. "You're getting good at snorting this stuff." Traci grinned as my right nostril sucked up the white line on our kitchen table.

"I like the way it smells. It smells almost as good as my grandmother's bread baking."

"I like the way it makes me feel." Traci balled up her fist and stretched her arms out. "Like I'm on top of the world!"

"I wouldn't go that far. I still think that cocaine is overpriced and overrated."

"Overrated!" Traci pretended to be alarmed as she began smearing the little pile of cocaine onto my gums.

"Traci, what are you doing?" I asked trying to talk through her fingers.

"Helping you to get higher. You will never say cocaine is overrated again."

I began to feel a rush and led the way to the bedroom.

"This reminds me of speed," I said, tumbling onto the bed.

Traci hugged me and kissed me. "It's better than speed," she insisted with her soft lips. "Way better than speed," she added, sucking on my tongue.

My heart was beginning to race; it was like I had drunk ten cups of strong coffee. It had never had this effect on me before.

"I only did speed a couple of times, but I didn't like it. I don't like to feel tense and speedy. And that's how I'm beginning to feel now," I said nervously.

Traci ran her fingers through my Afro. "Don't you love it though? Doesn't it make you feel like you've got everything under control? Like you can accomplish twenty things at once?"

"I think you gave me too much," I panted.

"Don't worry, you'll be OK."

"I don't feel OK. My heart is racing a mile a minute right now!"

Traci put her arms around me. "Just relax, Stevie, just relax, everything is cool."

"Everything is not cool! Don't you understand? I can't relax. How can I relax, when I might be OD'ing!"

Traci held me tightly. "You're not OD'ing, you didn't have enough to OD. Now don't panic. You can get through this."

My body felt stiff and my heart continued to race. Traci had failed to convince me. "Maybe you better call San Francisco General!"

"Are you sure?"

"Call them!" I gasped. "My heart feels like it's coming through my mouth!"

Traci stood up to go.

"No, Traci, no, don't leave me!" I shouted. I was afraid to be alone. It felt like I was giving birth through my throat!

"You said you wanted me to call General. The phone's in the kitchen." Now Traci sounded scared and confused.

"Never mind, I'll be OK, it's slowing down. I think the worst is over," I panted.

Traci wrapped her arms around me. "You scared me for a minute."

"I liked to have left here. I thought I was about to see my life passing in front of me."

"You're gonna be OK. Next time you'll be bragging about how high you were."

There's not gonna be a next time, I thought to myself. I'd had enough.

11

I'd just been turned down for a mailroom job at KTVU because I had too much education and not enough experience. The job hunt just wasn't panning out. My savings were practically gone. Grandma had sent me twenty dollars the other day, but I didn't want to ask her to pay my portion of next month's rent. Especially with her being retired. And besides, I didn't want to be dependent on my family.

It was damn near September, time to swallow my pride and go down and apply for food stamps. Like Traci said, a person with a college degree can get just as hungry as a grammar-school dropout.

Mothers fussed at children in different languages, the odor of raggedy hippies interfered with my breathing, and older people stared into the palms of their hands. It has come to this, I thought, sitting in the large, crowded welfare office, waiting for my name to be called.

I sat across from a big-boned eligibility worker with dark stringy hair and bags under her eyes who'd introduced herself as Mrs. Kimbroke. I started to tell her that I had almost majored in social work. Then I caught myself; I didn't need to come across as Mrs. Kimbroke's equal in this situation. So I waited quietly while she reviewed my application.

"You will receive forty-eight dollars' worth of food stamps each month."

"Is that all?" I asked.

"You will get a card each month, in the mail," she continued like a robot. "You will redeem your coupon for food stamps at an outlet in the Mission District. You should receive your first allotment in about fourteen days."

"Fourteen days!" I said. "Are you saying that it might take two weeks before I receive any food stamps?"

"Yes, if everything goes well."

I swallowed. "It's just that our refrigerator is almost bare." All we had at home were wilted vegetables, outdated bread and yogurt from Loving Foods, bottled water, and recreational drugs, I thought.

Mrs. Kimbroke raised her eyebrows. "You're not sharing food with anyone are you? Because, if you are, I will be forced to void this application."

"No, no," I pleaded, imagining that voiding an application might be routine for her.

"We would then have to base your grant amount on the resources of your entire household."

"No, we don't share food," I assured her. "Just the empty refrigerator."

Mrs. Kimbroke narrowed her eyes. "You do have your own clearly marked shelf in this empty refrigerator?"

"Of course," I continued to lie.

"Good, well, I'll get this processed as quickly as possible."

"I'm just not sure I can last two more weeks."

"You're not eligible for emergency food stamps because you've indicated that you have cash on hand."

"Seven dollars!"

"That's more than most people have. I see people with kids every day who are down to their last dime. You're lucky. You're young, you don't have any children, and you've got on a pair of nice, comfortable shoes."

"See, I told you it pays to be open," Traci said, hanging up the phone.

"What's going on?" I asked, looking up from the cutting board where I was slicing a potato to fry. I was always taught to peel potatoes, but Traci had convinced me of how important it was to eat the potato skins. She'd told me that there was this huge family in Mexico, and everybody had malnutrition but this one boy. The doctor was baffled until he learned that the boy was the only one in the family who ate the potato skins.

"That was Susan's boyfriend, Roger," Traci reported.

"How's he doing?"

"Fine, he just got his work accepted into a gallery."

"That's great."

"He said one of his paintings is going for five thousand dollars!"

"Wow!"

"He'll get half and the gallery will get the other half."

"I'd like to see his art."

"Well, you're in luck, because he's invited us over next Saturday night to party. He's going to show slides. He's supplying everything: food, drinks, drugs, music; all we've got to do is bring ourselves."

"Well, I'm not turning down free food. Not when I'm still waiting for my food stamps." Grandma had paid my September rent, but I was still broke.

"I heard that. And I sure as hell ain't turning down no free drugs, I'm sorry."

I felt myself tense up. It bothered me that Traci placed so much value on getting high.

Traci was cracking eggs to make the omelettes. We had just a little bit of cheese left. I liked that when it came to household stuff we were really equals. We shared the chores, we weren't into roles, and when we did have sex, we took turns making love to each other.

"So, Traci, what did you mean when you said that it pays to be open?"

"I mean like if we were hung up on race, our sorry asses would be stuck out in Hunter's Point or West Oakland or somewhere like that. But instead we're going to be in a SOMA loft, hobnobbing with artists."

"What's SOMA?"

"South of Market Area. It's mostly a gay men's scene; leather bars and glory holes, but quite a few artists have moved there recently. It's like up and coming."

"What are glory holes?"

"Clubs where men go and stick their dicks in holes in the walls and other men service them. It's the ultimate in anonymous sex."

"You can say that again," I said, glad that Traci hadn't served the omelette yet, 'cause the cheese would look nasty.

You can't judge a book by its cover, I thought, looking around at Roger's loft. The outside of the warehouse building wasn't hitting on anything. But his huge space with high ceilings and cement floors covered with oriental rugs was a different story. Roger had it furnished with antiques, plants, and interesting art.

Susan and Roger looked straight out of Banana Republic in their matching safari outfits. Susan's suntanned face and new shag haircut added to her outdoor appearance. Traci and I had coordinated our clothes too. She wore a white T-shirt and black jeans, and I had on a black leotard and white jeans. But Susan and Roger took the cake.

"This place is beautiful," I marveled.

"Glad you like it." Roger beamed, his arm around Susan.

"We're not early, are we? Where is everybody else?" I asked.

"Yeah, we called ourselves being fashionably late," Traci added.

"A few of our friends couldn't make it."

"A lot of people are out of town," Susan cut in.

"Anyway, we decided to just stick with you two and get to know you better."

"That's cool." Traci smiled.

"Yeah," I agreed, feeling honored.

We sat around drinking wine and shooting the shit while Roger farted around in the kitchen.

Roger brought out a tray of sushi and held it in front of me.

I stared at the assortment. "I thought that you were Chinese."

Roger laughed. "I am Chinese, but I don't have to eat only Chinese food."

"You're right, it's just that I love Chinese food."

"You've never had sushi before?" Traci asked.

I shook my head. Susan pursed her thin lips. "Come on, Stevie, try it, you'll like it. Start with the tuna," she pointed.

"OK," I agreed, reaching for a piece of something pink with rice wrapped around it.

"This stuff could grow on you," I said, washing down my fourth piece of sushi with white wine.

"Let's see where you paint," Traci said.

Roger ushered us into a far corner of the room where several paintings of vegetables and fruit sat on easels.

"That's what he's working on now." Susan pointed proudly to a painting of a head of lettuce with pink-tinged leaves.

"It's gorgeous," I said.

"Doesn't it remind you of a cunt?" Susan asked.

I almost choked on my sushi.

Traci nodded.

"I love women; everything I paint has to do with women. Female energy is the source of my creative expression," Roger informed us.

Susan turned toward Traci and me. "Are either of you familiar with Judy Chicago's work?"

"Stevie, you're from Chicago," Traci reminded me.

"Yes, and I am familiar with Judy Chicago's work. I saw the dinner party exhibit with my old roommate, Celeste," I said.

"Uhmm," Susan nodded respectfully. Even Traci came to attention. I was so glad finally to know something about something!

We settled back in the comfortable old loveseats while Roger showed his slides.

"Your paintings are fantastic!" Traci exclaimed. She and I were cuddled across from Susan and Roger.

"My sentiments exactly," I agreed.

"Thank you."

"Yeah, and there was something very sensual about all those

fruits and vegetables. Most men wouldn't be able to pull that off," Susan bragged.

"Susan should know, she's a student at the San Francisco Art Institute," Traci informed me.

"Roger really likes women as people, and I think that's rare," Susan said, running her fingers through his hair.

"My mother told me as a child that most men didn't really like women," I said. "At the time I didn't understand what she meant. You're lucky to have found a man who really likes women as people."

"Roger's not just into the image of women, he's into the essence of women," Susan bragged.

"That's deep," Traci said finishing her glass of wine. "Too deep to deal with sober."

"Would you like more wine?" Roger asked jumping to his feet. "What's your pleasure, wine, weed . . . or the white girl?"

Traci's eyes lit up.

"The white girl?" I asked, confused.

"Y'all know the white girl can always be a friend of mine," Traci smiled.

"Who's this white girl? What are you all talking about?"

"You'll see, Stevie, I'll go get her. She's really nice." Roger winked.

I'd put two and two together in my mind by the time Roger returned from the kitchen area with a cutting board containing a mound of cocaine.

"I figured, so cocaine is 'the white girl?' "

Traci nodded. "She's everybody's Miss America."

"Not mine," I said.

"Stevie's on a crusade against drugs these days," Traci said while Roger cut the cocaine with a single-edged razor blade.

"Do you eat red meat?" Susan wanted to know.

"Sure, when I can afford it."

"Well, red meat is full of drugs. They give all kinds of artificial hormones to cattle, you know."

"I'm not on any crusade; I'm just not into it. You all can go right ahead."

"That's cool."

"Yeah," Roger agreed, "but feel free to change your mind."

Many lines later, I was the only one who wasn't high. Susan had stripped down to her bra and bikini underwear. She'd had this bright idea that they should experience being high on the waterbed. I watched as she lay still on the waterbed while Roger made a ridge of the remaining cocaine on her thigh with a serving knife.

"If you want more, now, you gotta come and get it," Susan giggled.

"I want more," Roger laughed.

"I want more too," Traci added.

"For once, I'll be sexist, ladies first."

"Traci," I groaned, feeling jealous, but she ignored me and rubbed her nose up Susan's thigh; just inches away from her crotch. Traci licked the cocaine residue off of Susan's thigh.

My stomach tightened as I watched Susan sit up and kiss Traci on the mouth. Traci kissed her back, and the two of them fell into the bed, their bodies intertwined.

Roger reached over and put his arm around my shoulder. "I have to admit that they look hot together. But don't you feel sort of on the sidelines holding the jackets while your friends dance?"

"I can't believe this," I groaned.

"Well, Stevie, if you can't beat 'em, you might as well join 'em."

"Yeah, Stevie, jump into the mix." I stiffened as Susan reached out and grabbed my arm and pulled me onto the waterbed. I felt like I was lying on a bowl of Jell-O that hadn't quite set yet. Susan rolled on top of me while Traci lay next to me with her arm around my shoulder. I felt embarrassed to be in this position.

"Row, row, row your boat, gently down the stream," Susan sang as she rocked her pelvis against mine. "Merrily, merrily, merrily, merrily, life is but a dream," Traci sang along with Susan.

"This is crazy," I protested, denying the sensual feelings shooting through my body as Susan rubbed against me.

I lay there frozen, afraid to feel and unable to get up without a major display of force.

"The three of you look so beautiful together," Roger said prancing around like a fool with a rose sticking out of his mouth.

"Let me up," I said, struggling to rise up over Susan's warm body.

Susan pushed me down. "Oh, come on, Stevie, we were just beginning to have fun."

"Yeah." Traci tugged on my arm. "Can't you go with the flow for a change?"

"Yeah, if you can't go with the flow in a waterbed, where can you go with the flow?" Roger wanted to know. He plucked the rose petals and sprinkled them on top of us.

"Look, maybe, this just isn't my idea of fun, OK?"

"Is it true blondes have more fun?" Susan sang.

"Stevie, why don't you just loosen up; ain't nothing but a party. Stop going through life with the emergency brake on."

"Traci, I don't call not wanting to wallow around in a waterbed with someone I barely know, going through life with the emergency brake on."

"Someone you barely know?" Roger interrupted. "How can you say that? I thought we were your friends."

"Stevie, how am I going to get to know you, if you won't let me," Susan pouted, still pinning me down.

"I thought you were different, but it looks like I was wrong," Traci sighed.

"Different, what do you mean, different?" I asked suspiciously.

"Different from the average black woman," Traci answered.

I felt myself growing angry. How dare Traci talk like this in front of these people!

"So, what is the average black woman like?" I asked sarcastically."

"Repressed and uptight in certain situations."

"I think you're making a gross generalization."

"Well, I think you're living proof."

"Stevie, you better have your fun now, before Kate gets back and things return to status quo," Susan interrupted.

"What are you talking about? Traci, what does Kate coming back in January have to do with anything?" I looked at Traci. "We might want to get our own place by then."

Traci suddenly became interested in the folds of the waterbed.

"Go ahead, you may as well tell her," Susan insisted. "She's gonna find out when Kate comes home in January, anyhow."

"I want to find out now!" I shouted.

"OK," Traci hesitated. "Kate and I were lovers, OK?"

I gulped. "You and Kate were lovers?"

Traci nodded.

"How come you never told me?"

"You never asked."

"How would I have known there was anything to ask about? And what does she mean, things are going to return to status quo?"

"Well, Kate and I kind of left things open."

"What do you mean open? Like you might just pick up where things left off? Is that what you mean by open?"

"Kate and I believe in living in the moment. I can't say how I'll feel when Kate comes back in two weeks, until the time comes."

"Two weeks!" Roger and I shouted together.

"Kate's not coming back in two weeks, is she?" Susan asked, sitting up.

Traci sighed. "I just got a letter from Kate. She couldn't take it anymore. Turns out the guru's been making all kinds of passes at her and some of the other female students."

"I can't believe that all this time you never told me anything! All this time! How could you?" I said, feeling hot tears welling up in my eyes. "How could you be so dishonest and then have the nerve to dog me in front of strangers."

"We're not strangers," Roger cut in.

"I'm sorry, Stevie, I was just going with the flow. One thing just led to another. I never expected us to get so involved. And I wasn't sure how things would be between me and Kate when she came back. January always seemed a long ways away."

"You still should've told me!"

"Hindsight is twenty-twenty. I'm sorry, but right now, I've gotta be there for Kate."

My chest felt tight. My stomach was in knots. "Tell Kate not to worry, I've washed my fingers of you!" I shouted. Traci had a surprised look on her face, and Roger and Susan looked confused. I ran toward the door, hesitating only long enough to grab my jacket from the coatrack. I didn't stop until I reached the sidewalk. I was angry and scared and hurt all rolled into one. But it felt refreshing to be out in the foggy night air, despite the men dressed in leather and chains all around me.

12

Jawea was still away at Tai Chi camp, so I felt free to cry.

"Everything has turned to shit," I moaned to Artemis as I hugged her with one arm and the tear-stained pillow with the other. Artemis wiggled away from me. She could pick the worst times to be indifferent.

Suddenly, it became clear to me. I had to get out. I no longer had a place here. I didn't feel like being with Traci. I couldn't sleep in Kate's room. The straw mat, Indira Gandhi poster, and the stained glass hanging in the window no longer felt like home.

I started emptying drawers. When Traci came back, I didn't plan to be here. Maybe it was a crazy thing to do, to leave like a thief in the night, but I didn't care. I had my pride.

But where could I go at this hour? I must be crazy. I only had a few dollars to my name. I remembered my food stamps. At least I had them, I'd redeemed my coupon yesterday. Hadn't I observed people attempting to buy and sell food stamps yesterday on Mission Street? If worse came to worst, maybe I could trade them for cash. But that wouldn't help me tonight.

I decided to call the Haight-Ashbury Switchboard. I'd seen a flier that said they ran a shelter. I hated to have to go someplace like that with all of my stuff. But at least I only had one suitcase and a carry-on bag. And I didn't have anything really valuable to worry about. By Monday I could get Grandma or my parents to wire me some money for a one-way ticket back to Chicago. I dialed the number.

"I'm sorry, but we're full tonight. You have to get over here before six o'clock," the bubbly voice on the other end explained.

"It's just that I don't know where else to turn," I moaned.

"What's your situation?"

"Hopeless."

"Have you been battered?"

"No . . . not physically."

"Are you in fear of being battered?"

"It's never happened before."

"Is this your boyfriend or your husband?"

"Uhhh . . . It's my lover."

"Oh . . Did she threaten you?"

"She told me her old girlfriend is moving back here. I have to go. I can't be here when she gets home."

"Calm down. Do you have any money?"

"Just a few dollars."

"If you can get across the bay I think they might take a crisis walk-in at the Women's Refuge. You can call to see if they're full. But you'll have to hurry up. BART will stop running soon, and the last bus for Berkeley leaves the Trans Bay Terminal at midnight too. If all else fails, and you're really desperate, you could always sleep on a bench inside the Trans Bay Terminal. But it could be dangerous, especially for a young woman alone. You'd probably want to stay awake all night to protect yourself and your stuff. And, it wouldn't hurt to have some sort of a weapon on you, just in case."

A chill ran through me. "Thanks a lot." I swallowed. "You've been a big help. I better get off now, and start packing so I can get out of here before she comes home."

"I'll call around for you to locate a bed. Call me from a phone booth if you're out in the street. By the way, my name is Meadow."

I thanked Meadow and gave her my name and number.

I kept hearing Bob Dylan singing the lyrics of "Like a Rolling Stone" over and over in my head.

It wasn't just my pride that drove me around the apartment, hastily collecting my things, but also my fear of confronting Traci. I realized I was afraid of my own anger.

I heard the front door. "Oh, shit!" I gasped aloud. What if Traci walked in on me now? I wasn't quite finished packing. I held my breath.

"Anybody home? I'm back."

I let out a sigh of relief. It was Jawea, thank goodness.

I greeted her in the hallway.

"Hi, Stevie, my ride decided to leave tonight instead of tommorrow. So, we left after dinner and drove straight through."

"Welcome home." The word *home* stuck in my throat. "How was Tai Chi camp?"

"It was so powerful. Artemis, come here, Artemis. My form improved so much." Artemis continued to sit in the windowsill, not paying Jawea any attention.

"You got a nice tan."

"It was hot, and we practiced outside most of the time. Artemis always acts pissed when I've been away this long."

"That's good."

"Stevie, are you OK?"

"Why do you ask?"

"Your energy seems scattered. I don't know, maybe I'm so relaxed, it makes you seem tense. It's always an adjustment coming back to the city after a week in the country."

"Yeah," I agreed, staring off into space.

"Stevie, are you sure you're all right?"

"What do you mean?"

"Look at your arm! It's got big red splotches all over it! I think you've broken out into hives!"

"Oh!" I said, surprised to see the rash on my arm. "I broke out into hives the night before our debate tournament last year, I was so nervous."

"What are you worried about now? What's wrong?"

"I've decided to leave Traci."

"Are you shitting me?" Jawea asked, surprised.

"No, I'm serious." I looked Jawea in the eye. "How come you never told me about Traci and Kate?"

"It wasn't for me to tell," Jawea answered softly.

"Well, Kate's coming back."

"Yeah, in January, you knew that."

"No, something happened with the guru and she's coming back sooner, in two weeks."

"Oh, shit! Well, Kate can't just kick you out. That wouldn't be fair. We'd have to give you a month's notice."

"I don't want to be around Kate and Traci. It would be too humiliating."

"I can understand why you would want your own space."

"Who wouldn't?"

"Trace should have told you. Just like she should've told Nancy."

"Who's Nancy?"

"Just somebody Traci got involved with last year when Kate was away at an artist's colony."

I remembered the woman who stamped our hands at the dance. The one who'd asked if I was the newest link in Traci's chain of fools. "Does Nancy have freckles?"

"A ton of 'em," Jawea nodded. "How did you know?"

"We ran into her once."

"Oh. I'm afraid Traci's just not good at facing up to shit."

"Well, I have no choice."

Jawea slid down the wall and sat on the floor. "I'm sure this is no picnic for Trace."

I leaned against the wall. "Why not? I left her at Susan and Roger's place. She's probably over there screwing Susan right now before her time runs out."

Jawea laughed. "Time is not a big issue. Traci and Kate have an open relationship."

"Well, I'm closing the book on ours."

"You have to do what's right for you."

"Yeah," I nodded.

"So, what *are* you going to do?"

I sighed, "I don't really want to go back to Chicago, but I'm scared not to."

Jawea stood up and put her hand on my shoulder. "I can relate to being scared; that's real. I used to think that you were in your head too much. But that came from your gut, I can feel it."

"Yeah, me too."

"Stevie, we're all fucking scared. Most of the time, I'm scared shitless."

I'd never thought of Jawea as being scared.

My stomach churned as the telephone rang. I had finished packing, but I still didn't want to talk to Traci.

"If it's Traci, I'm not here," I shouted from Kate's room as Jawea ran toward the kitchen.

"Stevie, it's for you."

"Who is it?" I asked, walking into the kitchen.

"It's a man."

"It's not Roger, is it?"

Jawea shook her head. "Might be one of your brothers or your father. I'm not sure."

I reached for the phone. At least it wasn't Traci.

"Is everything OK? It must be after one in the morning back there," I said, walking toward Kate's bedroom with the telephone.

"No, it's only a little after eleven. Stevie, I hope that I didn't wake you up." This wasn't a voice I recognized.

"No, I'm awake. Who is this?"

"Sterling."

"Sterling?"

"Sterling Grant from KPIX, remember?"

"Yes, of course. My mind has just been somewhere else."

"I hope it wasn't too late to call. I thought you might still be up, since it's Friday night."

"I'm still up, don't worry."

"Stevie, I called to tell you about the Minorities in Media luncheon at Fort Mason tomorrow. It's a great networking opportunity."

"Oh."

"I'm sorry it's such short notice, but I forgot to call you before I went away. I was down in L.A. visiting my sisters."

"Sterling, thanks a lot for thinking of me, I really appreciate it."

"No problem. I said I'd look out for you. I hope that you'll be able to make it."

"Actually, Sterling, I can't make it. I'm going back to Chicago."

"Going back to Chicago for a visit already? Is your family OK?"

"They're fine. I'm going back to live."

"No!"

"Yes."

"Why?"

"Things just haven't worked out for me here. It's time for me to throw in the towel."

"Just because you haven't found a job yet? You can't get established overnight, you know."

"I just had a bad scene with my girlfriend. I can't really talk. She could walk in at any moment. I don't want to see her. I called the Haight-Ashbury Switchboard. They're trying to find me a bed in a shelter. If they can't, I might have to sleep in the Trans Bay Terminal tonight."

"Sleep in the Trans Bay Terminal! Over my gay body! Now, you listen to me. I have a car. I can be anywhere in this city in fifteen minutes. You are not going to any shelter tonight and you sure as hell are not sleeping in anybody's terminal."

"Thank you, Sterling. But maybe you could just give me a ride to BART."

"Did you hear what I said? You are not going to anybody's shelter or anybody's terminal, period!"

"Yes, sir." I couldn't help but feel taken care of. Sterling was acting like the big brother I never had. And I felt safer now that he'd confirmed that he was gay.

"You like San Francisco, am I right?"

"Of course. San Francisco will always have a place in my heart."

"Well, there's no reason for you to leave San Francisco just because your relationship has gotten funky."

"How about these reasons: For starters, I don't have a job. I'm broke, I'm on food stamps and Medi-Cal."

"That's exactly why you don't need to go back to Chicago."

"Come again?"

"You don't need to go back to Chicago in defeat. It would be like you were a failure."

"It's too late to salvage my ego. Besides, I can't stay out here. You don't understand. I have no money."

"*You* don't understand. I knew the first time I saw your face that you didn't belong in Chicago."

"What do you mean?"

"There is an openness in your eyes that Chicago can't fill."

"Thanks for the poetry. I know that some people are content just to hang out. But I've been hung out to dry. It's time for me to be realistic, not artistic."

"Stevie, excuse my language, but sometimes you have to fuck being realistic!"

"Easy for you to say, you've got a job and a place to stay."

"You can find a job. And you've got a place to stay, too."

"I told you, I can't stay with Traci anymore."

"You don't have to *stay* with Traci. She's not the only person in this town who can offer you a roof."

"What's that supposed to mean?"

"It means that you can stay on my couch till you get on your feet. No strings attached. I'll even empty out the living-room closet for you."

"That's very sweet of you, Sterling, but I couldn't—"

"My couch is very comfortable. It's not one of those uncomfortable sofa beds."

"I believe you, but I've learned to put more emphasis on

inner comfort than outer comfort these days. There's no such thing as no strings attached. There's always strings."

"Wow, nobody can accuse you of not being cynical."

"There's less chance of a misunderstanding that way."

"Well, somebody helped me get on my feet, once. And I believe that what goes around, comes around. A part of me would like to return the favor."

"A part of you?" I hated to sound suspicious, but I wanted him to make it plain.

"Yeah, and my ego is involved a little bit, too. Maybe having just seen *Rocky* is a factor."

"*Rocky?*"

"Yeah, this movie I previewed down in L.A. about a boxer who beats the odds. It was really inspiring. It'll be out next year."

"Well, not everyone can be a Rocky."

"No, but I believe you can be. And I'll always be able to take satisfaction in knowing that it was partly because of me. So, that's one reason I'm offering to take you in. Let's face it, Stevie, whatever people do, they ultimately do for themselves."

"You mean your motives aren't entirely unselfish?"

"Are you kidding? The fish ain't been biting lately in the romantic department. So, hey, I could use a shoulder to cry on or a creative mind to dream up a new strategy."

"Well, I think I have a reasonably strong shoulder and a pretty active imagination. At least this time the cards would be on the table. And heaven knows, I don't want to go back to cold winters and steamy summers."

"Come on, Stevie, where there's a couch, there's a way."

"Are you sure that you want to give up your couch? I mean, you really don't know me from Adam."

"Yes, I do too, honey, 'cause if you were Adam, you

wouldn't be sleeping on my couch, you'd be up in the bed with me!"

Sterling had taken the suitcase to the car while I was saying good-bye to Jawea. I'd already hugged the cat. It was almost midnight, and we still hadn't heard from Traci.

"Jawea, I'm glad I got to know you."

"I'm going to miss your energy."

"Tell Traci . . ." I felt a lump in my throat. "That I wish she had been honest with me. But I don't regret being with her." My eyes were suddenly clouded with tears. "Tell Traci that she was the bridge that got me across."

Jawea nodded. "I'll try to remember all of that."

"Take care, Jawea."

"You take care too." Jawea hugged me. "Remember, your energy will always be a part of this house."

Sterling reappeared on the stairs. "The car's all packed."

"Don't forget to stay behind your eyes," Jawea shouted as I headed down the stairs.

" 'Stay behind your eyes!' Wow, I can't offer you that kind of depth," Sterling chuckled as we got into his old T-Bird.

"That's OK, Sterling. Just be yourself."

"Well, I hope you like disco."

"I'm not all that familiar with it."

Sterling started up the car. "You will be, 'cause I'm a disco queen!"

I wondered what on earth I was getting into. At least Traci was the devil I knew.

fall/winter 1975

13

Sterling and I sat in his matching blue wing chairs sipping white wine. Lounging around in his bathrobe and bedroom slippers, he reminded me of Hugh Hefner.

"Stevie, it's when you're at your lowest that it's important to look your best."

I squirmed. I didn't know how to take his remark. It didn't sound like the thing to say to a person recovering from a love affair gone sour. I mean, it had only been three days, and I was still recuperating.

I took a swallow of the dry wine. "The last thing I'm concerned about right now is my appearance."

Sterling tilted his head back and raised his eyebrows.

"Well, we do have the children to consider."

"What children? You don't have any children, do you?" I was confused. It was hard to imagine "crumb snatchers" romping on Sterling's white-and-blue oriental rug. And there were no smudges on his Japanese-print couch or the raspberry-colored walls. His apartment was immaculate.

"I'm talking about the members."

"The members of what?"

"The gay children, honey. My friends. The children will be scrutinizing you. And if you don't look good, I won't look good."

"Your friends judge people by how they look on the outside?"

"Yes," Sterling answered without hesitation. "Our motto is, 'Friends don't let friends wear polyester.'"

I glanced down at my rumpled T-shirt and worn jeans.

"Well, at least I'm partial to cotton."

"Now, don't get the wrong idea, the children will give you points for having a good heart. But they will down you for not making the most of your natural assets." Sterling rocked to the rhythm of his words. "You're an attractive girl, Stevie. It would be a shame if you just let yourself go."

"Let myself go! I can't believe it! I look like a beauty-pageant contestant compared to some of the politicos in the women's community."

"I've seen how they look, believe me. God don't like ugly and neither do I." Sterling pointed at me. "Don't get me wrong, Stevie, I'm not trying to make you into a femme fatale."

"You're not?"

"Actually, I think you have baby butch potential."

"Baby butch?"

"Yeah, tomboyish, but cute"—Sterling rubbed his chin—"not deisel dyke. A bull, without the dagger, so to speak. I want women to just want to nuzzle you up against their bosoms. Take shit off of you like they would a little boy, because he's so cute. I think this image could get you over."

"Will it help me get a job?"

"As a matter of fact, yes. Stevie, you have to understand something." Sterling lowered his voice. "This is San Francisco, 'durling.' And it's very competitive. There are a lot of gentle people here. But it's still dog-eat-dog, honey. You can't afford to half-step. With a new hairstyle and a confident stride, you can project that you're the woman for the job in the bedroom as well as in the boardroom."

"Leave my hair alone. You sound like my mother."

"Honey, when the going gets tough, the tough get a new hairstyle." Sterling crossed his leg and patted his neatly trimmed 'fro.

"You don't like my natural?" I couldn't hide the irritation in my voice. Sterling probably wanted me to get some ultrafeminine, straightened style, like Diana Ross.

"I'm not against the natural on women. It's just that you have one that you appear to care nothing about. A cut would do you good."

"First of all, I haven't really been tripping on my hair. And secondly, I can't afford a haircut right now."

"Well, I'm sending you down to Vidal Sassoon's Training School."

"Sterling, I can't take money from you."

"Look, I'd rather spend a measly five dollars than watch you start looking like Buckwheat."

"Buckwheat! You're signifying now!"

"What are friends for, if not to pull your coattails when necessary?"

I stood in line waiting to be picked by one of the students at Vidal Sassoon. All of the other guinea pigs were white, except for one Asian.

I'd never had my hair cut by a white person before. What if he or she didn't know the first thing? What if no one picked me? The old anxiety crept back. The voice I'd heard riding on a bus—"I prayed for a boy because at least I didn't have to deal with *that* hair." Or the tired tape from my own mother—"How can you have the nerve to be tenderheaded with these naps?"

I was thankful that at least I had a hairpick in my purse. How could I live it down if the stylist's narrow-toothed comb popped in two, flying across the room?

To my surprise, two women pointed toward me simultaneously: A perky blonde and a stylish brunette. The women looked at my head longingly. Here I was afraid that I wouldn't be selected, and don't tell me they were gonna fight over me!

"Jane, I should give in and let you have her."

It was fine with me, I didn't have a preference.

"Are you sure, Megan?"

"Positive. This is only your second day. You can use the practice."

Now, I did have a preference. But Megan had already turned toward another customer.

"You're new?" I gulped.

"Yes, g'day," blondie smiled. "I'm Jane. I just came over from Australia."

"G'day, I'm Stevie," I mumbled. But I was afraid it wasn't going to be a good day for me and my hair. Maybe it wasn't too late to bolt.

"Well, Stevie, I'm anxious to forge ahead," Jane said cheerfully as she steered me toward a row of chairs.

I made up my mind that I would just have to wear a scarf until my hair grew back. Even if I looked like Aunt Jemima, it would be preferable to the haircut this woman was about to give me.

I slumped in the chair and Jane tied a smock around me.

"Shall we start with a shampoo?"

"No, I washed my hair a couple of days ago."

"Don't worry, the shampoo is included."

"It's not the money. It's just that with black hair, it's easier to cut dry. It changes shape when it's wet."

"That's right," a loud male voice cut in. I looked up at a tall, slim man with a dark ponytail.

"Here, comb it out with a pick first," the man instructed.

Thank goodness, somebody here knows shit from Shinola, I thought. Too bad he wasn't cutting my hair.

"Jane, have you ever cut a black person's hair before?"

I hoped the instructor would rescue me from this disaster about to happen.

"No, Peter, but I'm anxious to have the experience."

"Great," the instructor boomed. "I love your enthusiasm."

"Well, I'm anxious to have a good haircut," I cut in.

"Jane comes highly recommended."

"Yeah, but she's never cut a black person's hair before," I reminded the instructor. I might have to get funky if Jane messed my head up.

"Don't worry mate, I'm going to put my heart and soul into your haircut."

"You'll look marvelous," Peter insisted. "Remember, our motto is If You Don't Look Good, We Don't Look Good."

"OK, I'm gonna hold you to that."

Time had marched on. We'd chitchatted about the weather and the aborigines. Jane was still cutting, alternating between clippers and scissors. All of the other customers were gone. I closed my eyes. I didn't dare look into the mirror. This woman was a cutting fool.

But it was downright embarrassing. It seemed unfair that my hair took so long and poor Jane got the same money as the other stylists. She was probably regretting she'd ever picked me.

"This is so satisfying."

"What is?"

"Cutting your hair. I feel like an artist, like a sculptor."

"Oh," I said, afraid to believe my ears. "Here I was feeling sorry for you because it was taking so long."

"Don't be silly, mate."

To my surprise the instructor led a group of students toward us. The teacher pointed at my head. "This type of hair can be challenging."

I frowned. Nobody wants to have her hair called challenging. Just humiliate me to death.

"But the results can be stunning," he continued. I let out a sigh of relief, but I was still afraid to look. I couldn't trust white folks' opinions. Didn't Mama used to say, "White people will call a monkey cute"? Then again, I couldn't ignore the pleasant chorus of oohs and ahhs from the other students.

Jane thrust a big mirror in front of me. I dared to peep into it. My hair looked good. Better than good. It was totally happening! I turned and surveyed the back of my head. I was scared of Jane! She could cut her behind off!

"You did a really good job. I love it!"

The group of students applauded as Jane glowed with pride. I never thought a five-dollar haircut would lead to this much attention. To top everything off, Jane whipped a camera out of her bag. She explained that she wanted to put me in her scrapbook. I went on and smiled, big time. Too bad I couldn't afford a tip.

. . .

"You're a bad mamajama now!" Sterling yelled his approval over a Bette Midler song when he saw the cut.

"Am I bad?" I grinned. I turned around so that Sterling could inspect the back.

"Miss Thing, you are Superbad. That's a haircut and a half."

"You know, Miss Ann had never seen an Afro-American before today," I laughed. "Had just left the aborigines, day before yesterday." I clapped my hands. "But honey, she got to clipping and got to cutting, and the rest is history." I shouted over Bette's sultry, "Do You Wanna Dance?"

Sterling nodded. "Miss Ann got down, all right." He stretched his hand out and I gave him five. "She got all the way down!"

"In fact, this calls for the Zorro snap," Sterling insisted, snapping his fingers in a Z.

I celebrated my twenty-second birthday on one of those rare warm San Francisco nights. Sterling took me to hear this dynamite disco queen, Sylvester, sing. Two of the black "children," Lester and Derrick, joined us. We had all jumped clean, wearing gold chains, platform shoes, and colorful attire. Mama had mailed me a box of my clothes. And my family had sent me fifty dollars for my birthday. Anyway, the music was happening, and the North Beach Club was jam-packed with writhing, hot, sweaty bodies.

Of course, Sterling had given me the 411 on his friends. Derrick was cute and he knew it. He kept a perm in his hair and hoped you would think it was natural. He had a nice body. He was a letter carrier. Derrick and Sterling were occasional "fuck buddies," when they were both between lovers.

Lester was another story. He was chubby with a reddish complexion. He looked more like a teddy bear than a Castro clone. To be honest, his wrist could stand to be a little stiffer. And yet there was something solid about him. Lester was hoping to find a brotha. Unlike in Oakland, many black men in San Francisco would knock him down trying to get to a white man who reminded them of Clark Gable. Lester was the type who was always stuck holding everyone else's sweaters.

Lester wasn't interested in casual, anonymous sex (not that Lester was considered hot trade, anyway). He craved a long-term relationship. But that was hard to come by for a gay man in his twenties. Sterling said Lester would have better luck over in Oakland, where people were more settled.

Sylvester, dressed in bright flowing clothes, his face dripping with sweat, took his final bow. It had been an exhilarating show; the room was still abuzz with energy.

Hot Chocolate's "Disco Queen" blasted from the loudspeakers. Men danced together under a big, glittering silver ball. An older man with bushy sideburns walked over to Derrick and asked him what was going on.

"Ain't nothin' goin' on here, but the rent," Derrick said coolly, and turned away.

"Derrick's a golddigger," Lester whispered to me. "If Mr. Charlie don't wanna support 'her,' he better keep steppin'." Soon a hunk wearing a chain vest and tight jeans swept Derrick onto the dance floor.

Sterling looked on enviously. "Derrick thinks he's the chosen one. But most of the time, I get way more play than he does. Lester, remember that night at the Stud? My mood ring was a good color that night."

"Yeah," Lester agreed, "you were cooking with oil."

"And you know, Derrick can't hold a candle to me at the baths. They can't see how small his dick is in a club."

"You've definitely got him beat in the dick department."

"Y'all are terrible," I protested. "Are you forgetting that there's a lady present?"

"A lady? I thought you were a fag hag!"

"Forget you, Sterling."

"I just spotted the perfect man for Lester."

"Where?" Lester asked anxiously.

"Over there in that corner," Sterling pointed. The one with the glasses. He looks like that child in the cartoons. You know that boy that be with Bullwinkle."

"Poindexter," I said peering at the spectacled brother in the button-down shirt.

"Sterling, you cold," Lester frowned.

"He might be a nice guy," I cut in. "You need to look beneath the surface. Everything that glitters isn't gold."

"So long as I have my youth and good looks, I'm gonna be picky." Sterling pouted.

"You need to put more emphasis on inner qualities," I argued.

"I heard that," Lester agreed. "Plenty of men pass me up because I'm not considered fine. But that doesn't mean I don't have something to offer."

"Of course you do," I assured him.

"Let's face facts; men are visual," Sterling insisted. "And my pupils are dilating right now!" He said, cruising the place.

"It didn't take a psych major to tell us that," Lester groaned.

Sterling rubbed his finger. "It's been real, y'all. But my mood ring has changed colors." He strolled over to the bar and hovered next to a tanned, mustached hunk in a sleeveless undershirt and army fatigues. Sterling pulled out a cigarette, and the apple of his eye gave him a light. Sterling told me he only smoked cigarettes in clubs.

Derrick walked back to our table. He motioned toward the dude nearby with the chain vest. "John invited me over to his place. He lives in the Marina District. He even has a view of the water," Derrick bragged.

"Some folks have all the luck." Lester frowned. "Well, get enough for both of us."

"It was nice meeting you, Stevie."

"You too, Derrick."

"Later, Lester." Derrick tossed his head. "Tell Sterling I had love to get."

Lester and I danced together to K.C. and the Sunshine Band's "That's the Way I Like It." Sterling was boogeying nearby with the dude who'd lit his fire at the bar.

"Lester, you're a really good dancer."

"Too bad I don't get more practice," he sighed.

"Don't worry, your ship will come in one day."

"Yeah, but don't hold my breath, right?"

"You deserve someone special. It's quality, not quantity."

"Thanks, you're really sweet."

"I bet most of the men in here are too shallow for you. Look at them."

"I'm looking." Lester spun around on the dance floor. "I'm looking. I'm always looking."

"Check out that one over there gyrating in those shiny gold hot pants. He leaves nothing to the imagination."

"Honey, I can sho' imagine him without his shorts." Lester drooled as the guy bumped his groin against his dance partner to Donna Summer's "Love to Love You Baby."

"And look at that one in the torn cutoffs. You can see his butt."

"Where?" Lester panted like a dog. "Wow, if I could just have one night with him. I swear, I would die a happy man," he joked.

"What are those dudes in the ruffled shirts inhaling?" I asked.

Lester eyed the couple sniffing from a vial. "That's probably amyl nitrite. It's an upper. It's supposed to be an aphrodisiac."

Lester bought me a beer and we lounged against the wall.

"Clint, say hi to the birthday girl," Sterling said, hanging on to his new squeeze.

Lester and I shook hands with the muscular dude.

Sterling took a drag off of his cigarette. "What happened to Derrick?"

"He gotta pull," Lester reported.

"Clint asked me if I wanted to go to the baths. But I told him I couldn't ditch the birthday girl."

"I didn't know he had company," Clint said shyly. He tugged at the red bandanna around his neck.

"No, you go head on," I said. "I'm cool."

"No, that would be cold," Sterling protested. "Not unless you and Lester wanna hang out," he added hopefully.

"I'm enjoying Lester's company. But I don't wanna cramp his style."

Sterling looked surprised, as if he wanted to ask, What style?

Even Lester appeared at a loss for words. "I . . . I . . . don't have to cruise tonight. It's your birthday. We can hang out together if you want to."

"Sterling, just go. I'll be fine," I insisted. "If Lester hooks up with somebody, I'll check out a women's bar I read about in the *People's Yellow Pages*."

Clint winked. "She sounds like the kinda girl who can take care of herself."

"Gon' Ms. Birthday Girl, wit yo' bad self." Sterling stretched his palm out and we gave each other five. "Here I was worrying about you, and you hunting down your next piece of ass just like the rest of us." He smiled.

I knew that I was looking for more. But I didn't say anything.

After Sterling and his date had spaced the place, Lester said, "I wish I could dip Clint in chocolate. Then he would really be fine."

"That reminds me of one of my grandmother's stories," I said. "She was visiting family down South. And all the girls were talking about wanting to meet somebody fine. 'What happens to all the homely men?' Grandma asked. Her niece answered, 'Those are the ones we marry.'"

Lester took a swallow of beer. "Let me sip on that." He rested his elbow on the wall ledge and held his chin. "You know what? I'm gonna go over there and ask that brotha to dance."

"Who?"

Lester nodded toward the guy Sterling teased him about earlier.

"Poindexter?"

"Yeah."

"Really?" I asked surprised.

"Yeah, he looks like the marrying kind."

"I heard that," I smiled. "And if the brotha says yes, I'll go check out that club I mentioned. And leave you to your own devices."

Lester shook my hand warmly. "You got a deal."

"Knock 'em dead."

I wanted to be surprised, so I didn't look up for a while. But when I did, Lester was cutting up on the floor with Poindexter to Gloria Gaynor's "Never Can Say Good-bye." It was time for me to book.

Wild Side West was a club in the middle of Italian North Beach, but it had a cowboy theme. There were pictures on the walls of women riding horses, and a lot of the patrons were dressed in jeans, flannel shirts, and Frye boots. But nobody patted my shoulder and said, "Howdy, pardner."

I was the only black person in the dark, crowded, smoky club. This wasn't unusual for San Francisco. If I were going to make it here, I guess I'd have to get used to feeling like a fly in a pail of buttermilk, as Grandma would say.

I didn't come here to hold up the walls. So I decided to assert myself as soon as I spotted someone cute and had polished off a couple of beers.

I *had* to dance to LaBelle. I checked out a shapely brunette over in the corner. She was fashionably dressed, for a lesbian bar. She had on nice black pants and a pale-blue silk Indian-style top. At least she wasn't dressed like a rancher. I took a big swallow of beer and swaggered toward her.

"Would you like to dance?" I asked, wanting to rush her onto the small floor space to finish out the song.

The young woman smiled at me like she might be flattered. She tossed her head back and said, "Sure."

I was a happy camper. It was the first time in my life I'd ever asked a stranger to dance. And she'd said yes!

I put my heart into it and we jammed on into the next song.

We tore up the floor, rocking close to each other's bodies. The woman was even grinning up in my face the whole time. I thought she was cute with her turned-up nose and pouty-lips. So what if she was white? I could love 'em from snow to crow. Wasn't this a free country? And it didn't get any freer than San Francisco.

When the song ended, my dancing partner waved to some people coming in. She said she had to catch up with her friends. I thanked her for the dance like a perfect gentleman, and she was gone.

The next couple of tunes were tired. I couldn't see taking a chance on getting rejected behind some song that didn't even have it going on. Especially on my birthday. The woman I'd danced with was busy talking. And I didn't see anybody else that looked interesting. I decided to call it a night.

Walking along Broadway was really a trip. The streets were lit up with neon signs advertising naked women and sex acts. Barkers in uniforms outside the clubs tried to entice people to come inside.

"Completely nude, our ladies go all the way! Male to female, female to female. Come get it while it's hot!

"How about you, young lady? You won't see this back where you're from."

I just laughed and kept on stepping.

"Girl, I'm so glad i tracked you down," Sharlinda sighed after we'd exchanged greetings and discussed the weather.

"Your Mama said you out there living from pillar to post. Said you need to bring your butt back here to Chicago. What you out there for anyway?"

"I like it out here."

"You ain't got a pot to piss in or a window to throw it out. Everybody back here is working."

"You gotta job?"

"Yes, ma'am. I got on with Head Start in Milwaukee."

"Well, go 'head on wit yo' bad self."

"You could get hired here or with Model Cities or something. I'm a black studies major and they got me teaching, girl."

"How do you like Milwaukee?"

"I like that it's only a hop, skip, and a jump from Chicago. I got me a cute one-bedroom apartment. And I got my eye on a fine brotha across the hallway, too."

"I'm scared of you."

"What's happenin' with you in the dude department? Obviously that thing with Mr. Goodbar has fizzled out."

"Yeah, it's dead. But all I'm tripping on right now is getting a job and a place."

"Surrounded by all them fags, I guess you ain't got much choice."

I bristled. "Sharlinda, I'm not comfortable with that word."

"Listen at you. Don't nobody care what you comfortable with back in the Midwest. We tell it like it is."

"Well, I'm telling you how I feel."

"Okay, Miss Touchy-feely, I'm sorry. I ain't got nothing against gays. My favorite uncle is funny. I just don't want to marry one, you dig?"

I groaned. "So, Sharlinda, have you heard from Today lately?"

"Girl, I'm worried about the Beaver. No point in me beating around the bush."

"Well, make it plain."

"Today got involved with somebody."

"So?"

"They talking serious, girl."

"So, what's wrong with that?"

"Plenty."

"Is he a drug addict or an alcoholic? Does he beat her?"

"Well, no."

"Well, then what are you tripping about? I thought you said you weren't gonna beat around the bush!"

"I was just building up to a climax. Girl, Today is riding the bus."

"Riding the bus?" I asked, not having heard the expression used like that since college.

"Yeah, girl, she's up with a hoogie."

"Look, it's not the end of the world because Today is seeing a white dude. I mean, is his color the only thing you have against him?"

"You don't understand, Stevie. Sam's not only white."

"Mr. Charlie's name is Sam." I chuckled. "Well, what else is he?"

"You've heard that there's nothing worse than a stingy man, right?"

"Yeah, although I can think of worse things."

"Well, this is worse."

"What is he a murderer or a rapist?"

"No, he's poor!"

"Poor? What do you mean by poor?"

"I mean he's poor as in po'. He ain't got shit, OK," Sharlinda replied.

"White and poor, huh?"

"You got it." Sharlinda sighed.

I digested this information. White and poor; it wasn't even exotic. It conjured up thoughts of white bread and gravy,

Cheese Whiz and endless recipies involving Spam and Vanilla Wafer cookies. Hadn't I heard that a white poor person could never really ever rise above it, unlike black people? Their poorness got under their skin, their pasty white skin, which couldn't even tan decently. Poor black people were at least interesting, expected to be colorful, have attitude, be able to dance and sing like they meant it. And black people had a debt to collect, a score to settle. We'd been wronged, dogged royally in this country. A white poor person couldn't play a sympathy card. My grandmother had told me about a black man who seemed to begin every sentence, "Now if I hadda been born white." Grandma said he'd damn near be president of the United States if he'd been born a white man, to hear him tell it. But who could argue that a person born white didn't have a better shake in life, all in all?

"A business major and she ends up with trash." Sharlinda interrupted my thoughts.

"Sharlinda, money isn't everything. Haven't you heard the best things in life are free?"

"That *sounds* nice, but I'd rather have nice *things*."

"It's not about that out here. Plenty of folks have furniture made of crates and plywood and cinder blocks. They get their clothes from secondhand stores or even free boxes. And if they have a car, it's an old beat-up number. And nobody trips. In fact, people are worried about appearing too materialistic. They even have a name for it . . ."

"Yeah, stupid-ass white folks," Sharlinda groaned.

"No, downwardly mobile."

"Well, that might be cute if your daddy happens to be an investment banker. But if some folks start moving downward, they'll be picking cotton pretty soon. I mean, what was the struggle for, if you don't want shit? If white folks want to drop out and throw away everything, that's their business. And you can be a love child if you want to. But that hippy-dippy shit done played out in the rest of the country. Me myself, I want a piece of the damn pie!"

"Sharlinda, maybe the pie is sour. You think all these white folks are happy? These suburban housewives, popping Valium right and left, and these white men in suits with their three-martini lunches? I think a lot of them are as empty as all get-out."

"If they are, it's their own damn fault."

"The point is, maybe we can learn from their mistakes. Why adopt their bankrupt values?"

"You tripping, Stevie. White folks are miserable because it's just part of being white folks. They're a tired race of people. Let's face it, they never learned how to have a good time. They can't dance, they don't put any feeling in they songs, and most of them can't fuck."

"In that case, let's hope Today has found an exception."

"I wasn't gonna say it, but this makes me wonder about Today."

"What do you mean?"

"Girl, haven't you heard folks say, 'A white man is a step away from being with a woman?' "

"No, really?"

"Yeah, girl, so no telling what line she might cross next."

"Sharlinda, you need to quit."

"Girl, I'm just telling you what folks say."

"Give me your new number, I gotta run." I needed time to digest that.

14

Even the devil knew I needed a job by now. I couldn't be up under Sterling with no money much longer and hold my head up. We got along, but I still had to dance to Sterling's music. I mean that literally and figuratively. I'd grown to like disco, which was lucky, since he played it nonstop.

Sterling had a thing against football, said he didn't want any parts of it. Wouldn't even watch the Forty Niners play against the Bears. Sterling would've been a walking stereotype, except that he loved playing basketball. Sterling said he could talk as loud and smell as funky as the next nigga on the court.

But he was sure finicky about everything else. He even had his albums alphabetized. Sterling threw a hissy fit just because I'd put his Sylvester album in front of Donna Summer. I was reminded of what Grandma always said: "I'd rather be in my own shack, than in somebody else's mansion."

Nobody in their right mind would tell a job interviewer that they were gay. At least that's what I thought. But Sterling had convinced me that "coming out" at my interview with the Personal Change Counseling Center would be my ace in the hole. I couldn't believe I'd agreed to do it. But Sterling knew more about the do's and don'ts in this crazy town than I did. So, if he thought coming out would get me over, it was worth a try.

I faced my two interviewers, Ellen and Mitch, with what I hoped was a warm and confident smile.

I'd already glanced around the tasteful, comfortable office. I appreciated the wood. I concluded that I'd prefer to work in a Victorian house than a modern office building any day.

Ellen, the assistant director, was pleasant-looking, with long straight hair and a big face. She was babbling on about how they were looking for a receptionist who believed in taking responsibility for her own destiny. I couldn't help but feel relieved. Here I'd been worried that I might have to take a typing test.

Mitch, the director, said that he was an est member. He was around thirty, tall, muscular, and dark-haired. He reminded me of a wild-eyed intellectual.

"We believe that everyone should take responsibility for his or her own life," he insisted, tugging at his sideburn.

I nodded. No point in being controversial.

"Do you understand what we mean when we say that you are responsible for your own feelings?"

"I think so," I answered cautiously. I might think he meant one thing, but he might really mean another.

"We mean that no one else can make you feel anything," Ellen offered.

"No matter what they do?" I tried to make it sound more like a statement than a question. But I wasn't so sure I agreed. It seemed to me that people could trigger feelings in you.

"Ultimately, you choose your reaction," Mitch insisted.

"For example," he continued, "say you called me a 'conniving Jew.' "

I looked at Mitch and realized that he was Jewish. I was glad he hadn't used me as an example.

"I can choose to express anger," Mitch continued. "I could call you a dumb nigger, for example." I felt myself getting hot. They'd better hire me after putting me through this bullshit, I thought. Mitch was probably just looking for an excuse to call somebody a nigger and get away with it. He wasn't fooling me. I was a minute off his ass.

"Or Mitch could laugh it off."

"Yes, I could *choose* to laugh it off." Mitch smiled.

"The point is, I *choose* my reactions. I can choose to let you get to me. Or I can *choose* to see you as a pathetic soul not worth my energy."

I nodded in agreement. I wondered how I was going to work in that I was a lesbian. Despite my irritation, I needed a gig badly. Even a receptionist job that paid $600 a month.

"How much typing is involved?" I asked. It was better to have it out in the open. I was no typist. I knew the keyboard, had to in order to be a journalism major. But 30 wpm was about my top speed.

"We're not concerned about your typing ability."

"You're not?" I asked with relief.

"No," Ellen continued. "We're interested in the kind of energy you project. We want someone who is in touch with his or her feelings."

Ellen gave me a soulful look. I remembered to make eye contact. White folks love it when you look them in the eyes. Otherwise, they think you're sneaky. I learned that in social psychology class. But in the South it was different. Black folks were taught to look down out of deference when talking to white folks.

"And someone who's willing to disclose his or her feelings," Mitch added, staring me down. "Disclosure is very important here."

Well, I'd like to disclose that I think y'all are full of shit, I thought to myself. But instead, I cleared my throat and said, "Well, I'm a lesbian."

"She's a lesbian too!" Ellen blurted out.

"You'll be hearing from us very soon." Mitch winked at me. "I'm really feeling psyched about your disclosure."

"And your energy," Ellen chimed in.

I knew that the job was as good as mine, if I could survive working with these crazy white folks.

I walked home from the interview, through the Upper Haight and into the Castro. It was windy, which was nothing new, but the sun was shining. I had a little pep in my step because I thought I'd finally be offered a job.

"Say, baby, say!"

I wasn't used to being bothered, so I was surprised. Most of the men in this neighborhood were only studying other men. I turned around in front of the Castro Theater and glanced into a milk-chocolate-colored baby face. I was thinking maybe this cute, husky brother got off at the wrong Muni stop.

"Baby, you look like my third wife."

I kept walking. I knew he was probably jive. But I was curious. He looked too young to have been married three times.

"So, how many times you been married?" I called over my shoulder.

"Twice," he answered. I heard his feet running to catch up with me.

It took me a minute to get it. "Very funny. You've got an interesting line, but . . ."

"But what?" He asked, hot on my trail.

"But I ain't biting."

"You trying to tell me to go fish somewheres else?"

"Yeah, if you wanna catch anything."

"Baby, I used to could sell hot water sandwiches. Why y'all got to be so hard on the brothas these days?"

I ignored the question but I couldn't help but smile. The "Negro" was almost refreshing after my interview with those woo-woo's this morning. I mean, at least brothaman was for real, in a jive sort of way.

"You know, baby, if I wasn't allergic to white women, I wouldn't be bothered with you. I'd let you gon' about your business."

I slowed down. "Humph," I chuckled, "that's a good one. Allergic to white women? Well, brotha, you're suffering from a rare disease in this town."

"Yeah, and I can't even qualify for Medi-Cal."

"That's too bad," I said, turning up Sterling's street. This dude was good for a laugh or two, but now I was ready to get rid of him. To my irritation, the brotha continued to walk alongside of me.

"Stop following me."

"Baby, we going to the same pad."

"No, we're not."

"Yes we are too, Miss Stevie."

I was startled. "How do you know my name?"

"I know all about your behind."

I felt nervous. Who was this fool? And how dare he get cute?

"How do you know my name?" I demanded, trying to mask my fear.

"I'm Buster, Sterling's baby bruh, you dig?"

"You're Buster?" I asked, remembering that Sterling said his younger brother was really a trip.

"That's right, I'm going out to dinner with Sterling tonight."

"Well, why did you have to act so mysterious?"

"You thought I was just another jiveass nigga out here in the streets, didn't ja?"

"Maybe I still do. You just happen to be Sterling's brother."

"Now you wanna show your drawers. Well just remember, you ain't the only one from Chicago."

"So?"

"So, don't get funky. Be nice to baby bruh. Because you act a fool and the next thing you know your shit'll be set out there in the street. Girl, you'll be living outdoors."

I turned at the bottom of the stairs and rolled my eyes.

"Really, you have that kind of power over Sterling?"

But I wasn't tripping. I remembered that Sterling had said Buster had to be taken with a grain of salt.

Buster snapped his fingers. "All I've got to do is say the word."

"Oh, please, gimme a break." I walked up the stairs. "What time are you supposed to meet Sterling?"

"Six o'clock, straight up."

I glanced at my watch. "It's six o'clock now. Why don't you unlock the door?" I asked, checking to see if Buster had a key to the apartment. "So I won't have to go digging into my shoulder bag."

"Ain't that a blip, I forgot to carry my key with me."

"A likely story." I shook my head. "Buster, you're starting to lose some of your power."

Buster smiled and followed me into the apartment. "Come on, baby, let's be friends. I bet we got some karma we've yet to resolve."

I didn't answer, I just thumbed through the mail to see if I had anything. There was a postcard from Paris. I turned it over. It was from Celeste! She said she missed me. That she was teaching art, and there was a little girl that reminded her of me. "Of course she's my pet," she wrote. I got a warm feeling. I missed my girl Celeste.

"Thought I was just a go-ta-work-come-home-whus-fuh-dinna-go-ta-bed-kinda nigga, didn't ja," Buster said over my shoulder. "Didn't know I could whup that New Age shit on you. Didn't know I was hipped to unresolved karma? Did ja?"

"No, but let's resolve our karma right now. It's been real, but I'm going to the bathroom."

"Before you do that, why don't you bring me a beer?"

I sighed. "They're in the refrigerator."

"What kind of hostess are you? Ain't you forgetting your home training? I could see if you was from L.A. But you from Chi town."

"Now I live *here*. So get it your damn self."

When I returned from the bathroom, Buster was settled back on the couch, sipping a brewskie.

"I wonder why Sterling isn't here yet," I said.

"I wonder why the nigga painted this room pink."

"It's raspberry," I corrected him as the phone rang. I left to answer it. Maybe it was a job offer. No such luck; it was Sterling calling to apologize for sticking me here with Buster.

"I know my brother can be a trip."

"You ain't never lied. You should've heard him bragging about how one word from him and you'd set me out on the street."

"You should've said, 'nigga puh-leaze.' Believe me, you have nothing to worry about. I can barely tolerate having that jive turkey in my house."

"Thanks." I sighed. Sterling and I were solid. Had I doubted that for one minute?

"Just don't let Buster start drinking, or you may never get rid of him."

"It's too late," I said, cringing. "He's not an alcoholic, is he? 'Cause, he's already got his mitts on a beer."

"No, but he has a tendency to get loud when he's had a few."

"Aren't you coming home soon?" I asked hopefully.

"No, that's why I called. I'm stuck on a shoot down here in Watsonville. All the way the hell near Santa Cruz—farmworkers' strike. Tell Buster I'm sorry, I'm gonna have to take a rain check."

"You wanna tell him yourself?"

"No, I've gotta go. I can't really stay on the phone."

"Sterling can't make it. He's stuck in Watsonville on a shoot. He said he'll hook up with you another time."

"Another time?" Buster looked disappointed. I guess I didn't think it would faze him.

238

"Yeah, he has to take a rain check."

"There might not be another time. He knows I'm leaving Monday."

"You're going on a trip?"

"I'm moving to Alaska."

"Alaska, wow. Why Alaska?"

"Why not Alaska? I need to stack up me some dead presidents."

"So, it's all about the paper?"

Buster nodded. "I'ma be working on the pipeline, making some long green."

"It's gonna be cold up there."

"That's cool, 'cause money's got all kinds of friends. Heat is one of 'em."

"Well, if I don't see you again, good luck." I almost twisted my mouth to say, It was nice meeting you.

"Stevie." Buster swallowed and looked at me with his big dark eyes. "If you not doing nothing, how about me and you getting down with some Creole food tonight?"

"I don't think we've hit it off well enough to make it through a whole dinner together."

"Look, I was just giving you a hard time. It wasn't personal. I don't tease people unless I like 'em."

"Well, you didn't really know me. I mean, you still don't. And I guess life is hard enough."

"Look, I apologize. It's one of my last nights here, and it would be nice to have some company. And besides, it's my Mama's birthday." Buster's voice cracked. "It's the fifth one since she passed."

"I'm sorry," I mumbled, remembering that Sterling told me his mother had died in a car crash on the Dan Ryan Expressway back in Chicago. After her death, Sterling's father had moved to the Bay Area with Sterling and Buster. Sterling's two sisters had gone to L.A. to live with an aunt. His father was a porter on the railroad. He lived in San Pablo, over in the East Bay.

"I guess I just don't wanna be alone tonight," Buster said softly.

I nodded and reached for my sweater.

"This gumbo will sho' clear out your sinuses," I said, inhaling the spicy, greenish brown mixture. "None of that red mess, this stuff is authentic." I took a swallow of beer. "Makes you wanna slap the judge!"

"Gumbo got you speaking in tongues, huh?" Buster joked.

"Well, let's not get sacrilegious."

"I can't help myself. This jambalaya is preaching." He smiled, sucking on a crab leg.

I glanced around the cozy little Creole restaurant with red-check tablecloths. "This is nice. I'm glad I came."

Buster turned up his beer can. "You ain't came yet."

I groaned. I thought he wanted to talk about losing his mother. Instead he was talking foolishness.

"Buster, how old are you? I know men mature slower than women, but damn."

"I'm twenty-two. How old are you? That rhymes, I'm a poet and I know it. If I had a boat, I'd row it."

I sighed. "I'm the same age."

"We're a match then."

"Too bad you and Sterling couldn't get together, especially with it being your mother's birthday and you leaving and all."

"Dig up, it may have been a blessing in disguise. Most of the time we hook up, we just end up getting on each other's nerves anywho. We don't see eye to eye on certain things. You know what I'm saying?"

"Like what?"

"Mainly his lifestyle."

"Why can't you just accept it? I don't notice you over there sprouting wings."

"Look, he's my brother and I want what's best for him, you dig?"

"Who's to say what's best for somebody else?"

"Word up, I just believe a man should be a man."

"You mean like John Wayne?"

"Hey, dig up, I can be a sensitive dude. But I still like women."

"That's you. Maybe everybody isn't cut from the same cloth."

"Hey, baby, I can't help it. The thought of two men getting it on just turns my stomach, you dig?"

"Then take some Pepto-Bismol. Besides, you don't have to think about it."

"In San Francisco, it's hard not to." Buster pointed with his thumb toward two slender men gazing at each other at the next table. He lowered his voice. "They put it all up in your face."

I raised my voice. "Nobody flaunts their sexuality any more than straight people," I scoffed. "Who ties tin cans to cars and honks the horn because they've gotten married?"

"Hey, which side are you on?"

"I'm on the side of fairness."

"Sounds to me like you might be a little 'happy' yourself."

"What do you mean?" But I knew "happy" meant "gay."

"You know," Buster said, wiggling his wrist. "Are you a member, as Sterling would say?"

"Are you ready for the check?" the waiter smiled.

"I guess I'm not sure, to tell you the truth," I responded.

Buster frowned. "What do you mean, you're not sure?"

"I was involved with a woman and it didn't work out. But she's the only woman I've ever dealt with."

"You know what I think?"

"What do you think?"

"I think you just ain't never had no good dick before."

"I'll bring you your check," the waiter said, and rushed away.

"I beg your pardon!" I snapped.

"Well, excuse me. I should've said, I don't think you've met the right man yet."

"Maybe it's you who hasn't met the right man yet."

"Stevie, I won't even dignify that with a response. I just wish we had more time. If I wasn't moving to Alaska Monday, I could help you."

"Help me do what?"

"Help you find out what you really need."

"You've got a lot of nerve. I hope you don't think it's you."

"Look, girl, you can't hurt me with your little digs. I can see right through them. We've got chemistry between us. Don't you feel it, too?"

"You make me laugh. If that qualifies as chemistry, then, I stand corrected."

"A sense of humor is very important, don't you agree?"

"Yes, a similar sense of humor."

"I'm finding our conversation fascinating." Buster pointed to the check. "Let me pay this bad boy. And what do you say we continue this discussion at my estate?"

"Surely you jest."

"Well, then let's continue this conversation in my room at the Y."

"You stay at the Y?"

"Yeah, the Residence Club on Powell Street. It's right on the cable car line. I'm sure you've passed it."

"I'm sure I have. And I plan to keep right on *passing* it."

"Once again, I'm gonna let something slide. Pretend like I didn't even hear it."

"Well, I better be going."

"So soon? The night is still young, as they say."

"It's been a long day. The food was great. Thank you for dinner."

"You're welcome. You'd be surprised how many girls don't even say 'thank you.' They just think they're entitled. I don't mind giving, don't get me wrong. But it doesn't cost anything to show appreciation."

"You're right. Well, good luck in Alaska."

"You sure you don't want me to walk you home?"

"I'm cool, I'll just jump on Muni. Can't get much safer than the Castro."

"Yeah, better you walking through that neighborhood at night than me."

"Well, you do have a cute butt. Maybe you'd get a taste of what women have to put up with."

"Humph." Buster squirmed uncomfortably. "I would have to hurt one of them sissies."

"Personally, it gives me a warm feeling to be surrounded by men at night and not have to worry about my safety."

"Not all men who hit on women are dangerous. Sometimes we just don't know how else to express ourselves."

I stood up to go. "Well, maybe you should take lessons."

Buster took my hand. "Will you be my private tutor?"

I pulled my hand away. "Sorry, I need more job security than you can offer. Good night and good luck."

"Well, can I at least get a hug good-bye?"

I shrugged. I'd never have to see Buster again, so I leaned over to give him a quick embrace.

But when I smelled his Brut cologne, it reminded me of how long it had been since I'd held a man's body. To my surprise, it stirred something inside of me.

Sterling came in late, waking me up, laughing like a hyena. He had the nerve to twist his mouth and say he'd just come back from the baths. I rubbed my eyes in the lamplight and sat up on the couch.

And you know what I was thinking? It seems like nobody was even studying the fact that it was their Mama's birthday. Buster hadn't said nary a word about it during dinner. And here I thought he'd wanted a shoulder to cry on.

"The baths?" I yawned.

"Yes, and it was so hot." Sterling popped his fingers. "Got me a hot thang tonight! Stevie, you should've seen him. He was so fucking fine. He was such a gorgeous hunk. Looked just like the Marlboro Man."

"So he was white?"

"Yeah, but he was fine."

"You know I've noticed, you hardly see two brothas together in the Castro."

"Stevie, this ain't chocolate city. San Francisco is only around ten percent black. And we're a minority within a minority. You look like a damn fool waiting around for a black lover."

Sterling pointed his finger at me. "But I'm not a snow queen, if that's what you're trying to signify."

"Snow queen?"

"That's what they call brothas who are only into white boys. Folks, usually white trade, who are into Asians are called rice queens."

"What do they call white men who are into black men?"

Sterling hesitated. "Size queens." He laughed.

When the phone rang, I'd just finished reading the Sunday paper. I was feeling a little lonely and almost bored enough to do the crossword puzzle. I was hoping it was good news, like a job offer, even though it was Sunday morning. I would've settled for a call from Mama. But I was disappointed when I heard Buster's voice.

"Sterling is shooting hoops in Golden Gate Park."

"Actually, I called to talk to you."

"What about?"

"What you doing?"

"Reading the paper."

"Stevie, I still want to help you. I know that we don't have much time. But a little time is better than *no* time."

"Help me do what?" I sighed.

"Discover your true nature. I can make it rise. Baby, let me be your baking powder."

"If you're trying to seduce me, your technique isn't working."

"Stevie, let's get real. You need a man."

"No, I don't."

"Yes, you do, and I'm just what the doctor ordered."

"You are so jive. I can't believe we're even having this conversation."

"You're trying to sound confident. But underneath it, you've got doubt. Is Buster what I need? Could he be my knight in shining armor?"

"Excuse me, but I *need* to get back to my crossword puzzle."

"I could rock you here. I could rock you there. I could rock you out of this atmosphere."

"Nigga, puh-leaze."

"A woman can't take you where you need to go. She might have male energy, but she's still in a woman's body."

"So, I like women's bodies."

"Why settle for a substitute? Why pour saccharine when you can sprinkle sugar?"

"Buster, your technique still isn't working."

"So, would you prefer to be wined and dined?"

"To badgering? Yes."

"You mean you would let me have the pleasure of your company again?"

"I don't know if I'm up for all that."

"Why do you hate men?"

"It's not that I dislike men. You've helped me to realize that."

"Hey, I finally got through to you, huh? What can I say?"

"It's just that I dislike you."

"Why do you wanna be so cold?"

"You need a little cooling off."

"You think I just wanna get in your pants, but that's not true. I just wanna be with you. Will you come with me on a hike? I'll bring us a lunch, wine and all."

"I don't think so."

"Come on, Stevie, it's my last full day in the Bay Area. I

want to spend it with you. Come on, just say, yes, and I'll do the rest."

Finally, his flattery got to me. The brother was basically harmless. He was more entertaining than anything else. And I could use the exercise.

"Where do we meet?" I asked.

Buster looked athletic in his royal blue jogging suit. And even though it was an overcast day, his skin had a warm glow.

"I go up there to think." Buster pointed to a big hill. "You can see everything from up there."

We hiked toward a mountain. It looked close, but Buster said it was three miles away. I was glad to be out in nature, walking under redwood trees and climbing golden hills. It was a perfect day for hiking, cool and crisp. But it was still ass kicking, climbing up the winding trail.

After about two miles, we rested under a tree. Buster searched frantically through his backpack.

"I can't believe I forgot the dope. Blam! What are we gonna do now? You don't happen to have a joint on you, do you?"

I shook my head.

"Blam! I can't believe I forgot it!"

"Hey, we're out here in nature. What could be a bigger high?"

"Well, I guess you're right, John Denver."

"I wouldn't mind having his money."

"Dig up, we ain't got the munchies, but let's go 'head and grease."

"Cool with me," I nodded.

Buster dug in his backpack and handed me a sandwich.

"Thanks."

We washed down the turkey sandwiches and potato chips with swallows of white wine.

"This Almaden wine is on the money, huh?"

"Uhm hmm, it's good," I agreed.

"See, I know how to throw down. Some niggas would've broke out with a bottle of Night Train."

"That's true."

"You know, Stevie, I might be black as a crow and talk more shit than a radio. But I don't mean no disrespect. I mean, in regards to your nature."

"You do talk mucho shit, but actually, you're the color of my grandmother's brownies."

"And, baby, I taste just as good."

"There you go again, talking shit."

"Anyway, dig up." Buster looked me in the eyes like he was about to confide something. "You know, I can almost understand a woman turning to another woman."

"You can?"

"Yeah, 'cause I know women have been dogged by men. Maybe a woman just wants to be loved. She's looking for tenderness and understanding. She's afraid that she can't find that in a man. So she turns to her own sex. Women, I can understand." Buster nodded. "But there's no excuse for two rusty niggas to climb into bed together."

"Not in the world according to Buster."

"You got it."

"Look, I haven't been really dogged by men." I shrugged. "I guess I just like women."

"OK, OK, we found something we agree on." Buster raised his plastic wineglass. "We both like women." I tapped my glass against his.

We'd finished eating and were back on the trail again.

"You know, Stevie, the problem with most girls is they're looking for wallets. Take my ex-girlfriend, Charmaine. I took her out last New Year's Eve to this club where my main man, Larry, is the bouncer. OK, so brothaman let's us in for free. And then my other partner, Raphael, is at the bar, gives us a bottle of free champagne. And I'm a happy camper, 'cause I'm only a part-time loader at UPS, you dig?"

"I heard that. Hey, they got any openings?"

Buster shook his head. "They done just hired for the Christmas season."

"Well, finish the story."

"OK, I'm all smiles and shit, but then I notice Charmaine's looking like she done just lost her favorite pair of earrings. I say, 'Baby, is something wrong? Ain't you having a good time?' You know what the bitch had the nerve to say?"

"I don't like the word *bitch*."

"You know what the nice young lady had the nerve to say?"

"What?"

"Everything is beautiful, except you ain't spent no money on me yet."

"You know that's how a lot of women are raised to think. If a man cares about you, then he'll spend some money on you."

"Well, I don't go for a handful of gimme and a mouthful of much obliged. So, my New Year's resolution was to ditch the bitch. I mean the nice young lady. And by Valentine's Day, Miss Thing had sho' nuff talked herself out of a box of chocolates."

"Well, Buster, on the other hand, there are plenty of men who are looking for service providers."

"Hey, I can do wash, I can cook, and I can clean. I'm looking for a fifty-fifty love. I'm not into playing games anymore. That's what I was about back in high school. All I wanted to do then was get over."

"Don't you *still* want to get over?"

"Yeah, but now I'm more discriminating. When I was young, I'm shamed to admit it, but my motto was 'pussy ain't got no face.' "

"You must've been a real charmer."

"Nowadays, I'm looking for more. Don't get me wrong, looks count to a point. That's the first thing most men notice. That's why you caught my eye. But looks can only take you so far and then other shit has to kick in. Like sincerity."

"Beauty is only skin deep, but ugly's to the bone. Beauty always fades away but ugly holds its own," I recited.

"Guess what, Stevie?" Buster panted. "We're here! We made it to the top of the mountain!"

We stood in silence, surveying the Bay Area below. I noticed the sound of my own breathing.

"Look," I pointed. "You can see three bridges. It's amazing. And look at all the sailboats."

I glanced over at Buster. I was surprised to see tears rolling down his cheeks.

"Buster, are you crying?"

"No, I'm cool," he sniffed. "Something must've got in my eyes. Probably just allergies."

But then I saw him tremble. "Buster, you *are* crying! What's wrong? You can tell me."

"I come up here and talk to my Moms. I'm usually alone. I didn't know I'd get this affected."

I put my hand on Buster's shoulder for a moment. "I understand."

"You ever lost anybody close?"

"No, not really."

"Then you don't *really* understand."

"I guess you're right. I suppose I've been lucky."

"Hell, yeah, you've been lucky. You don't know. I would give anything just to see her again. Even just to pick up the phone and talk to her. Just one more time. Do you know Sterling blames me for our Mama's death?" Buster blurted out.

"Blames you? Why do you say that? Didn't she die in a car accident?"

"Yeah."

"You weren't driving, were you?"

"No, she was the only one in the car. It was icy. Her car skidded, and ran into a concrete divider on the expressway."

"Then how could Sterling blame you?"

"Moms was on her way to pick me up at football practice. I'd forgotten my bus fare," Buster added sheepishly.

"It's still not your fault. You were young. Things like that happen. It was fate."

"She never wanted me to play football. Said it was too rough."

"But you really wanted to play?"

"Pops was the one who pushed me into it. He said he already had one sissy, he didn't want two."

"That's heavy."

"Stevie, I know everybody thinks their mama is the greatest."

"Not everybody thinks that, Buster."

"But, my Moms *was* the greatest. She was strong, but she was also gentle."

I looked out at the bay. "I read somewhere, 'There's nothing stronger than gentleness and there's nothing gentler than real strength.' "

"That's beautiful, just like Moms. She had class, but at the same time she was totally down-to-earth. She spoiled all of us." Buster's voice cracked. "But especially me, her baby son. She'd run through hell in gasoline drawers for me."

I put my arm around Buster's shoulder. "When I was little she used to braid my hair," Buster sobbed. "When my head would be between her knees, I'd be in my favorite place in the world."

"My Grandma's lap used to be my favorite place in the world," I cut in.

"I wasn't no sissy, though. You know how black boys always have braids when they're little."

"Yeah," I assured him. "My mother braided my brothers' hair too."

"Would you believe, I still have my little braids. You know, how some folks have a bronze shoe? Well, I have my braids in an old cigar box."

"You kept them all these years?"

Buster nodded.

"Wow."

"When we were growing up, Moms was never too busy to scratch and oil our scalps. She'd say, 'Want me to look at your scalp?' Remember the days of Dixie Peach?" Buster smiled.

I nodded. "I can take you back to Mange."

"Dog Mange! You done really shown your drawers now. I'd forgot about Mange. I can still picture that brown bottle with that smelly-ass shit. Moms would rub it in my sisters' heads. She was determined to grow them some hair. Used to smell up the whole damn house. But Moms said that was a small price to pay for them to have French rolls."

"You know I got a sample of styling lotion from Vidal Sassoon. It's in my backpack. I wonder if it works on our hair? They did a good job cutting mine."

"Yeah, they did."

"Buster, you want me to look at your scalp?"

"Really, here?"

"I can braid your 'fro."

"You sure you won't feel like a service provider?"

"I offered, didn't I? Besides, you provided the food. And haven't you heard, 'There's no such thing as a free lunch'?"

"Braiding would condition my 'fro."

"You don't mind me doing it out here in public?"

"I don't care what these white folks think. There's no shame left in my game. I done already boohooed."

I ran my fingers through Buster's natural. "My mother would say, 'You have a nice grade of nappy hair.' "

"In other words, you ain't got to comb a bunch of beads."

"Sit your butt down and lean back."

"Stevie, I can't believe it. I'm finally getting between your legs!"

"Shut up before I pop you with this comb."

"Remember, a man's head is very sensitive."

I parted, scratched, oiled, combed, and braided while Buster's shoulders warmed my thighs.

When I finished braiding Buster's hair, he suggested that we go back to his room and smoke a joint. I hesitated because I knew where weed could lead. And I wasn't sure I wanted to go there.

"Stevie, you're the only girl I've ever felt really comfortable with, that I could really talk to. I wanna get next to you before I go."

I felt my heart race. I was drawn to something in Buster.

I gulped, "I guess we could see what happens."

"We can make it happen."

Buster and I kissed while sitting on the creaking bed in his nondescript room. His bags were packed and ready to go. We were both high on reefer. Barry White's deep, sexy voice rang out from the clock radio.

Buster stroked my face. "Baby, I wanna take you down."

"I've never really enjoyed sex with a man before," I confessed. "I mean, the last few times, it was okay."

"With me it'll be different," Buster whispered. "All I care about is pleasing you."

"I like a slow hand," I confided, tugging on one of Buster's braids.

"You got it." Buster winked. He stroked my breasts through my T-shirt. I felt my nipples harden. "You're really turning me on," I said.

He reached under my shirt. I unfastened my bra. Buster cupped my breasts in his hands.

I pulled off my T-shirt. Buster sucked my breasts. His tongue felt good on my nipples.

Buster looked up. "Whatever you want, you just tell me, you dig? I mean, I won't get my feelings hurt behind you telling me a little to the left or down instead of up."

"Well, some men are on an ego trip and I don't wanna come off like a traffic cop."

"Hey, I'd rather take directions than for you to be lying

there frustrated, baby. This ain't no one-man show. We're in this together, you dig?"

"You're being so sweet."

"Baby, your sweetness is my weakness."

I stroked Buster's cheek. "The first time I had sex, I was young and scared and just not ready physically or emotionally. I certainly wasn't relaxed. And looking back, I'm sure I was afraid of opening myself up to a man. Not to mention that it hurt."

Buster kissed me and wrapped his arms around me. "There's no reason a man can't be gentle. A lot of young dudes don't realize that. But the last thing I wanna do is hurt you in any way."

I remembered about birth control. That had been a big plus about dealing with Traci. I didn't have to worry about getting pregnant.

"You know, I'm not on the pill or anything."

"Don't worry, I got a rubber. I gotta fresh pack of 'em."

I smiled. "We'll probably only need one."

Buster laughed and hugged me. We rolled around on the bed and my body writhed with anticipation. The weed was really kicking in, and I was hot. Booties began flying every which way and we started coming out of our clothes.

I ran my fingers up and down Buster's chest. "You don't mind me asserting myself do you?"

"Hey, I'm in seventh heaven. Why should I have to do all the work?"

I slid my wet tongue up and down Buster's ear.

"Baby, you blowing my mind."

I tugged the little nappy hairs on Buster's chest. Then I rubbed my breasts against his body. It felt warm and exciting being up against him.

Buster rewarded me with a long kiss. I sighed as he rubbed his hard penis up and down my naked thighs. His juice moistened my skin.

"You know, my first boyfriend was too big. And so was Myron, for that matter. In retrospect, we should've used K-Y jelly. Maybe we should use something now. It's been a long time."

"You think we'll need it?" Buster asked.

I looked down at his erect penis.

"Maybe not, thank goodness you're not real big."

"Oh."

"I meant it as a compliment."

"Oh. I'm not too small though, am I?"

"No, of course not, you're not too small, you're perfect," I assured him.

Buster managed a smile.

I hugged him. "There's no one else I want inside of me," I whispered.

We kissed and touched and teased each other. Buster played with my clitoris, and I put the rubber on his penis. My vagina contracted. I was ready to let Buster in. His slow, gentle thrusts felt good inside me. He rubbed my clitoris and I called out his name.

I spied Sterling bouncing a basketball out on the pavement as I walked toward the house. I was still basking in the afterglow of my orgasm.

Buster had asked me to ride with him and Sterling to the airport the following night. Of course I wanted to see him off, but I didn't want to cut into Buster's time with his brother.

Buster had insisted that he wanted me there, and that Sterling wouldn't mind. I had told him I'd run it by Sterling.

"Let me see the ball?"

Sterling held the ball away from me. "Ain't no *C* on it," he teased. "You want it, you gotta take it. He started bouncing the ball and doing some fancy footwork. Sterling was impressive for a minute. But Sterling didn't know what he was up against. I got the ball away from him.

I dribbled the ball expertly. Sterling finally got it back.

"Hey, where did you learn that?" he asked, wiping his brow.

" 'Negro,' my brother plays for Iowa State. And I'm the one who taught him how to make his first basket. I had a basketball jones way back in grade school. If I were a man I'd probably be in the NBA by now," I bragged.

"Well, excuse the hell outta me."

"I gotta ask you about something," I said, following Sterling into the crib.

"What about?" Sterling asked, opening the refrigerator.

"Buster."

"What about Buster?"

"I wanna tag along with you when you drive him to the airport tomorrow night. Is that cool with you?"

Sterling popped open a can of beer. "Yeah," he nodded, "but why?"

"Buster wants me to. And I want to."

"Stevie, Buster doesn't even know you."

"Yes, he does." I didn't divulge that Buster knew me in the biblical way. "Buster and I went out to dinner the other night. And we went on a hike today. So, he does know me."

Sterling looked surprised. "You had dinner with Buster and went on a hike together? When did all this happen?"

"Friday night and today."

Sterling thoughtfully sipped his beer. "And you still wanna be in his company? Are you studying to be a psychologist or something?"

"Buster has his good points. Anyway, I told him I didn't want to cut into your time together, but he said you wouldn't mind."

Sterling shrugged his shoulders. "Well, you're welcome to come along. Believe me, you won't be interrupting a Kodak moment or anything. We'll probably shake hands and that's it."

"You know, Buster thinks you blame him for your mother's death. And he's hurting behind it."

Sterling's face got tense, but he was silent.

Suddenly, I felt scared. "I'm sorry if I was out of line. I mean, I know I'm living under your roof and all. If you want me to hold stuff back, then I will. But we can't really be close if I can't be real with you."

Sterling sighed. "No, I want you to be real. And you were mighty real. But Buster still had no right dragging you into this. I don't appreciate him airing our dirty laundry. It's our family's business."

"Maybe so, but my grandmother used to say, 'Dirty laundry washed in the dark seldom comes clean.' "

"Look, I know that my mother's death wasn't exactly Buster's fault. But he was a fuckup, and she catered to him. So it was hard not to blame him at first. Maybe I should just blame the weather."

"Yeah. So you're not still mad at him?"

"I guess I've resented Buster for a long time. It wasn't enough that I got good grades, played clarinet in the school band, and got a scholarship to U.C. Berkeley."

"What reason was there to resent Buster?"

"My father always threw him up in my face. He was the athlete, had the girls."

"I can see how that would be hard. Especially with him being younger. And not to mention that you were tripping on being gay."

"Tell me about it. Anyway, Buster ends up getting a football scholarship to San Jose State and flunking out after two years. At least I got my degree."

"You and Buster are individuals. And you're both adults. It's time to quit comparing."

"You don't know what it's like to have my father's foot on your neck all your life."

"Sterling, you're special, no matter what your father thinks."

"I heard that." Sterling smiled.

The rain was coming down hard and the windshield wipers were busy. Sterling said it was the beginning of the rainy season. "It doesn't play out here," he warned. "You'll damn near need an ark before it's over."

I sat quietly in the backseat of the car while Buster and Sterling talked about how cold it was going to be in Alaska and how much long green you could make. And then Sterling pumped up the volume, and we all started rocking to Evelyn "Champagne" King singing "Shame." I popped my fingers, 'cause "Shame" was one of my favorite jams.

Sterling pulled up to the curb of the San Francisco International Airport. "You're not parking?" I asked. It had never crossed my mind that we were going to say good-bye to Buster on the sidewalk. I'd envisioned at least a kiss at the gate.

"There's no need to park. It's too much of a hassle." Sterling was already out of the car, running for the trunk in the pouring rain. Buster turned and squeezed my hand. It felt warm even though his hand was cold.

"I'll get out," I said.

"Here you go, man." Sterling passed Buster the duffel bag.

"Can you handle everything?"

Buster nodded. "Thanks, man." They gave each other the black handshake.

Sterling cleared his throat. "I bought you a little going-away present, man. I wasn't sure who you were rooting for these days. Well, here." Sterling pulled a Chicago Bears cap out of his right coat pocket and a Forty Niners cap from the left one. "Either one of them will cover up those braids."

For a minute Buster appeared speechless. "Thanks, man," he swallowed. "I really appreciate it."

I watched Buster hug Sterling, and it did my heart good.

"All right now. Take it easy." Sterling rushed back toward the car.

"Don't tell Sterling I'm a Raiders fan," Buster winked.

"Your secret's safe with me."

"Thanks for everything. You're the most sincere girl I ever met. But I still think you're too much woman to waste on another woman."

I frowned at his backhanded compliment. "Forget you."

Buster stared into my eyes. "Stevie, I'll never forget *you*."

Suddenly, everything seemed out of focus. My chest felt open and my knees weakened. I leaned forward and kissed Buster's full lips. He kissed me back and my legs felt wobbly.

"I just wanted to give you another reason to remember me," I said hoarsely.

"Let me get outta here, before I change my mind about leaving."

I watched Buster drag his bags through the glass doors. He

was gone, and I was left wondering what it all meant. A car horn interrupted my thoughts. "Don't you have sense enough to come in outta the rain!" Sterling shouted, his head hanging out the window.

I slid into the front seat.

"What the fuck is going on?"

"Buster and I hooked up. I tried to tell you."

"You mean y'all got it on?" Sterling raised his eyebrows.

"Yeah, we did."

"Stevie, what the fuck has gotten into you!"

"You mean besides your brother's dick? Sterling, why are you going to Hollywood? You pick up men at the baths and God knows where else."

"Honey, I just take care of business."

"So, you should understand attraction."

"I can understand anybody wanting a piece."

"I thought so."

"What I can't understand is this flip-flopping. You don't see no sign outside my window, saying House of Damn Pancakes. Do you?"

"No."

"Stevie, you don't wake up one morning, and just say, I think I'll be straight today."

"It just happened, OK?"

"Well, don't let it happen again. You have to get your identity straight—I mean clear." Sterling smiled. "You have your reputation to consider."

"I do?"

"Yes, you're building a portfolio."

"Why can't I be open to whatever feels right?"

"Because, then the next thing you know they'll be calling you bisexual."

"That's so bad?"

"Stevie, everybody hates bisexuals. Lesbians will think you're just a straight woman experimenting at their expense. And heterosexuals will see you as a nymphomaniac."

"Well, what's the solution?"

"You've either figured out you're really straight after one experience with a woman and you'll never look at another woman again."

"I can't agree to that."

"Let me finish. Or you can be a lesbian who just got attracted to a man. Quiet as it's kept, it happens sometimes. My cousin Jackie in L.A. says lesbians digress occasionally."

"You mean like a recovering alcoholic falling off the wagon?"

"Exactly, but you can still maintain your lesbian identity and nobody's the wiser."

"Why do I have to maintain anything? Why can't I just be myself?"

"Sounds catchy, but I think you'll discover it's a gay world, after all."

15

I got the job at the Personal Change Center! I was alone when they called; Sterling was at work. They say success means nothing if you don't have anyone to share it with. So, I called Mama.

"Mama, I gotta job!"

"Which one?" she asked skeptically. Her dry tone took a little bit of the wind out of my sails.

"The receptionist job I told you about at the Personal Change Center."

"Oh, the one with those nut cakes."

"I can deal with them. I'm just happy finally to be working."

"How much did you say it pays?"

I hadn't said. "Six hundred dollars a month, plus benefits."

"They're paying garbagemen more than that. And you're young, benefits aren't that important."

"I'm not tripping on the money. It's more than enough to make ends meet. I've been surviving on a lot less."

"To think, after four years of college you'd settle for a receptionist job. Just letting your education go down the drain."

"Mama, it's a foot in the door. I don't plan to be a receptionist forever."

"What *do* you plan to be?"

"I plan to use this gig to get established. I'm still gonna keep my eyes open for jobs in the media. I might even go to graduate school."

"If you get a master's degree, then maybe they'll let you be a secretary," Mama said sarcastically.

"Mama, it's tough out here. You can't just pop your fingers and get a glamorous job. They've got Ph.D.'s waiting tables and driving cabs."

"Anybody with a Ph.D. who's dumb enough to wait tables or drive a cab deserves to have his degree taken away."

"You don't understand. There are people who'll take almost any job just for the privilege of living in San Francisco."

"All I can say is they need to throw a net over the place."

"Now at least I can start looking for an apartment."

"Yeah, I guess you don't want to wear out your welcome in that fellow's house. You know how temperamental sissies are. Sterling might just come home one day and start redecorating and decide you don't match the new pillows."

"Mama, you oughta quit."

"You know they can get hysterical at the drop of a hat."

I sighed. "How's everybody?"

"David hurt his knee in basketball practice."

"Is he okay?"

"Yeah, the doctor says it wasn't serious. But he has to sit out a few games. Your other brother jumped up and joined the marines.

"What about his asthma?"

"It hasn't been acting up. So, they let him in this time."

"Why would Kevin want to join the service?"

"Everybody can't play basketball. This way Kevin can get an education and see the world."

"Yeah, he can go to exotic places and meet exotic people and kill them."

"Vietnam is over."

"Yeah, but you never know when they'll get involved in another one."

"I'm not for killing. But I'm not gonna knock his decision. They're doing more killing right here in Chicago. They've been pressuring Kevin to join a gang."

"Oh no."

"Oh yeah, it's getting rough out here. Kevin's friend Taureen just got shot last week in the arm. He's got a cousin in the gangs. Kevin says it was a revenge shooting."

"Is Taureen all right?"

"Yeah, he's OK. But you know he's scared. He never knows when it might happen again."

I sighed. "How's Daddy?"

"Better, now that Kevin has enlisted. They've had a few runins. Kevin's no white tornado around the house. And he likes to stay on the phone when he's not out in the streets. Ray resents him, and when he's had a few drinks your father is Chief Snorting Bull. But the doctor told him he better lay off alcohol."

"Hope it didn't go through one ear and out the other," I said.

"Time will tell."

"How's Grandma?"

"She's right here. But she gave us a little scare last night. Thank the Lord, when she woke up this morning her bed wasn't her cooling board and her sheet wasn't her shroud."

"What are you talking about?"

"I'll let her tell you."

"Grandma, what happened?" I asked, concerned.

"Chile, I liked to left here last night."

"What do you mean, Grandma? You've hardly known a sick day in your life."

"Well, the old gray mare ain't what she used to be."

"Come on, you're still frisky as a filly."

"Well, last night, I didn't think I could gallop another further."

"What happened?"

"I thought my heart was going to give out. I was in the middle of ironing."

I felt scared. "Are you okay now? Did you go see a doctor?"

"I'm fine. I took some Alka-Seltzer and everything is hunky-dory."

"Maybe it was just indigestion."

"That's all it was. Today I'm fit as a fiddle."

"It still wouldn't hurt for you to go get a checkup, though."

"You know I don't fool with doctors. My grandmother lived to be a hundred and seven and never saw a doctor in her life."

"Grandma, this is a different era." I almost reminded her that her grandmother had been a slave. But instead I told her about my new job.

So far, I liked the gig. Probably at this point I'd like any job. But I actually enjoyed dealing with people who wanted to grow.

And the reception area was pleasant and comfortable. It used to be the living room of a stately Victorian. It contained enough wood to be considered quaint and enough of a draft to remind you that you were in San Francisco. Unfortunately, the fireplace no longer worked. So I wore my bulky knit Mexican sweater most of the time. And if I still was too cold, I turned on the space heater.

I was the only person of color on staff, except for Carolyn, who was Chinese. She was the bookkeeper, and only came in once a week. The Personal Change Center was one of several organizations she worked for.

Carolyn had a baby, named Jeffrey, but she didn't show you his picture or brag about a new tooth or a first step. The only way I knew about him was the director mentioned something in relation to Carolyn being on maternity leave last year. That's when I found out she had a husband and a child. I asked Carolyn how come she didn't talk about her baby.

"I want him to go to Stanford and become a doctor or engineer. Until then, no reason to brag."

Carolyn was like that, cut-and-dried, no nonsense. I'm not saying she wasn't a good mother, but let's put it this way, I wouldn't want to be her child.

The telephone interrupted my thoughts. "Personal Change Center, may I help you?" I could barely hear the faint voice at the other end. "Could you speak up a little louder, please?"

"My name is Bonnie MacGregor and I'D LIKE TO SIGN UP FOR THE ASSERTIVENESS TRAINING GROUP!" the woman shouted.

I reached for a folder. "I'm sorry, but that group is full."

"This is the second time I've tried to get into Assertiveness Training and it's been full. Oh shit! This really pisses me off."

"Would you be interested in another one of our groups?"

"Just forget it. This just isn't my day. And to top it off, I'm out of Valium."

"Well, I'm sorry I couldn't help you."

"It's not your fault. What else have you got?"

"Let's see, there's one space left in the Pre-Orgasmic group. I mean, if that would be appropriate."

"Yeah, go ahead and sign me up. What the hell, maybe I'll learn how to assert myself in bed."

Carolyn walked into the reception area lugging her briefcase. Although she was only pushing thirty, she looked matronly in her drab pants and top.

"Have a nice weekend."

She shook her unstylish bob. "Relatives coming from China."

"I guess you'll be doing a lot of cooking then."

Carolyn shook her head again. "Uncle own restaurant, go out every meal."

"I heard that."

"What your weekend plans?"

"I'm going to be looking at an apartment, down in the Haight tomorrow. I might end up living right near the corner of Haight and Ashbury. Imagine me living where it all happened!"

Carolyn groaned. "Decent people don't live in the Lower Haight."

"Where do you live?"

"Richmond District, very respectable."

I'd gone with Traci to Peg's Place, a lesbian bar on Geary Street. Traci had said it was in the Richmond District.

I bet Carolyn didn't know about her local lesbian watering hole, I thought. But who was I to burst her bubble? "Yeah, but it's flat, out in the Richmond." I frowned. "No hills, no views."

"Don't need views if you have inner peace." Carolyn pointed to her head. "Best views inside here."

· · ·

Sterling washed dishes and I swept the floor. He liked to wash dishes so that he could use Palmolive. He swore it softened his hands. What can I say, we were into roles. After a childhood spent being the only girl, I was all too happy to be relieved of dish duty to sweep and mop and take out the garbage instead.

"I've got my eye on this fine-ass Mexicano, darling. Muscles like you wouldn't believe. Works in the mailroom."

"Latino, huh?"

"Sí, señorita. If they fine, they mine."

"I have a feeling you move fast and you might need the entire mansion to entertain. I don't want to cramp your style."

"You're not, so don't even trip. Take your time looking."

I felt relieved that Sterling didn't want me to take just anything. "They wanted a hundred and sixty dollars a month for a studio, and it was a dump!" I complained as I slid the broom under the kitchen table.

"Honey, sometimes it's harder to find an apartment in this town than a job or a lover," Sterling declared.

I sighed. "The killer was, there were ten people ahead of me. I couldn't even get it if I wanted it. I'm young, black, haven't established any credit."

"You gotta uphill battle."

"Carolyn says no decent people live in the lower Haight, anyhow."

"Don't tell me you came to San Francisco to be surrounded by decent people?"

"Hell no," I laughed, sweeping up the trash.

I awakened from a nightmare and sat up on the couch. I recalled my dream. "I'm really a good person! I'm really a good person!"

I'd shouted. "No, you're not!" An angry mob had insisted. "You're a lesbian!" Then they scurried away, grabbing their children as if fleeing a plague.

I wondered why I hadn't told the people in the dream that I wasn't a lesbian. I didn't see a lesbian when I looked at myself in the mirror. I just saw me. I was attracted to men. I'd even received a postcard from Buster. He wrote that everything was cool. He was working hard and making good money. Buster told me to "stay sweet" and to tell Sterling, "hey." I missed him. Buster had shown me that I could be satisfied by a man.

But I still felt torn. I didn't want to go back to Traci. But I hadn't forgotten that holding a woman's body had felt like floating on a magic carpet. And sucking a woman's breast had calmed me more than soft music and candlelight. I wanted some more.

Later that day, I was at my desk, bright eyed and bushy tailed. The women were coming in for the first meeting of the Pre-Orgasmic group. Most of them seemed nervous and a little stiff. They were all white, in their twenties or early thirties, except two of them were considerably older. My heart really went out to them. All those years without "getting a nut," as Sterling would say.

Suddenly, this hip young woman with long blonde hair came bopping in, smiled at everybody, real comfortable-like. Turned out she's the facilitator. She looked to me like she could have multiple orgasms, the way she radiated. Everybody was gazing at her and you know they were all thinking, I hope she can help me.

I spoke to the blonde. "Hi, I'm Stevie. I'll be leaving, but the door automatically locks."

The group leader smiled and said her name was Cynthia and in the same breath asked, "Don't I know you?"

I looked at her, puzzled. She looked familiar, but damn if I could place her. I wouldn't have minded knowing her; she was kind of cute.

"Didn't we dance together before, at Wild Side West?"

I shook my head. I'd only been to Wild Side West once. I only remembered dancing with one person, and she wasn't blonde.

"I colored my hair; I used to be brunette. Now do you remember me?"

I remembered her now, but I felt embarrassed, so I barely nodded. I could see women looking at me with new interest. A few were smiling. A black woman who'd danced with a white woman was their friend. It was like I was Casper, the friendly ghost.

"Oh yeah," I mumbled. "It's a small world."

"I thought you were beautiful."

I felt a surge of attraction. I couldn't help but blush. Hopefully, my brownness covered it up.

"Still do, as a matter of fact," Cynthia carried on shamelessly in front of her group members. "Don't any of you worry," she reassured them. "I have experience with guys too. I'm bisexual. This group is for women of all sexual preferences, just like the flier said. I know a lot of you are straight."

"Yeah," an older housewife type groaned. "Men are such lousy lovers."

"I've heard there are no frigid women, just clumsy men," a serious young woman wearing a polyester pantsuit and Coke-bottle glasses added hopefully.

Cynthia smiled. "Well, most men need to be trained. But

first, you have to discover what feels good to you. That's what this group is about, doing it for ourselves."

I watched as the new recruits trooped in behind Cynthia.

I decided not to leave after all. Why not catch up on some paperwork, read the personnel policies, and straighten out the brochure table?

Two hours later, I was thumbing through the annual report when the conference room door opened. "Remember, you have to take responsibility for your own orgasms."

The air bristled with excitement as the group of chattering women entered the reception area.

"And also, remember to draw your vulvas for next week. And don't forget your clitorises."

I stifled a laugh as the newly confident army marched out.

"You're still here?" Cynthia winked.

"I just had some work to catch up on."

"All work and no play makes Stevie a dull girl."

I glanced around the room. We were indeed alone. "I like to play."

Cynthia walked toward me seductively. "Oh yeah?"

"Yeah."

"You wanna play with me?"

"What do you mean?"

"Damn, Stevie, we were on a roll."

"It's just that we're at my work."

"So?"

"I just thought it'd be nice to be more comfortable."

"Fuck comfortable."

"OK, repeat the question."

"You wanna play with me?"

"If you think you can handle it," I answered boldly. I was

surprised by my own bravado. But I felt a rush of adrenaline. No more Ms. Nice Guy, I chuckled to myself.

Cynthia pursed her lips. I could finally relate to Sterling. I just wanted something hot.

"I think I can handle anything you can dish out."

"Whoa," I raised my eyebrows. "I'm scared of you."

"Don't be, I don't bite. Unless you like that sort of thing." Cynthia winked.

"I'm not into pain."

"What are you into?"

I gave Cynthia a soulful look. "Right now, I'm into you."

"What do you wanna do about it?"

Go for it, I told myself. This is no time to be coy. But my throat felt dry and I couldn't find my voice.

"You wanna get it on with me?"

I was speechless but I managed to nod.

"Then let's get it on!"

Cynthia put her arms around me and I kissed her. I felt another rush of adrenaline when I tasted her tongue. Cynthia sucked my earlobe and made me shiver.

My heart was beating fast. It was like a movie. This was so unlike me. I couldn't believe that I was doing whatever I was about to do; especially at the office. It was so daring, so brazen, so hot!

"Come on, Stevie, sock it to me."

Cynthia had brought out the dog in me. I flicked off the light switch and backed her up against the wall. I rubbed my body up against her like my high-school boyfriend did to me in my basement.

Cynthia sighed. "I love being woman-handled by you."

I kissed her, long and hard. She ran her fingers through my

natural. I cupped Cynthia's plum-size breasts through her crinkly cotton shirt. I ran my thumbs across her firm nipples.

Cynthia helped me to pull off her top. She moaned when I lowered my lips onto her saluting breasts.

I rubbed my pelvis against hers while sucking her breasts.

"Yes! Stevie, you are turning me on! I am getting so turned on!" she gasped. Cynthia pulled my Afro so hard that I thought of reminding her that it wasn't a wig.

I ran my fingers down Cynthia's thighs. She kicked off her Birkenstocks and loosened her drawstring pants. I pulled them off, revealing a nice bush. She wasn't wearing panties and that was all right with me.

I couldn't get my clothes off fast enough.

I squeezed next to Cynthia on the couch.

"Look at us," she pointed. "We look so beautiful together."

I admired the contrast of our nut-brown and peach-ice-cream—colored bodies. Her blonde hair draped over my breasts.

"I wish somebody could take a picture," Cynthia cooed.

"It's cold in here, let's warm each other up," I suggested. I climbed on top of Cynthia and our vaginas made squishy sounds as I rubbed into her.

My hot fingers felt her soft, moist bush. I played with it for a while. Cynthia moaned as I inched my hungry finger inside of her.

I wasn't sure how many fingers she took. But when my middle finger moved easily, I inserted my index one as well.

"Yes! Yes!" Cynthia shouted. "It feels so good to have you inside me! It feels so good!"

I fondled Cynthia's clitoris while I finger-fucked her. She guided my hand. I worried that Cynthia thought I was inept. Then I remembered that she believed in taking responsibility for her own orgasms.

Suddenly, the building began to shake. I paused. I'd heard of feeling the earth move during sex, but this was frightening.

"Don't stop! Don't stop!" Cynthia begged.

"But the windows are rattling!" I protested.

"It's just an earthquake."

"Just an earthquake!" I shouted.

"It's not the big one," Cynthia panted. "Trust me, I'm a native. Don't stop, I'm just about to come!"

I continued to play with her, but I jumped when I felt a sudden jolt underground. Cynthia's body jerked into spasms as the earth shook for a few seconds. I could hear my heart racing.

Cynthia hugged me. "Don't worry. It was no more than a three-pointer."

"I've never been through an earthquake before."

"You'll get used to them. They're usually pretty mild."

"It was a nerve-wracking experience," I confessed.

Cynthia kissed me. "Thanks for hanging in there. I had a great orgasm. Let me make love to you now."

"That's okay. I'll take a rain check. I'm still a little shook up. I don't think I can really relax right now. There might be aftershocks."

Cynthia patted my shoulder. "I understand, it's your first earthquake. You need to process it."

Sterling was so proud that I'd actually "gotten me some." "It's a happy day!" He declared as he went around dusting the living room while I vacuumed. "Cynthia's orgasm registered much higher on the Richter scale than that earthquake," Sterling insisted.

"You act like I won a lottery or something," I shouted over the sound of the vacuum cleaner and the disco music.

Sterling attacked a cobweb with his feather duster.

"Admit it, don't you feel better? Less clogged up."

"OK, I admit it, I'm human."

"You worked it, girl!" Sterling yelled, popping his fingers with one hand while he dusted the windowsill with the other. "You knew how to ride! You got it up and down and then you got it from side to side!" he added, dropping his duster and doing a series of snaps.

"Sterling, you know you're the first man I've ever known who could see dust," I marveled.

"I've been like this ever since I can remember. Being able to see dust was probably the first sign that I was gay."

16

Bonnie was early for the Pre-Orgasmic group. She was putting the final touches on a crayon drawing.

"What do you think, Stevie?" I glanced up from my desk at the paper Bonnie held in front of me.

I glimpsed the picture of Bonnie's vulva and turned away. I was a little embarrassed to be staring at a drawing of her genitals. It seemed disrespectful. The woman was old enough to be my mother.

"My clitoris isn't too big, is it?"

I hesitated. "You're a better judge than I am. I mean, at least you've seen it. Not that I want to see it. I mean, nothing personal. I'm sure it's very nice."

Bonnie giggled, "I meant as clitorises go."

I glanced at the picture again. It looked like a hairy pyramid with a red jelly bean inside of it.

"I'm no expert." And you're no artist, I thought to myself. "But I think it's probably in the normal range."

"I just didn't want to overemphasize it and have people in the group think, you know, I was showing off. Although I doubt Fred could find it if it were a Mack truck."

"Well, show him the drawing."

"He's only interested in the Forty Niners."

"At least your clitoris is red and the Niners have red uniforms."

"I'll point that out to Fred," Bonnie laughed.

Cynthia surprised me with a kiss on the cheek. I looked up from my novel. I'd been so engrossed in Zora Neale Hurston that I hadn't heard her come back into the office.

I smiled and laid *Their Eyes Were Watching God* facedown on the desk. "What's happenin'? Your group isn't over yet is it?"

Cynthia shook her head and leaned over me with her chin resting in her palm. Her peasant top revealed her cleavage.

"The women are looking at themselves," Cynthia reported. "I thought I'd give them a little privacy." She hoisted herself on top of the desk. Her short denim skirt showed off her legs.

"Looking at themselves how?" I asked with mild concern.

"They've stuck plastic speculums inside their vaginas. They're examining their cervixes with flashlights and mirrors."

"Sounds so clinical," I teased.

Cynthia shook her head. "It's really empowering for them. So many women are intimidated by pelvic exams. And some doctors are such assholes. They think they're fucking gods, with their big hands and cold metal speculums. A lot of them make women feel stupid if they ask questions."

"I've never even thought about looking at myself like that," I admitted.

"Maybe you should be in there. I have an extra speculum. I don't think they would mind if you joined them for this."

"I'm not about to gap my legs open in a roomful of folks, I'm sorry."

"What do you mean? We're all women. I'm surprised to hear you talk this way. Wouldn't you like to see your cervix?"

"I used to sell *Our Bodies Ourselves* in the campus bookstore. So, I'm up on the downstroke."

"But, you've only seen pictures. Don't you want to see the real thing?"

"I don't have a burning desire to."

"I wonder if your cervix is darker than the other women's in the group."

I felt embarrassed. "Don't be ridiculous."

Cynthia touched my arm. "I didn't mean any offense. I just thought you could add a little color to an otherwise pale evening, that's all." Cynthia stroked my hand lightly with her fingers.

I relaxed a little. She hadn't meant any harm. She'd just made a stupid remark. "Look, I'm not tripping anymore. I just don't feel like playing show-and-tell. But, I wouldn't mind seeing my cervix sometime in private, if you wanna give me a speculum."

"Do I get to watch?"

"Sure," I shrugged. "You're my lover." I was surprised to hear myself utter those words. After all, we'd only been together two weeks. I didn't want to scare Cynthia.

But she smiled and kissed my lips. So, I guess it was cool with her.

When the last student had gone, Cynthia and I went to Cordon Bleu. It was a hole-in-the-wall, but the Vietnamese food was great. It felt romantic, gazing into each other's eyes in the candlelight while feasting on five spice chicken. We could hear the clanging of the cable cars every now and then in the background.

"I'm starting a Pre-Orgasmic group in the East Bay next week," Cynthia announced.

I glanced around the small, dark restaurant. I felt self-conscious discussing sexuality in public. Thank goodness, the few people remaining appeared engrossed in their own non-English conversations.

"Where in the East Bay?" I asked.

"Oakland, at the Women's Health Center. It'll be interesting, because there should be a mixture of women. I'm really psyched about it. I'll be back in my old stomping grounds."

"You're from Oakland?"

"Bump City, born and raised."

"They call Oakland Bump City?"

"Yeah and Oaktown."

"Is your family still over in the East Bay?"

"My brother, Tom, is a Hare Krishna. He wears orange and plays drums on Telegraph Avenue in Berkeley. He sleeps in People's Park. My sister and her boyfriend follow the Dead around the country. Paula calls me when they're at the Coliseum."

"I'm almost afraid to ask. But what about your parents?"

"They're Quakers."

"Quakers?" I asked, visualizing the man on the Quaker Oats box.

"Yeah, plain, decent, justice-loving folks. I went away to college in L.A. as a form of rebellion. But technically I'm still a member of Friends Church in Berkeley."

"Do your parents know you've been with women?"

"Yeah."

"Do they accept it?"

"My parents are gentle, tolerant people. They raise llamas up in Mount Shasta."

"Wow, I've seen pictures of llamas."

"They run pack trips. We'll have to go sometime."

"Yeah, sounds exciting."

After we cleaned our plates, Cynthia and I split a fried banana and coconut ice cream dessert. Cynthia sucked on her spoon. "You should've heard some of the comments the women made about their drawings."

"The ones of their vulvas?" I asked.

Cynthia nodded. "One of 'em broke down in tears. She'd never even touched herself sexually before. She always felt dirty down there. Said her husband told her, he'd rather eat quiche than eat her cunt."

I rolled my eyes. "Real men don't eat either one, huh."

Cynthia shrugged. "Another woman shared that she'd like to be affectionate just once and it not have to lead to sex. And a third woman said her boyfriend always wants to have sex after a fight."

"He hits her?"

"I don't think they fight physically."

"When black folks say a fight, we pretty much mean physical. You folks don't distinguish between an argument and an ass-kicking."

"You're right, most white people don't. I'll have to remember to ask Mindy if he hits her. Would you believe that half the women in the group don't even masturbate?"

"I'm sure they do now. After you've whipped them into shape."

Cynthia laughed. "Masturbation is their homework." She stroked my hand. "You masturbate regularly don't you, sweetie?"

I hesitated. No one had ever asked me if I masturbated at

all, let alone regularly. "I do occasionally," I said sipping my tea. "You know, when I'm not with anybody."

"Having sex with a partner is not a substitute for masturbation. You should masturbate at least once a week, whether you have a partner or not."

I held Cynthia's hand and kissed it. "But it's more fun with somebody else."

"It's up to you to make it fun with yourself," Cynthia commanded.

I saluted her. "I promise to do better." But not until I get my own place, I thought.

"Today is Lester and Poindexter's two-month anniversary!" Sterling announced as they walked into the kitchen. "Who says gay men don't have long-term relationships?"

I looked up from the newspaper. "Congratulations," I smiled.

"Thanks." Lester made it over to a chair. I sipped my coffee across from him at the table. "I hope he turns out to be the one for you."

"So far so good." Lester winked. "He treats me right. He's got a J-O-B and he's even cute without his glasses."

"Right on! What's he do?"

"There you go getting all analytical." Sterling frowned and leaned against the refrigerator and crossed his arms.

"I just asked what kind of work the brotha does. What's so analytical about that?"

"Lester said the 'Negro' was working. Why can't you leave it at that? You ain't gotta scrutinize his occupation."

"I think you doth protest too much. Lester, what's his real name and what does he do?"

"Winston, and he's a mortician."

"A mortician?"

"Yeah, he's just starting out in his father's business out in Bayview."

"Well, it's honest work," I pointed out.

"Lester said he was looking to settle down," Sterling reminded me. "And Winston sounds like the settled type."

"Hope it works out."

Lester sighed. "Me too."

Sterling came to the table, and searched through the newspaper. "Gimme 'Dear Abby.' "

"Here."

"Y'all got anything to eat?" Lester turned his attention to the refrigerator.

"There's still some fried chicken left. And I can heat you up some greens, black-eyed peas, and a piece of corn bread."

Lester's face lit up like a Christmas tree.

I handed Lester a full plate. "The corn bread will be warm in a minute."

"Thanks, Stevie."

"You welcome."

"Honey chile, you sho' can burn!" Lester complimented me with a chicken leg hanging from his mouth.

"Thanks, cooking runs in my family."

"Speaking of cooking, heard you got something 'cooking' with Miss Ann?" Lester winked.

I rolled my eyes at Sterling, not that I really minded him putting my business out. He gave me an impish smile.

"We're mixing our spices, but sometimes I wish the flavor was deeper." I sighed.

Sterling looked up from the paper. "There you go, Stevie, you just been up with the child for a hot minute and already you wanna get deep. You need to learn the importance of being superficial," Sterling insisted as the doorbell rang.

"Hey, I know what you mean about wanting to connect on a deeper level," Lester said. "I mean, lesbians don't usually have that problem as much. But you can imagine how it used to be for me dealing with these shallow-ass men. No pun intended."

"On that note, I'll answer the door," Sterling said sarcastically.

"And I'll see about the corn bread."

I was surprised when Sterling returned with a slight, dark-haired white woman with an intense look and sharp features.

"This is Peggy, a neighbor; she's got a petition," he announced.

Peggy nodded and ran her hands through her long, stringy hair.

"I told her I wasn't about to sign it. But she said she saw a woman coming in and out of here, and wanted to talk to you."

Peggy gazed hopefully in my direction.

"What's your petition for?"

"It's about men having sex in the park around the corner. I'm afraid even to let my kid play there, even in the daytime."

"That's too bad," I answered. I couldn't get behind casual, anonymous sex, especially where kids might see it. My only casual encounter hadn't been anonymous or in public. Cynthia and I had at least known each other's names and occupations. And we'd both been interested in seeing each other again.

"Yeah, that's funky," Lester agreed. "Kids oughta be able to play in the park," he added, washing his corn bread down with a gulp of soda pop.

Sterling folded his arms and cocked his head to one side.

"I didn't know there were any real kids left in the Castro."

The woman sighed. "This neighborhood didn't used to be like this."

"Didn't used to be like what?" Sterling glared.

"There used to be a lot more families. Now that the rents are going up, who can afford to live here?"

"Well, now you know how it feels to be in the minority."

"Be nice, don't act ugly," Lester reprimanded.

"Look, gay men have fixed up these Victorians. We're the ones who turned this neighborhood into a showplace," Sterling retorted.

"That's true," I agreed. "But she does have a point. Kids should be able to play in the park."

"Why would anyone with kids want to live in the Castro, any damn way? That's what I want to know."

Peggy's eyes narrowed. "We have a right to be here," she shot back at Sterling. "I was born and raised in the Castro. My parents were Irish immigrants. This was a real neighborhood, with mom-and-pop stores and Scout troops before they turned it into a sex playground."

"Look, we don't have anywhere else to go. San Francisco is a mecca because we're oppressed everywhere else. Shouldn't there be a place for us?"

"Sterling has a point," Lester agreed. "Straight people can show affection in public and nobody says doodley-squat."

"Affection, I don't mind affection. But my son saw two men groping each other's crotches on the street."

"They got hookers on the corner in the Tenderloin who are just as outlandish," Sterling countered. "Maybe, you're just anti-gay."

"Maybe she's just anti—lewd behavior," I said, defending Peggy.

"Right on, sister!" Peggy shouted. "Some of my best friends are gay men."

"Some of my best friends are colored," Sterling groaned.

"Now, Sterling, let's play pretty," Lester polished off another piece of chicken. "Sounds like the woman is just against folks having sex in the park in broad daylight."

"Damn straight, I am. My gay friends are not promiscuous. I know a couple who's been together for ten years. I support the rights of consenting adults behind closed doors."

"Can't everybody afford no hotel."

"Sterling, why can't they go into the privacy of their own bedrooms?" I asked.

"You don't want to bring everybody up in your place. You might not even know their names."

"But yet you're willing to have sex with them?"

"Sex is one thing, bringing somebody in your crib is another."

I shook my head. "I'm sorry, but I can't relate."

"Me either," Lester sucked thoughtfully on a chicken bone. "I'm a gay man, but I guess I have different values."

"So, you'll sign my petition?" Peggy asked anxiously.

"Yeah," Lester nodded.

Sterling sighed and began wiping crumbs off the kitchen counter.

Peggy turned to me. "What about you?"

"I'm presently looking for a place. I'm still up under his roof. But I'm gonna go ahead and sign it, too. Sterling, are you gonna put me out on the street?"

"Not because of political differences. Unless you plan to vote Republican."

Peggy eagerly shoved the petition in front of Lester and me. There were only a couple of names on the page.

"You're looking for an apartment, did you say?"

"Yeah, and it hasn't been easy."

"My husband and I rent out a cute little cottage over in the Mission."

"Wow, you do?"

"Yeah and it's really nice. We haven't even put a sign in the window yet. Our tenant just gave notice. She's moving to Seattle."

"What part of the Mission?" Sterling demanded. "Stevie doesn't want to live just anywhere. She's poor but proud."

I cautiously awaited Peggy's answer. The Mission District was a colorful, mostly Latino area, with a growing counter culture. In addition to great Mexican restaurants, Catholic churches, and thrift shops, there were coffeehouses, a women's bookstore, a lesbian bar, and a movie house that showed independent films. But some parts of the Mission were rough and had a high crime rate.

"It's in the nicest part of the Mission. It's almost in Noe Valley. I won't have any trouble renting it. It's above Dolores Park."

"That's a good area," Lester agreed.

"I like it around there," I added. I was beginning to get excited. "What's it like?" I asked.

"How much does it cost?" Sterling wanted to know.

"It's a studio, but it's got a separate kitchen and a nice backyard."

"A backyard in San Francisco. You mean it's got a blade of grass," Lester marveled.

"And flowers," Peggy nodded.

"Well, how much does it cost?" I asked cautiously. "I don't bring home a big salary, but I'm very responsible. I'd be a good tenant."

"Yeah, Stevie can't afford it if it costs an arm and a leg," Sterling chimed in.

"Leslie was paying a hundred and fifty dollars a month. I guess I'd rather get a good tenant in there than raise the rent."

I let out a sigh of relief. "I can afford a hundred and fifty a month."

"If the place ain't falling apart, she'll take it," Lester smiled.

"I'll want a fifty-dollar cleaning deposit."

"What about first and last?"

"If you want it, you can give me fifty dollars to hold it and a hundred fifty when you move in. Forget about first and last, if you're willing to paint."

"No problem," Lester spoke up.

"Yeah," Sterling agreed. "We'll have a paint party."

"Thanks," I said. "Sounds like a plan."

"You saved me an ad in the paper. You saved me the hassle of talking to a lot of folks. And I really hate to reject people."

I couldn't believe what might have fallen into my lap. But I wanted to see the place first, before I became a grinning fool.

Cynthia and I clapped enthusiastically in Berkeley's Black Repertory Theater. I was happy. I had it all, a job, a lover, and I'd just put a deposit on my cute cottage.

But I still cared what people thought, especially black folks. So, I was wearing a frilly blouse. Thank goodness, Cynthia's long hair made her look feminine despite her suspenders.

The executive director stood onstage with her cast in the old converted dry cleaners. "Thank you very much." The attractive matriarch beamed. "Now, if you liked this play, tell your friends about it. And, if you didn't like this play"—the director raised her eyebrows—"tell them about it anyway. 'Cause, they just *might* like it." She waved good night. "May God bless you."

Cynthia and I walked down Shattuck Avenue toward her Chevy Impala. The cars were parked diagonally. "I'm really glad that we saw that play," I said. I'd suggested it after reading a review.

"Yeah, me too," Cynthia agreed.

"Thanks for driving."

"You wanna drive back?"

"All the way across the bridge?" I gulped. I'd driven Cynthia's car a couple of times; once to take her home after she had her wisdom tooth pulled, and last week after a Gil Scott-Heron and Brian Jackson concert. I'd refused the joints being passed around, wishing to avoid all those collective germs. It was a good thing, because Cynthia wound up too high to drive.

"Driving across the bridge would be good practice for you."

"Cool," I agreed. Cynthia threw me the keys.

We sat in the parked car, holding hands and listening to KJAZ.

"I'll have to tell the members that this production is worth crossing the bridge for."

"The members?" Cynthia looked puzzled.

"Sterling and his friends. The gay children."

"Oh. By the way, what were you whispering to me about during the play?"

"I was telling you to quit leaning on me. You were practically nibbling my ear. I'm not into showstopping."

Cynthia frowned and let go of my hand. "I didn't know you were so closeted."

"Call it what you want. I just wanted to enjoy being around my people without folks cutting their eyes."

"It was a racially mixed audience."

"Well, I was mainly tripping on the black folks. I wasn't in the mood to rock the boat."

"I don't understand why you were so uptight. People were engrossed in the play. They weren't noticing us."

"You'd be surprised how quick folks can come to attention. Sometimes they have eyes in the backs of their heads."

"You sound paranoid."

"Hey, I don't care if you are a white girl from Oakland. I still know black folks better than you do."

Suddenly, a squad car pulled alongside of us. What do they want? I wondered. We weren't doing anything illegal.

"My registration is current," Cynthia assured me.

The lone policeman walked over to the passenger side.

"How does he know it's your car? I'm sitting in the damn driver's seat," I muttered.

The officer motioned for Cynthia to roll down her window.

"Are you all right ma'am?" he asked, after she lowered it part way.

"Of course. What do you mean?"

"I was just concerned. You've been parked here for a while."

"So what? I'm just having a conversation with my girlfriend. Is that illegal in Berkeley?"

I glanced at the policeman out of the corner of my eye. He looked under thirty, but I still didn't trust him. I knew not to get funky with the police. He might go upside my head with his nightstick. Where I was from they didn't call them billy clubs, they called them nigga beaters. And they didn't call them that for nothing.

"I thought she might be a male."

My mouth flew open. "A male!" I repeated.

"So, what if she were?" Cynthia snapped.

"Well, after that thing with Patty Hearst, we're just being real careful." The policeman sighed. Patty Hearst had been captured recently near San Francisco along with a woman SLA member. The two other SLA members, Bill and Emily Harris, had been arrested in the city.

"Sorry to have disturbed you," the officer continued to address Cynthia. "Have a nice evening, ma'am."

"I can't believe it!" I exclaimed after he left. The two brothas in the SLA died in the fire in L.A. Who did he think I was?" Cynthia was quiet, like she was in a daze.

"It's so racist!" I shouted. "McNab automatically thought you might be in danger, just because you're white and I'm black. Never mind the fact that Bezerkley is known for crazy-ass white folks. You could've been holding me hostage."

"I just can't believe it," Cynthia marveled.

"Yeah, in Berkeley of all places," I agreed.

"I just can't believe he called me ma'am!"

"Huh?" I asked confused.

"I'm only twenty-seven years old and that pig called me ma'am!"

"I can't believe you're tripping on *that* instead of his racism!" I shouted.

Cynthia leaned her head back against the vinyl seat. She let out a long sigh. "I'm sorry, honey. I was in my own world." Cynthia made a face. "I'm so vain."

"Yeah, you probably thought this song was about you."

I told Sterling about the incident with the fuzz as we ate tuna sandwiches in the kitchen. He rolled his eyes and shook his head. But Sterling was less understanding about my irritation with Cynthia.

"I expected more from a white girl from Oakland," I explained. "But solidarity took a backseat when the cop called her ma'am."

"To be honest," Sterling waved his hands, "I can't blame the chile for not wanting to be called ma'am at twenty-seven."

I shook my head. "I still have reservations about being with a white woman."

"At least you gotta Miss Ann that looks like something," Sterling said between bites. "I'm glad you're not the type that'll be up with anything, just so long as it's white."

"I'm not that shallow. I just wonder if Cynthia can ever really empathize with my experiences as a black woman."

"Y'all ain't got married at Glide *yet*."

Traci had told me that Reverend Cecil Williams, the pastor of Glide Methodist Church, actually married gay and lesbian couples. It wasn't legal, but it still had spiritual significance for some people.

"Just go with the flow," Sterling advised. "I'll take hot sex over empathy any day. Most white folks are racists to some degree. You think I scrutinize the politics of every dude I deal with? Just because I'm black, I gotta show three IDs to get in some of these gay bars," Sterling informed me.

"You would expect better from people who know how it feels to be discriminated against," I said angrily.

"Humph, don't fool yourself." Sterling tilted his head and sucked in his teeth. "The only reason some of these dudes gimme the time of day is because I'm their flavor of the month."

"Well, I couldn't be bothered with them."

"Don't get me wrong, there are some good ones," Sterling said dreamily. "And, you know, I have a superficial side, myself."

17

Cynthia and I sat wrapped in each other's arms in her Potrero Hill apartment watching the sunset.

"I can see a ship," I pointed. "Is that Oakland over there?"

"Yeah."

"Don't you just love looking out on the water?"

Cynthia nodded. "I'm a water sign."

"Which one?"

"Pisces."

"I'm a Libra. I wonder if we're compatible."

"You sure can turn me on."

"Thanks."

"Stevie, you're so polite."

"You don't think I'm *too* polite, do you?"

"I think it's kind of sweet."

I held Cynthia's hand. "Remember, you said you were bisexual."

"Yeah."

"Are you one of those bisexuals who needs to have both a male and a female lover to feel balanced?" I asked.

I personally believed that I could be faithful to either sex if

I were in a committed relationship. I didn't like sexual labels, they weren't individual enough. But, I wanted to know what being bisexual meant to Cynthia.

"No, I don't have to have a male and female lover at the same time. I can be attracted to both men and women sexually. But women are my primary focus. I just labeled myself as bisexual so that the women in the group would figure I could relate to them."

"So, if we got seriously involved, you wouldn't feel the need to get with some dude?"

"If we get seriously involved, hopefully I won't feel the need to get with anybody else sexually, male or female. You're the only one I'm sleeping with right now, in case you're interested."

I was interested, and I was happy to hear it. "So, are we just having a fling or are we in a relationship?" I asked boldly.

Cynthia leaned over and turned on a lamp. "Let's satisfy each other's needs for six months and then we'll talk about a relationship," she replied.

I shrugged. "Lately, I've been in a faster lane than I'm used to," I confessed.

"What are you used to?"

"A respectable courtship."

"I can't believe you. You are like from another era."

"What era?"

"You remind me of a character in *Our Town*."

"Which one?"

"George, when he tells Emily how important it is to have someone care about your character?"

"I remember. *Our Town* is a great play. But I still don't like being compared to the people in it. They were so Republican, so white, so New England. I mean they went straight from a milkshake to marriage. I think I'm a little racier than that." I fingered Cynthia's turquoise bracelet. "I had you calling out my name the other night, didn't I?"

"Thank goodness, you have another side."

"That's a nice bracelet. Where did you get it, Santa Fe?"

"Yeah, I liberated it from one of those tourist traps."

"You stole it?"

"I just wanted to see if I could get away with it. It was part of my rebellion. It gave me a cheap thrill."

"You steal things?"

"It was just a lark. I can count the number of times I've ripped off shit in my whole life on one hand. Haven't you ever stolen anything?"

I shook my head.

"Not even a candy bar when you were a kid?"

"My brother David did once, and my mother made him take the money out of his piggy bank to pay for it. And apologize."

"But you never did?"

"We were raised to think stealing was wrong."

"Stevie, you are so wholesome. If it weren't for your lovemaking and the way you talk, I would swear you were a white person trapped in a black person's body."

"Believe it or not, most black people don't steal," I shot back.

"Honey, I was just teasing. You're in your head too much."

"You're the one who's studying to be a shrink."

"But my MFCC program integrates mind, body, and spirit."

"I just didn't appreciate your stereotyping."

"Except the part about your being good in bed, I bet."

"Contrary to popular belief, some of us 'colored folk' are complex individuals."

"I know that. But you know what? Right now, I don't have the energy for anything more complex than wild, passionate sex."

I sighed. I was still tripping. I wasn't really feeling hot and bothered.

Cynthia leaned her body against mine.

"I'm sorry, sweetie. I didn't mean to bum you out. Do you forgive me?"

"All right," I said as I felt her body heat mixing with mine. But I still felt like I was putting the cart before the horse as I followed Cynthia into the bedroom.

"Stevie, wake up, it's raining!"

I yawned. "Isn't winter the rainy season?"

"If it's raining here, it's probably snowing in the Sierras!"

"So what if it is?" I rolled back over.

Cynthia grabbed my shoulder. "That means we can go skiing!"

"Skiing? I've never been skiing in my life. Besides, everybody who ever went skiing on TV broke something. Remember when Dick Van Dyke broke his leg?"

"I'm talking about cross-country skiing. There are almost no injuries. It's just like walking. It's the best exercise. I love it! And you'll love it!"

"But isn't it expensive?"

"It costs a lot less than downhill skiing. We don't have to buy lift tickets. And we can do it for dirt cheap. We can stay at the Sierra Lodge."

"OK, I'm game."

"Oh goody!" Cynthia bounced on the bed. "We'll have to call and make reservations before they fill up."

She leaned over to kiss me.

I pulled away. "I haven't brushed my teeth yet."

"Ok, then, I'll kiss your other lips."

Cynthia planted kisses up and down my naked body. I tingled with excitement when her head finally sank between my thighs.

I'd just walked out of Macy's department store in Union Square and was lugging a bag with my new ski jacket and sweater. I knew I was splurging, but Sterling had encouraged me. He said I had an image to uphold. "How many black folks are on the ski slopes? You have to be a credit to the race."

Call me middle class, but I wanted my stuff to look nice. I wanted my clothes to be coordinated even if my body wouldn't be. Let's face it, I'd never really had the true middle-class experience. Father coming home in a suit, carrying a briefcase. Mother wearing pearls while she did her dusting. The cookie jar always full, and kids getting to go away to summer camp. Secretly, I'd envied the sterile white families on *Father Knows Best*, *Donna Reed*, and *Leave It to Beaver*. I couldn't hang with them long, but I couldn't help but fantasize about people who could solve their problems in thirty minutes with nobody getting whipped.

I was almost at Market and Powell, by the cable car turnaround. Two men suddenly backed me up against the wall, in broad daylight, flashing badges in my face.

"Macy's security," one of them barked.

My mind was a whirlwind as I looked into the two scowling pink faces. I realized that they'd followed me for several blocks. I knew I hadn't stolen anything. In fact, I'd spent a big chunk of my first paycheck in their store. I hadn't even lingered; they had no reason to suspect me, except that I was young, black, and carrying a large bag of their merchandise.

The huskier of the two detectives pointed at my bag. "Let's see what you got in there."

"What do you want? I just finished spending all kinds of money in your store."

"Can you prove it?" The other one asked.

I bristled. "The only reason you're stopping me is because I'm black! You have no reason to suspect me."

I noticed that people were rubbernecking.

"Let's see the receipts."

"Sistah, legally, you don't have to show them shit!" A brother in dreadlocks shouted.

"I'm going to show you the damn receipts. Just to prove to you that every black person leaving your store with a large bag isn't a thief."

I rummaged around, hoping that my receipts hadn't blown out. Or that the salesclerk hadn't forgotten to give them to me. I found the two receipts and shoved them at the men.

"Y'all treating the sistah like she's in South Africa or some damn where," the dreadlocked brother shouted. "Having to show her pass and shit."

"Now, satisfied?" I yelled. "I wish I hadn't spent a dime in your damn store!"

"Boycott Macy's!" the brother shouted.

"Girlcott Macy's!" a tough-looking white woman in leather echoed.

The detectives turned away sheepishly, but neither of them apologized.

One of them mumbled, "We're just trying to do a job here."

But that was just a cliché, same as *Father Knows Best*.

I was on the phone. I had just finished telling Grandma about being treated like a criminal by Macy's.

"And you had me thinking it was different out there."

"It is, and it isn't. I mean, generally that's true. But some people say things are just more subtle."

"Well, there was nothing subtle about what happened to you."

"I second that emotion. But I still try to deal with people as individuals. It's hard, though. But otherwise I guess I'd be walking around in a rage all of the time."

"White folks will sho' try you."

"Yeah, I've been tested."

"And here you thought you were rich and white."

"What are you talking about? I just got off of food stamps last month."

"Didn't you twist your mouth and say you were goin' skiing?"

"Yeah, so?"

"So, when did you become rich and white?"

"It's cross-country skiing, Grandma."

"You ain't fixing to try and ski across the whole country, are you?"

"No, you just ski on flatter ground than with downhill skiing."

"I thought going down hills was the point."

"There will be some hills, they just won't be real steep."

"Well, I hope you get your money's worth. Who you going with?"

"A friend."

"One of us?"

"No."

"You ain't fixing to spring a white husband on us, are you?"

"I'm not hardly thinking about getting married."

"Ain't no romance involved."

"It's a girlfriend, Grandma."

"That don't mean nothing these days. Especially out there where you at."

"Ha, ha, very funny."

"Well, be careful, running with white folks."

"Grandma, I'm tired of tripping on race. I don't want to be careful. I just want to be myself!"

"Gone with yo' bad self, then. Some folks gotta learn the hard way. They might smile up in your face, but sooner or later you'll find out. White can cover a multitude of faults. And I ain't just talking about the snow."

"You would know, Grandma, since you have so much contact with white people," I said sarcastically.

"I'm just trying to protect you from unnecessary pain."

"If you protect yourself from pain, you also protect yourself from pleasure."

"You go 'head on then. Maybe you a pioneer. Probably we need pioneers. But when they do you dirty, you can always come running to me. I'd never leave you hanging out to dry."

18

I stared out the car window at the falling snow. It was a trip going from passing a palm tree–lined street in San Francisco this evening to goo-gobs of snow in the Sierras tonight. I was reminded that it was winter back in Chicago. Cynthia rubbed my thigh. "Don't the mountains look gorgeous?

"Uhm hmm."

"We have two whole days ahead of fabulous skiing!"

When we hit Emigrant Gap, we paid a guy to put chains on Cynthia's car. While we waited, I told Cynthia about how they'd treated me outside of Macy's.

"That was really a bummer. But you've gotta let it go."

"It's hard to let it go, 'cause racism is always there waiting to pounce. Sometimes, just when you least expect it, then, boom."

"Well, you don't want to become paranoid, do you?"

"No, but I don't want to have blinders on either."

"Look, I'm not saying there's not a lot of shit out here. Don't get me wrong."

"What are you saying?"

"I'm just saying you have to stay open to the magic that's

out here too. Or else you'll never experience rainbows in the sky and all that other good stuff." Cynthia smiled.

"I wouldn't want to miss out on all that," I said a little sarcastically.

"Don't you feel you deserve to be happy?"

"Yeah, of course."

"Well, then visualize peace and harmony and pink balloons."

I shook my head. "Maybe if I were blonde, it would make more sense."

I awoke after a night of snuggling in one of the twin bunks in our Spartan cubicle. I looked at Cynthia lying next to me, wiping the sleep out of her eyes.

"I dreamed about you last night," I smiled, sitting up in bed.

"I bet I was good, too," Cynthia yawned.

I nodded. "You were giving me a Pap smear."

After a hearty breakfast and packing a bag lunch, I was ready for the slopes. It was exciting picking out my poles, boots, and skis, and waxing the skis. Cynthia fastened my gaiters onto my ski boots. They were supposed to keep the snow from getting into my socks and shoes. She and I told each other how good we looked and quickly brushed each other's lips. "You're gonna love it. I'll meet you back here for lunch around noon."

I waved good-bye to Cynthia in front of the lodge. I stood holding my skis and poles, watching her take off in the winter wonderland. I still had a few minutes before I needed to walk over to the ski instruction area.

"Excuse me, are you Jean Stevenson?"

"Yes, are you the teacher? I was just headed over that way."

The chubby man shook his bald head. "There's an emergency phone call for you."

"From who?" I asked, concerned. I wondered if something had happened to Sterling. He was the only one who knew how to reach me.

The man handed me a scrap of paper. It said, "Evelyn Stevenson called."

"Do you have a phone I can use?" I asked, feeling scared as I followed him back inside.

"Over there," he pointed. I set my skis and poles against the wall.

I was a nervous wreck by the time Mama accepted the charges.

"It's your grandmother."

"What's wrong? What happened?"

"She went into pneumonia yesterday."

"Pneumonia! I just talked to her and she was fine."

"Turns out she's had walking pneumonia for weeks. We took her into emergency last night."

"Well, at least she's in the hospital. She'll get better."

"I just came back from the hospital." Mama's voice shook. "Jean, the doctors don't think she's gonna make it."

I swallowed. "Oh, no!"

"They're only giving her a fifty-fifty chance to live through the night," Mama said tearfully.

"Through the night!"

"She's pretty weak. She's in intensive care."

"Can she talk?"

"Yes, but her voice is faint."

"I want to come home. I have to be there. I'm gonna get out of here and hop a plane as soon as I can."

"Well, call us when you know your plans. Someone will meet you at O'Hare. And Jean, don't forget to pray."

"OK."

I hung up the phone, dazed.

"Aren't you signed up for a beginner lesson?"

"Yeah, I did," I stammered.

"I'm Joe, looks like you're the only one who's a beginner today. You have me all to yourself." He looked like an average Joe.

"Hey, something's happened. I just got some bad news. I don't think I can do it now."

"What kind of bad news?"

"My grandmother might be dying. I have to go to Chicago."

"I'm sorry to hear that. Are you thinking of driving down to the airport right now?"

"My girlfriend is skiing. She's meeting me back here for lunch. I guess I'm sorta stuck until then. Is there any way out of here? Is there a bus I can take?"

"Waiting for your friend would be the quickest way. The next bus doesn't leave until tomorrow morning."

I groaned.

"Take a deep breath," the ski instructor ordered.

To my surprise, I was able to.

"I don't like to give advice, but since you're pretty much stuck here for the next several hours, why not do the lesson?"

"How can I think about skiing when my grandmother could be dying?"

"You don't have to think about it. You just have to do it."

"I guess there's no guarantee that even if I left this minute I could get there in time."

"I think skiing would ground you."

"I just feel like I should be *doing* something."

"Doing something physical can be therapeutic."

"I still have to call the airlines."

"I don't think the airline situation is going to change in the next hour or so." The instructor put his hand on my shoulder. "But your state of mind could change."

"I just need something to hold on to right now."

Joe handed me my poles. "Try these."

"OK," I sighed. "Let's go."

Carrying my poles in one hand and my skis in the other, I ventured into the sunny, snow-covered world. Having the sun shining when you're feeling down just makes it that much harder, I thought.

"Stevie, are you a total beginner?"

"I've never been on a pair of skis before in my life."

"Let's snap on your skis."

I stood gripping my poles. I gazed apprehensively at the snow-covered slopes. Yet the thought of learning something new gave me a glimmer of hope.

"I've heard that cross-country skiing is easier than downhill skiing," I said.

"It actually takes more energy, but it's easier to learn."

"Cynthia said it's just like walking."

"Let's just practice walking a little bit, then."

"OK."

I gingerly moved my feet toward a slight incline. Suddenly, I began to slip. I dug my poles desperately into the snow, but it was no use. I fell to the ground, my skis a twisted mess.

I felt frustrated and helpless. I'd fallen on the ice plenty of times growing up in Chicago. But that was different. I'd always been able to get up. Because kids are cold, they cracked up when you fell. But usually my pride was hurt more than anything else.

"I must look like a fool. I sure feel like a fool. Why aren't people laughing at me?" I asked as folks skied nonchalantly by.

"Nobody's laughing because all of them have fallen about a million times. And they know that if you don't fall, you don't learn to ski. By the way, what other people think of you is none of your business."

"I'll have to remember that one." I struggled again to get up. "Damn, I feel like a paraplegic!" I moaned, attempting to raise myself, using the poles. But it was hopeless. I couldn't even begin to straighten my legs out.

"This is really ridiculous!" I muttered as Joe stood by quietly. "It's just like walking, all right. Yeah, if you're about nine months old."

"The first lesson you need to learn in skiing is how to fall."

"Well, I think, I've passed with flying colors. Now, if I can learn how to get up, I'll feel like a genius."

"OK, turn to your right on your knees. Plant your poles in the snow in front of your face." I did what I was told.

"Now, uncross your feet and raise yourself up."

"I did it!" I shouted, struggling to my feet.

"If all else fails, you can always unsnap your skis and get up that way."

"Now you tell me."

"OK, let's just walk a little again. Let's head over to the beginner's area; notice my stride."

I tried to move my arms and legs the way Joe did. I must look like a penguin following him, I thought.

"Look, you're skiing!"

"Yeah, I'm actually skiing!" But then I remembered Grandma and felt sad. Who cared if I was skiing when Grandma might be dying this very moment? And I wasn't even there to tell her I loved her.

Then, I slipped again and fell.

I pulled myself up again, and got up the way Joe had taught me. But it took a lot of effort.

"You're doing fine."

"This is hard work, though, this falling and getting back up."

"Yeah, but it's worth it. You'll see."

"If you say so."

"I do say so. Now, I'm going to show you how to go up this incline so you can ski down. And that's when the real fun begins."

"How can I have fun when my grandmother might be dead?"

"Would you rather sit around and worry?"

"I guess not."

"Well, turn your skis outward like this to go uphill."

Wouldn't you know it, I slipped again. I fell into the snow, sideways. My hand even hurt a little. I didn't even try to raise myself up this time.

"I don't need this bullshit today!" I shouted. "This was a bad idea!"

"Get up the way I taught you."

I sat up in the snow. "I feel so helpless," I cried. "I feel so damn helpless." I sobbed. "I might not even have a chance to tell her good-bye. I didn't even get a chance to tell her how much I loved her."

"Just let it out. I told you this could be therapeutic," Joe said.

"I'm cold," I shivered. I could see my breath.

"Well, try getting up the way I showed you."

"Forget that, I'm unsnapping these bad boys."

"You were doing great. You have to practice getting up."

"I don't have to do anything but stay black and die! And I can happily live the rest of my life without ever skiing again. Besides, I have never known any black person who skied. So nobody will ever expect me to ski. It isn't like being black and not being able to dance. I mean, skiing will never even come up."

"Who cares what other people expect of you? Do you want to live your life based on other people's expectations?"

I didn't answer.

"I'll tell you an AA story."

"What does Alchoholics Anonymous have to do with skiing?"

Joe ignored my question. "This guy asks God, 'Can you grant me the courage to change the things that I can change?' And God says, 'I can do that.' Then the guy asks God, 'Can you grant me the serenity to accept the things I cannot change?' And God says, 'I can do that.' Then the guy asks God, 'Can you grant me the wisdom to tell the difference?' "

"What did God say?" I asked with curiosity.

" 'Keep coming back.' "

I turned sideways and struggled to stand up on my poles. I almost slipped, but I managed to stand up.

"OK, I'm ready."

I followed Joe, slanting my skis as I trudged uphill.

I took a big breath. "Look, I'm at the top of the mountain."

"You're at the top of the beginner's slope. Soon, you'll laugh at what you called a mountain."

I gazed down at the powdery, white snow. "Well, I'm not laughing today."

"Stevie, bend your knees and drag your poles. Do your wedge to slow yourself down, if you need to. And just sit down if you get scared."

I took another breath and headed downhill.

I bent my knees. I dragged my poles. I did my wedge. It was thrilling. There was no denying it. It reminded me of riding a roller coaster.

Grandma had always said, "You can't keep a good woman down."

I wished she could see me now, sailing through the snow, maneuvering through this cold, white world.

When I reached the bottom, I looked back with wonder.

I'd already prayed and called the airlines when I saw Cynthia. I could get a red-eye flight out tonight.

Cynthia hugged me. "I'm sorry about your Grandma. That's a real bummer."

"Yeah, I just hope she pulls through. If we leave after we finish eating, I'll have plenty of time. I'm already pretty much packed for cold weather. I can just take what I have here. Besides, I've still got clothes back in Chicago."

"Wait, a minute. You're not expecting me to give up this weekend and drive you back to San Francisco today, are you?"

"Cynthia, time is of the essence."

"There's no guarantee that you can get there in time, no matter when you leave."

"I know, but I have to find out. It's a chance that I have to take. Otherwise, I might never see her alive again."

"Is your grandmother even able to communicate?"

"Yeah, she's not in a coma."

"OK, let's say she pulls through. I mean pneumonia isn't always fatal, even in old people."

"I have faith. She's a fighter."

"If she does pull through, then you would have gone

through a lot of changes for nothing. I mean can you really afford to go back there now? What about your rent next month? Didn't you put down a fifty-dollar deposit?"

"Yeah, but I just might have to lose my deposit. I can't afford not to go. Sometimes you just have to step out on faith and take your chances."

Cynthia sighed. "Is that being fair to Sterling?"

"I might be able to borrow the rent from my parents. Besides, that's between me and Sterling."

"Well, leaving today is between me and you."

"Look, I need you to be there for me right now."

"Sorry, but I'm not available to be there for anyone in the first six months."

"That's cold. I mean, what about emergencies?"

"I don't consider this an emergency."

"You don't?" I bristled.

"No, and for me to drop everything to rescue you wouldn't be fair to me. You're not the only one with needs, Stevie."

"You've already skied. It's not like you haven't skied at all. And even if you went back out there for a while and we left in a few hours, I could still make my flight."

"You are sure manipulative."

"I'm just trying to compromise."

"Look, I just can't be this emotionally involved this soon. You're requiring too much energy."

I couldn't believe that Cynthia was being so unfeeling. I thought she had more heart. "Is it my fault that my grandmother might be on her deathbed?"

"No, but is it my responsibility? I came up here to ski. I work hard and I need to play hard. And Stevie, playing with you turns me on. But rescuing you doesn't."

"I feel like you're kicking me when I'm down. I'm sorry that something 'real' intruded upon your playground."

"Skiing is a passion of mine."

"Look, I can understand why you love skiing. But skiing will always be here. My grandmother may not. Believe me, it's hard to feel at somebody's else's mercy. If it weren't someone I loved, I wouldn't put myself in this position. I wouldn't swallow my pride."

"I feel like I'm being mind-fucked."

"Just forget it then. I'm not gonna kiss your ass. I'll get back to the Bay Area some other way. Explaining myself to you is just like throwing pearls to swine!"

"What's that supposed to mean?"

"Let's face it, the quality just ain't there."

"You know what I think? I think you're too self-absorbed to see anybody else's needs but Stevie's. Maybe you'd be better off alone."

"I think you're right. I would be better off being alone than being with someone and feeling alone," I answered quietly and headed for the phone.

"I'm having trouble with my car. I think it's just the starter. I'm gonna run it over to Grand Auto. Maybe I can borrow Derrick's ride."

"Whatever you can do, Sterling, I'd appreciate it. The bus won't get me back in time to make my flight."

"Don't worry, I'll get you down here by hook or by crook."

"I hate to ask this of you. You've already done so much."

"Look, baby girl, don't trip. Sometimes it's actually easier to give than to receive. I might need you before it's all said and done. People need people. Cynthia must not be part of the women's community. They're usually known for being there for folks."

"She's into looking out for number one."

"And let's not forget, she's bisexual," Sterling added.

I lay on my bunk reading in our cubicle, in an effort to distract my mind from my worries while I waited to hear from Sterling. I presumed Cynthia was out on the snow. We hadn't crossed paths since our big argument.

I'd spoken to Mama again on the phone. She said that Grandma was hanging tough, but she still wasn't out of the woods yet. I'd succeeded in getting so absorbed in Toni Morrison's *The Bluest Eye* that at first I hadn't heard the knock at the door.

I tensed up; maybe it was Cynthia. But I wasn't sure she'd knock. Maybe she wanted to apologize. I hoped it was Sterling coming to pick me up. Maybe it was a staffer telling me I had a phone call. What if Grandma had died?

I held my breath. "Come in."

Traci, Jawea, and another woman stepped inside the door.

"What are you doing here?" I asked with astonishment.

Traci gave me an exaggerated scared look. "Sterling told me about your grandmother," she said.

Jawea hugged me. "I've missed you, woman. Sorry about your grandma."

"Thanks."

Traci cleared her throat, "Stevie, this is Kate. Kate, this is Stevie."

I nodded at the small, hippie-looking woman with long, straight, dark hair. She smiled hesitantly.

"I called to invite you to our Annual Bah Humbug Party. And to tell you that Brenda sent us a flier about a Black Women's Support Group she's starting. I work on Saturdays."

"Brenda from the Berkeley Women's Center?" I asked, remembering the sistah with dreadlocks.

Traci nodded and handed me a rolled-up piece of paper.

"What happened to Sterling?" I asked, confused.

"He couldn't make it," Traci explained. "We're here to take you to the airport."

"You are? You came all the way up here to give me a ride?"

They nodded.

"Sterling said he'd been trying to get his car started when he ran in to answer the phone. He wasn't sure if he could even get it to Grand Auto. Hey, that's when I said, I owe her one."

"We remembered how close you were to your grandma," Jawea added.

"Thanks," I said as tears welled up in my eyes.

"Can I get a hug now?" Traci asked. I held my arms out to her, and when we connected I felt like I'd finally let go of the past. Kate even put her hand on my shoulder.

"Sweetie, I brought you a rescue remedy." Jawea produced a small bottle.

"Thanks, I really feel supported."

"That's what community is all about." Jawea smiled.

"Kate, it's strange meeting you under these circumstances."

She shrugged. "When Traci asked to borrow my van, I just wanted to be a part of the effort."

"The bug needs a tune-up. I didn't want to chance it through these mountains," Traci explained.

"I really appreciate your help. I mean, it's not like you even know me," I said to Kate.

"I know your energy," she replied. "You lived in my room last summer. And you were lovers with Traci. We've shared some important karma."

"Look," I blushed, "I didn't know you all were still together when Traci and I got involved."

"Is that book good?" Traci pointed.

"It's great."

"Whatever happened was meant to happen," Kate insisted. "We learn the lessons we need to learn."

"Open your mouth," Jawea demanded.

I did, and she squeezed a dropper full of her herbal remedy under my tongue.

"Don't swallow for thirty seconds."

I made my getaway without seeing Cynthia. Kate drove, and Traci rode up in front with her.

"Jawea, I don't know if your rescue remedy will keep me from worrying about money. I just found the cutest cottage and now I've gotta take rent money and give it to the airlines."

"Don't come from scarcity," Jawea answered. "You have to believe in abundance. You have to believe that the universe will provide."

"I'll buy your airline ticket," Kate piped up.

"No way, you've already bent over backward. I was just voicing my problem, that's all."

"And I was just voicing my solution."

"I couldn't take your money."

"Do you have an issue around receiving?" Jawea asked.

"I don't know."

"I think you have a poverty mentality," Traci suggested.

"Look, Stevie, I have a trust fund. Money is easy for me to give. In fact, it's one of the easiest things. This is a situation that can let me use my money in a way that makes me feel good, and helps me resolve some of my issues."

"You don't want to deny Kate the opportunity to resolve her issues, do you?" Jawea asked.

"No, but how about if I pay you back?"

"Fine, if that's what you have a need to do."

"I do. Thanks a lot. And don't worry, I'll pay you back as soon as I can."

"I'm not worried about getting the money back. Besides, I know your credit is good. I got Traci back, didn't I?"

Kate put her arm around Traci's shoulder as she drove. I wasn't even jealous.

We munched on bean burritos as we approached the Bay Area.

"By the way, how's Artemis?"

"I think she misses you," Jawea said between chews.

"I miss her too, especially when I'm on the phone."

"She's been in a weird space lately, wouldn't you say?"

"I think she's just been separating her energy from everyone else's. I think she's just been processing," Traci replied. "That reminds me," she continued. "Kate told me a while back that she would be content just to bump into me."

I licked refried beans off my lips. "Bump into you?"

"Yeah, can you believe that?" Traci groaned.

"Weren't you all living together at the time?" I asked.

"Yeah," Kate answered with food in her mouth. "But, I was thinking about moving into the ashram over in Oakland."

"Anyway, I freaked out and told Jawea. And Jawea said that I just wasn't fucked-up enough for Kate."

"Kate has been with some fucked-up people," Jawea explained."

"They weren't fucked-up, they were just unevolved."

Jawea raised her eyebrows. "A woman whose idea of music is the theme song from *The Brady Bunch* is just unevolved?"

"Anyway, so I say, 'Kate, Jawea says you don't want to be with me because I'm not fucked-up enough for you.' "

"And Kate says, 'Traci, you're plenty fucked-up enough for me. You're just not fucked-up in a way that interests me anymore.' "

"Oh," I gulped, surprised they'd be so candid in front of me.

"Hey, but check this out. I didn't get defensive. I just took the shit in. And then I said, 'Kate, I need time to process what you just said, before I respond.' "

"Then, I said to myself," Kate cut in, "'Traci might not be perfect, but at least she's willing to process. And then I saw her aura. And it was so beautiful."

"Stevie, did you want to be talking about your grandma?" Jawea asked politely.

"No, it's been good to be distracted. I'll have plenty of time to worry on the plane. I just wish I could see people's auras."

19

Mama and Daddy picked me up at the airport. David was on a basketball road trip with Iowa State, and Kevin was stationed in Georgia. Mama looked tired. Her body felt stiff when I hugged her.

"How was the flight?" Daddy asked as I kissed him on the cheek. What difference did it make how the flight had been? Obviously I'd gotten here in one piece, I thought.

"Fine, how's Grandma?"

"She's still weak, but she's hanging in there," Mama reported.

"They took her out of intensive care," Daddy added. "So that's a good sign."

"She's out of intensive care! That's great!"

Daddy grabbed my bag. "The doctor expects her to pull through."

I let out a sigh of relief. "I prayed for her on the plane."

"I'm glad you haven't forgotten how to pray. Remember the Lord in thy youth," Mama recited.

"I was so worried that I'd hear bad news when I got here. I feel so relieved," I said as we walked through the airport.

"Well, your grandmother's not out of the woods yet."

"Evelyn, why do you always have to be so negative?" Daddy groaned.

"I'm not being negative. The doctor says the next twenty-four hours are critical."

"Well, I have a lot of hope," I cut in. "But how'd Grandma end up at County?"

"They were the only ones who would take her."

"But, doesn't she have hospitalization?"

"Yes. But that's still where she ended up."

"Black folks have a funny way of ending up at Cook County Hospital, no matter what."

"It's called institutionalized racism, Daddy."

"You hear that, Evelyn? It's institutionalized racism. Now, you heard it from a college graduate."

"Speaking of institutions, did you bring something to wear to church?"

"Let the girl go to the house and rest. She's had a long flight."

"No, take me straight to Grandma. I'm here on a mission."

"Well, tell your grandmother I'll come see about her after church."

"OK, Mama."

"You know, Jean, they've even got black sections of the cemetery here," Daddy said. "They just ain't got signs. They don't bury a black person just anywhere. You should've seen how far we had to drive to bury my buddy Red's father once we got to the cemetery. There wasn't a blade of grass either."

"Maybe they just bought a cheap plot," Mama suggested.

"There you go, Evelyn, still making excuses for the white man. Jean, it looked more like a construction site than anything else. They had work going on all around us. There's no way Daddy Red could rest in peace." My father groaned as we entered the underground parking lot.

Cook County Hospital was a huge, old, brick monstrosity. It had a strong, no-nonsense Chicago appearance. Grandma was on a ward. I couldn't believe she didn't even have her own room. I was told to wait for several hours until visiting time. I napped in a chair in the waiting room.

It was like a scene from a movie. A long room lined with beds, each with a couple of chairs around it. Some were occupied by visiting loved ones. The patients were mostly old, asleep, or in different stages of agony.

I passed a man dressed in his Sunday suit holding a Bible. He stood over a bed and loudly commanded Satan to leave an old woman's body.

Another man tried to sell me copper bangles. "They'll cure whatever ails you."

"Not today," I mumbled.

If that were the case this place would be empty, I thought.

I continued along the row of beds, searching for my grandmother's name. When I spied it, I rushed to Grandma's bedside. For the first time in my memory she wasn't a tower of strength. There were tubes coming out of her, and she was coughing up a storm. Her chest was rising up and down. I saw a pitcher of water at her bedside table.

"Grandma, it's me, Jean," I said before putting a glass to her trembling lips.

She peered at me through two cloudy slits. I wasn't even sure she recognized me. Grandma tasted the water and spoke.

"My baby done come see about me," she said as her chest rattled. "They had to call you in from the ski slopes."

"You heard that song, 'Ain't No Mountain High Enough?' Well, nothing could keep me from getting to you, Grandma."

"Well, I sho' have caused a uprising."

"Don't even talk like that. I'm just glad you're doing better. They say you weren't talking much yesterday."

"Ain't had nothing much to say."

"Still got your spunk, I see."

"I'm so tickled to see you, I'd dance a jig, if I could."

"I'm happy to see you, too."

"And here I was worried that my girl was pulling away from me."

"Pulling away from you. What do you mean?" I asked, sitting down close to her bed.

"Who's this white girl you went skiing with? What is y'all's story?"

"A friend."

"What kind of friend?"

"What do you mean?"

"I might couldn't hide peppermint candy from you. Well, you can't hide nothing from me neither."

"When the chips were down, I couldn't count on Cynthia. So, I'm through with her."

"I always said, I wouldn't trust one of 'em behind a broom straw."

"Well, another one loaned me the money to fly out here to see about you though, Grandma."

"Now, you know I always did say good and bad folks come

in all colors, too. And if it weren't for good white folks, Lord knows, we'd be in worse shape than we are now."

"Amen to that."

"Now, let's get back to that white hussy."

"She wasn't all bad, Grandma. She was just selfish. But it's an ill wind that blows no one any good. I reconnected with some folks and I got a chance to ski."

"Well, good things can come through bad sources. That reminds me of a story."

A pretty Filipino nurse greeted us and placed a thermometer in Grandma's mouth.

The nurse shook the thermometer. "Your temperature has gone down. How do you feel, Mrs. Dickens?"

"I guess I'll make it."

"I'm sure you will, Mrs. Dickens. You're a trooper."

After the nurse left, Grandma continued in her feeble voice.

"There was an old woman named Aunt Mandie, and she was on her back porch praying out loud for some food."

I'd heard this story many times before and would gladly hear it again. But I didn't want Grandma to overtax herself.

"Are you sure you're up to talking?"

"If you don't hush up. I ain't no vegetable yet."

"Well, go 'head on with your bad self."

"All right, so, two white boys passing by heard Aunt Mandie and one said to the other, 'Listen at that dumb darkie. She's stupid enough to think that God will send her some food.' The other boy had an idea. And the two of them ran to their houses and sneaked into their refrigerators and cupboards. They fixed a box of their parents' best food and took it and set it on Aunt Mandie's porch. The boys hid and waited for her to find it. Pretty soon, Aunt Mandie comes out and shouts, 'Lord have mercy, thank ye Jesus! The Lord done sent me this here food. The boys fell out laughing. 'Yassuh,' Aunt Mandie declared, 'the Lord sent it, but the devil brought it!' "

I laughed like I hadn't heard that story a hundred times. After all, it was one of my favorites.

"Jean, what do you mean, you're through with that white girl?" Grandma raised her eyebrows. "What are you through with?"

I felt nervous. Was Grandma asking me to come out to her?

"Grandma, here I thought you were at death's door, and all you wanna do is get up in my business."

"You act like you got something to hide."

"Are you sure you want to know?"

"Chile, ain't nothing new under the sun. I can deal with anything you can dish out."

"OK, Grandma," I swallowed. "Cynthia and I were involved. I was also with Traci, before her." I held my breath. "Are you shocked?"

"Do I look shocked?"

"It's hard to tell, you're sick."

"It would take a lot more than that to shock me. No wonder Evelyn turned pale as a ghost when I asked her if you were grinning up in some man's face out there."

I hesitated. "Can you accept me?"

"It's not up to me to accept you or not. Only person has to accept you is you. You'll always be Grandma's girl, no matter what."

"Are you saying that your love is unconditional?"

"I don't need no fancy words to describe it. I just know that Grandma's love is a fierce love, as my gay friends who come into the chicken stand would say."

"You have gay friends, Grandma?"

"I have friends who happen to be gay."

"And here Mama said if I told you, you'd have a stroke."

"Your mama is so old-fashioned. Baby, I'm a old rat in the barn. I've seen and heard it all."

"Mama's worried about my soul. She's afraid I'm going to hell in a handbasket."

"Heaven forbid that God would want you to be happy."

"Don't you fear God, Grandma?"

"How can you love what you fear?"

"That's a good question."

"Chile, folks think God created them just so they could be miserable."

"I used to think of God as sort of a pissed-off Santa Claus. But, it's like in that play *For Colored Girls Who've Considered Suicide When the Rainbow Is Enuf*. You can find God in yourself." I continued, "I guess, if you love yourself, then you'll find a loving God, and if you hate yourself, then you'll find a hateful God. They say you can't love anybody else until you love yourself. And maybe that even includes God," I added.

"Chile, you said a mouthful."

I sighed. "You know, Grandma, it's been really confusing. You see, I've been attracted to men and women. I don't want to be like a pancake, flip-flopping back and forth. I mean, I wish I could figure out which way I'm destined to go."

"Chile, maybe your nature is a journey and not a destination."

A couple days later, Grandma felt better and I returned to San Francisco. I had to get back to work and move into my new place. I was also eager to check out the Black Women's Support Group that Brenda was facilitating. The flier said that sisters of all sexual orientations were welcome.

Grandma used to say that she'd done been all through life and she'd done been many a fool. But, she'd say, "I ain't never been the same fool twice." And then she'd wink and say, "All who believe that stand on your head."

Grandma was right. My sexuality has been a journey. And I'm still on the road.